MONKEYFACE

Stephen Gilbert was born in Newcastle, County Down in 1912. He was sent to England for boarding school from age 10 to 13 and afterwards to a Scottish public school, which he left without passing any exams or obtaining a leaving certificate. He returned to Belfast, where he worked briefly as a journalist before joining his father's tea and seed business. In 1931, just before his nineteenth birthday, Gilbert met novelist Forrest Reid, by that time in his mid-fifties. Reid's works reflect his lifelong fascination with teenage boys, and he was quickly drawn to Gilbert; the two commenced a sometimes turbulent friendship that lasted until Reid's death in 1947. Reid acted as mentor to Gilbert, who had literary aspirations, and ultimately depicted an idealized version of their relationship in the novel *Brian Westby* (1934), also available from Valancourt Books.

Gilbert's first published novel, *The Landslide* (1943), a fantasy involving prehistoric creatures which appear in a remote part of Ireland after being uncovered by a landslide, appeared to generally positive reviews and was dedicated to Reid. A realistic novel, *Bombardier* (1944), followed, based on Gilbert's experiences in the Second World War. Gilbert's third novel, *Monkeyface* (1948), concerns what seems to be an ape, called "Bimbo," discovered in South America and brought back to Belfast, where it learns to talk. *The Burnaby Experiments* appeared in 1952, five years after Reid's death, and is a thinly disguised portrayal of their relationship from Gilbert's point of view and a belated response to *Brian Westby*. His final novel, *Ratman's Notebooks* (1968), the story of a loner who learns he can train rats to kill, would become his most famous, being twice filmed as *Willard* (1971, 2003).

Gilbert married Kathleen Stevenson in 1945; the two had four children, and Gilbert devoted most of his time from the 1950s onward to family life and his seed business. He died in Northern Ireland in 2010 at age 97.

Andrew Doyle is a playwright and stand-up comedian. His plays include *Borderland* (national tour for 7:84 Theatre Company, Scotland), *Jimmy Murphy Makes Amends* (BBC Radio 4) and *The Second Mr. Bailey* (BBC Radio 4). His most recent solo stand-up show was *Whatever It Takes* at the Soho Theatre, London. He has a doctorate in English Renaissance Literature from the University of Oxford where he also worked as a lecturer. He has previously written the introductions to several works by Forrest Reid and Stephen Gilbert for Valancourt Books.

By Stephen Gilbert

The Landslide (1943)*

Bombardier (1944)†

Monkeyface (1948)*

The Burnaby Experiments (1952)*

Ratman's Notebooks (1968)*

* Available from Valancourt Books. † Forthcoming.

STEPHEN GILBERT

MONKEYFACE

With a new introduction by

ANDREW DOYLE

VALANCOURT BOOKS

Monkeyface by Stephen Gilbert
First published London: Faber & Faber, 1948
First Valancourt Books edition 2014

Published by Valancourt Books, Richmond, Virginia
Publisher & Editor: James D. Jenkins
20th Century Series Editor: Simon Stern, University of Toronto
http://www.valancourtbooks.com

ISBN 978-1-941147-04-7
Also available as an electronic book.

All Valancourt Books publications are printed on acid free paper that meets all ANSI standards for archival quality paper.

Cover by Tyler Böhm
Set in Dante MT 11/13.2

INTRODUCTION

Monkeyface was a turning point in the career of Stephen Gilbert. His debut novel *The Landslide* (1943) had garnered enthusiastic notices, was published in both London and New York, and later translated into French. His next novel *Bombardier* (1944) sold sufficiently well to justify a second edition. When *Monkeyface* was published in 1948 Gilbert had hoped to build on this momentum and fulfil his lifelong ambition to become a successful novelist. Many critics found much to praise in this unusual tale of a monkey-boy from a desolate South American forest raised in the suburbs of Belfast. Writing for *The Listener*, George D. Painter described Gilbert's protagonist as "a charming character" and praised him for producing a novel "as sincere and attractive as it is painful".[1] A reviewer for *The Northern Whig* went so far as to detect "flashes of brilliance" that showed Gilbert to be "a true artist".[2] Yet the revenue from sales barely covered the author's advance. *Monkeyface* was, in Gilbert's own words, "a flop".[3]

The novelist Glenn Patterson has rightly described *Monkeyface* as "[o]ne of the strangest of all Belfast novels, by one of its most overlooked writers", and it would seem that Gilbert was entirely aware that he had become a victim of his own ingenuity.[4] "I wrote the book I meant to write," he defiantly stated in the fourth volume of his unpublished autobiography. "It isn't I who have failed. It is the public."[5] From his perspective *Monkeyface* was a success, but there is no doubt that he still hoped to attain a wider readership.[6] His fourth novel *The Burnaby Experiments* (1952), his most enigmatic to date, sold fewer than a thousand copies. "It has dropped into the world noiselessly," he later wrote, "like a dead leaf falling into a pool of black, stagnant water".[7] It was not until 1968 that he produced his bestseller, *Ratman's Notebooks*, a lurid story about a young man who trains rats to perform criminal acts on his behalf. There followed a hugely profitable film adaptation directed by Daniel Mann under the title *Willard* (1971), which gave rise to a sequel *Ben* (1972) for which Michael Jackson recorded the theme song. When *Ratman's Notebooks* was reissued in paperback under the title *Willard*, it went on to sell over a million copies.[8] Gilbert was unhappy with the new title; his intention had been that the lead character should remain nameless. Such was his disappointment that by the time of his death in 2010 he had seen neither Mann's adaptation nor the 2003 remake starring Crispin Glover.[9]

Monkeyface, like *Ratman's Notebooks*, bears many hallmarks of the science fiction genre. In particular, it fits into a tradition of storytelling about the close relationship between apes and humans. Even before the advent of evolutionary biology, the connection had been noted. As early as 1772, Lord Monboddo was advancing a theory of language evolution based upon the premise that "man in his natural and original state" had existed in an "abject and brutish" condition.[10]

This idea is satirized in Thomas Love Peacock's novel *Melincourt* (1817) in which an orang-utan known as Sir Oran Haut-Ton—"a specimen of the natural and original man"—stands for parliament, and in the opening chapter of Charles Dickens's *Martin Chuzzlewit* (1843) there is a reference to "the Monboddo doctrine touching the probability of the human race having once been monkeys".[11] Other nineteenth-century novels portray whole communities of intelligent monkeys living in isolation. James Fenimore Cooper's *The Monikins* (1835) depicts one such group living on the fictional Leap Islands near Antarctica, and Léon Gozlan's *Les Émotions de Polydore Marasquin* (1856) tells the story of a castaway in "Apeland" who eventually becomes king of the indigenous creatures by disguising himself in the skin of a mandrill.[12] This idea of intellectually developed simian tribes is also to be found in later works such as F. C. Constable's *The Curse of Intellect* (1895) and John Collier's mischievous comedy *His Monkey Wife* (1930).[13]

In *Monkeyface*, Gilbert adopts this premise to explain the origins of his central character, Bimbo. Kidnapped as a baby from an unspecified location in South America by the explorer Theodore Browne, Bimbo is reared in captivity in the fictional village of Belmore, apparently situated on the outskirts of Belfast. After his kidnapper's disappearance, it is his brother Sebastian—referred to throughout as "Mr. Browne"—who assumes responsibility for raising the monkey-boy. Early in the novel he is impressed by

Bimbo's powers of mimicry, and coaches him to repeat Loyalist political slogans such as "Up Ulster" and "No Surrender", an example of Gilbert's satirical treatment of the mindlessness of sectarianism.[14] It is not until Bimbo is introduced to Miss Martha Sutton, a local teacher, that his intellectual potential is fully appreciated. She insists on enrolling him in the school and, as a result of his ongoing contact with human beings, he is eventually "civilized" and develops a mastery of speech. However, Bimbo's capacity for friendship with human children does not prevent him from experiencing a struggle of identity. Irrespective of Miss Sutton's efforts to see him assimilated into the community, Bimbo feels an instinctive yearning to return to his origins. In this respect, Bimbo anticipates the character of Caesar in Rupert Wyatt's *Rise of the Planet of the Apes* (2011), a film which bears more than a passing resemblance to *Monkeyface* in terms of both theme and characterization.

During a visit to London Zoo in 1842, Queen Victoria famously declared an orang-utan to be "frightfully, and painfully, and disagreeably human". Needless to say, the findings of Charles Darwin and Alfred Russel Wallace provided all the explanation that was necessary for these anxieties, and it is no surprise to find Darwin's *On the Origin of Species* (1859) making an appearance in *Monkeyface*. Searching among Dr. Theodore Browne's papers for "some clue to his identity", Bimbo happens upon a heavily annotated copy of Darwin's book which, he hopes, "might explain the whole problem". However, Bimbo finds no satisfactory answers in the theory of evolution by natural selection. In spite of his efforts, he remains a taxonomically ambiguous figure. In the opening chapter the narrator asserts that "the creature was an ape", a point reiterated in Theodore's classification of Bimbo as "some species of anthropoid ape". This identification is a misnomer; apes do not have tails, and Bimbo's tail is one of his most prominent features. Furthermore, Bimbo's facial characteristics have an almost human quality reminiscent of the ancient Greeks. As a friend of Sebastian Browne observes in Chapter 3, Bimbo's ability to mimic human speech is "[a]lmost a proof of the theory of evolution".

Although early indications appear to signify that Bimbo could be an example of an intermediary species, a heretofore undiscovered "missing link" or, as John Wilson Foster suggests, "an alternative line of primate evolution", the text lends itself to a different interpretation, one perhaps influenced by the strict Presbyterianism of Gilbert's upbringing.[15] In Chapter 23, Bimbo reads notes outlining a specifically religious hypothesis written by his captor Dr. Theodore Browne:

> But why should Man be the ultimate achievement? It would be sad indeed to think so. Perhaps God is always experimenting, *has* always been experimenting. Is there really any proof of the Darwinian theory of evolution? Might it not be that God, when he creates a new species, places it first in some garden of Eden where it can go through the nursery stage unmolested by other creatures, who would naturally wish to destroy beings better than themselves? What definite evidence is there that any of the main species are descended from former species, that the primates have a common ancestor? The whole case for evolution is circumstantial.

This notion of God as "an experimental scientist" is Gilbert's chief variation on the traditional monkey-as-human subgenre of science fiction. Bimbo's goal, then, is to return to his "garden of Eden", to rejoin his race of superior beings.

That said, the success of *Monkeyface* depends upon the reader's empathy for Bimbo, and Gilbert has accentuated his human qualities in order that this might be achieved. Much of the novel takes the form of a school story, and Bimbo's attempts to secure friendships, as well as his rivalries and insecurities, are all recognizable aspects of childhood experience. Bimbo is at the centre of the reader's consciousness from the outset—the story opens with Bimbo in his cage—and although the novel is not written in first-person, Gilbert employs linguistic mannerisms that simulate Bimbo's own unfamiliarity with human society: a cameraman is described as holding "what appeared to be a box in the air in front of his face", Christmas crackers are "coloured tubes", and trains are "powerful animals with violent emotions". Accordingly, Bimbo's child-like sensibilities are reflected in Gilbert's imagery: when Bimbo admires the "bright dresses of the girls" at a party the spectacle is "like seeing a flower-bed with all the flowers walking about", and when he clears his throat he believes his coughs to be "alive . . . very angry and hot", scratching him "with their nails" as they fight to escape. Such techniques ensure that the reader's emotional identification with Bimbo is sustained throughout the narrative.

Taking this into account, it can be seen why Gilbert's emphasis on Bimbo's early infancy in South America is so essential to the story. His most significant memory is that of his mother's "kind brown face, the warm arms which had encircled him and pressed him close". Bimbo now inhabits a world without such affection, and his need to reclaim this lost, idealized existence is a typical motif of Gilbert's work. *The Landslide* depicts the resurrection of primeval creatures from a bygone "golden age", and the unnamed narrator of *Ratman's Notebooks* is forced to suffer the indignity of having to work as a subordinate in a company once owned by his deceased father. That social decline is a recurrent theme in Gilbert's work is perhaps inevitable given his own circumstances. After the death of his father in 1934 the family moved from Kensington Park in East Belfast to a relatively modest terrace house, 12 Kansas Avenue, just off the Antrim Road. Having grown accustomed to an affluent way of life, the family were forced to make many changes; the car was sold, along with many items of furniture. "Tea isn't high tea anymore," Gilbert wrote in his autobiography. "Just tea, with bread, jam and margarine. Mother watches us all to make sure nobody spreads the jam or the margarine too thickly."[16]

It was around this time that Gilbert became a director of his father's seed company, Samuel McCausland Ltd, an occupation that was to endure for the rest of his working life. His career was interrupted by military service; Gilbert was a gunner in the 3rd Ulster Searchlight Regiment and recounted his wartime experiences in *Bombardier*. It was his concern for the foundering business that prompted him to apply for early release from the army. He worked tirelessly, but nonetheless managed to find time to maintain his writing. His younger son Tom, whose bedroom was across the corridor from his study, recalls that the sound of his typewriter could be heard "every morning before going to work and every evening after returning from work". This practice would appear to be confirmed by an untitled poem written by Gilbert in September 1943:

> From eight till six of every day
> I am a seedsman and can say
>
> The value of the samples shown
> By farmers of the seed they've grown.
>
> But every evening after tea
> I change into a different me.
>
> I go upstairs and shut my door,
> And write a thousand words—or more.[17]

Gilbert's mentor, the novelist Forrest Reid, felt strongly that the "different me" ought to be prioritized. Reid had persuaded Gilbert to enter the seed trade in the belief that he would have "an easy time of it", at least in relation to his all-consuming efforts as a reporter for the *Northern Whig*.[18] At the time, Gilbert "took everything that Forrest Reid said as gospel" and followed his advice.[19] Later, when it became clear that the demands of running his father's business were damaging Gilbert's literary career, Reid changed his mind and condemned this dual vocation as an attempt "to serve God and Mammon".[20] Gilbert was later to concede the point: "My service to Mammon . . . has kept me from serving literature".[21] His ultimate goal, "to leave business and become a whole-time writer", never came to fruition.[22] That said, he enjoyed a highly successful career in the seed industry and fulfilled his lifelong ambition "to marry and have four children—two boys and two girls".[23]

It was Reid who had introduced Gilbert to Charles Kingsley's *The Water-Babies* (1863), a novel which may have influenced the writing of *Monkeyface* given its evolutionary theme. In a letter to Reid dated 31 May 1932, Gilbert writes favourably of the novel and comments particularly on its endorsement of "the idea that monkeys are det[er]iorated humans".[24] As the fairy points out in Chapter VI, there is "a downhill as well as an uphill road; and, if I can turn beasts into men, I can, by the same laws of circumstance, and selection, and competition, turn men into beasts".[25]

This explains why the trout in Kingsley's novel were once salmon; their latter-day unsightliness is their comeuppance for years of indolence, cowardice and greed.[26] Espousing what Arthur Johnston describes as a form of "moral Darwinism", Kingsley makes it clear that Tom's evolution as a water-baby is determined by the relative nobility of his behaviour.[27] In this way, the novel works as part science lesson, part cautionary tale, as we see Tom's progress hindered by the growth of "prickles, just like a sea-egg" all over his body, a punishment for stealing sweets.[28] Like most narratives based on degeneration theory, *The Water-Babies* takes a moralistic approach. Kingsley appears to adopt the Neoplatonic idea that a rebarbative appearance is an outward manifestation of moral dissolution, a concept that recurs in the study of physiognomy. One is reminded of the figure of Pietro Bembo in Baldassar Castiglione's *Il Libro del Cortegiano* (1528), who proclaims that ugliness equates to evil, and beauty to good: "I brutti adunque per lo più sono ancor mali, e li belli buoni".[29] In *The Water-Babies* we see this principle restated in the narrator's assertion that "people's souls make their bodies".[30]

There are intimations of this concept in Gilbert's *The Landslide*, in which the lead character's grandfather proposes that human beings have lost their telepathic powers as a consequence of their moral failings and have become "dumb animals".[31] Gilbert was acutely sensitive to ethical concerns, and his novels are replete with examples of characters being punished for their misconduct. It is perhaps to be expected that such ideas would find their way into his work given his religious background. Indeed, one of his earliest memories was a gift from his grandmother: an ominous "blood-red" card bearing the legend "BE SURE YOUR SIN WILL FIND YOU OUT" which had been mounted on the wall by his bed.[32] His parents had taken on a considerable financial burden in sending Gilbert to public school in the hope that he might become a minister, and yet the experience made him an agnostic.[33] At the time he was writing *Monkeyface* Gilbert had little doubt of the nonexistence of God—he did not reconvert to Christianity until 1960—and yet Dr. Browne's "garden of Eden" hypothesis is overtly theistic in nature. The kind of moralistic evolution and devolution we see in *The Water-Babies* evidently appeals to Bimbo; he is attracted to the notion of God as "the Divine Artist" who has created this new race to supplant humankind, bringing him "one step nearer to His vision of perfection".

However, whereas Kingsley's novel sees monkeys as less attractive—and therefore degenerated—manifestations of the human form, Gilbert's novel questions the anthropocentric nature of such judgements. As Bimbo examines his reflection in a mirror he concludes that he is "a definite improvement on Man", and it is clear that his intelligence far exceeds those of his school friends. Moreover, he is innately good. He balks at the human activity of hunting for pleasure; the sight of mounted deer heads in Sebastian Browne's home leaves him "much more shocked than if he had discovered Mr. Browne in the middle of a cannibal feast". In response, he makes his friend Hugo promise never to shoot another living being except in the eventuality of war. Bimbo is continually depicted as morally superior to human figures of authority; he is able to rise above the ego-driven pettiness of his teacher Miss Price, and eventually outwits the avaricious Mr. Browne. In addition, the debate about Adam and Eve in Chapter 12 serves as a reminder of humankind's postlapsarian condition.

That *Monkeyface* should focus on the corruption inherent in humanity should come as no great surprise. As Northern Irish secretary of the Campaign for Nuclear Disarmament, Gilbert was all too aware of the self-destructive impulse of his species. "What is the good of writing novels," he once asked, "if the whole human race is on the verge of annihilation?"[34] His autobiographical writings reveal the extent of his preoccupation with original sin. The first volume opens with a quotation from the apocryphal Second Book of Esdras (Chapter 7, verses 46-48):

> I answered then and said, This is my first and last saying, that it had been better not to have given the earth unto Adam: or else, when it was given him, to have restrained him from sinning.
>
> For what profit is it for men now in this present time to live in heaviness, and after death to look for punishment?
>
> O thou Adam, what hast thou done? for though it was thou that sinned, thou art not fallen alone, but we all that come of thee.

The profound sense of guilt that dominates all four autobiographical volumes apparently never abated, and was derived from what Gilbert perceived to be his own moral shortcomings. He claimed to suffer from a limited capacity for empathy, and yet in spite of this trait—or perhaps because of it—he was a dedicated humanitarian. With this in mind, it is feasible to see *Monkeyface* as a repudiation of so-called "civilization" and its exploitative, malicious nature. Unlike Adam and Eve, Bimbo's race has not fallen. His attempt to rejoin his family in their "garden of Eden" is at once a wish-fulfilment fantasy and an allegory of redemption. Above all, *Monkeyface* is a challenge to the assumption that humankind must be God's "ultimate achievement".

ANDREW DOYLE

March 13, 2014

NOTES

1 George D. Painter, review, *The Listener* (27 Jan 1949).
2 Review by "C.", The Northern Whig (6 Nov 1948).
3 Stephen Gilbert, unpublished autobiography, undated typescript (Special Collections, Queen's University Belfast, uncatalogued), vol. IV, p. 1b.
4 Glenn Patterson, "Glenn Patterson's Top 10 Belfast Books", *The Guardian* (28 March 2012).
5 Autobiography, op. cit., vol. IV, p. 1b.
6 Gilbert's hope that his writing might be commercially viable is made clear in an undated autobiographical fragment: "I had always wanted to be a writer—a novelist really, preferably a popular novelist". Stephen Gilbert, autobiographical fragment, undated typescript (Special Collections, Queen's University Belfast, uncatalogued), p. 3.
7 Autobiography, op. cit., vol. IV, p. 83a.
8 These sales figures are recorded among Gilbert's private papers. See Stephen Gilbert, unpublished journal, typescript (Special Collections, Queen's University Belfast, uncatalogued), p. 5.
9 I am indebted to Tom Gilbert for providing this information.
10 Letter from Lord Monboddo to James Harris dated 31 December 1772, reproduced in William Knight (ed.), *Lord Monboddo and Some of His Contemporaries* (London: John Murray, 1900), pp. 71-74. See p. 73.

11 Thomas Love Peacock, *Melincourt* (London: Hookham, Jun. and Co., 1817), p. 67; Charles Dickens, *The Life and Adventures of Martin Chuzzlewit* (London: Chapman and Hall, 1844), p. 5.

12 James Fenimore Cooper, *The Monikins: A Tale* (London: Richard Bentley, 1835). For the English translation of *Les Émotions de Polydore Marasquin* see Léon Gozlan, *The Man Among the Monkeys: or, Ninety Days in Apeland* (London: Ward, Lock, and Tyler, 1873). For Marasquin's mandrill disguise see pp. 125-126.

13 F. C. Constable, *The Curse of Intellect* (Edinburgh and London: William Blackwood & Sons, 1895); John Collier, *His Monkey Wife: or, Married to a Chimp* (London: Peter Davies, 1930).

14 This mistrust of sectarianism is clearly reflected in Gilbert's unpublished novel *The Bloody City* (1971), the original draft of which depicts an assassination attempt against the Unionist firebrand Ian Paisley. See Stephen Gilbert, *The Bloody City*, unpublished manuscript (Special Collections, Queen's University Belfast, MS45/2/14).

15 John Wilson Foster, *Forces and Themes in Ulster Fiction* (Dublin: Gill and Macmillan, 1974), p. 215.

16 Autobiography, op. cit., vol. III, p. 29.

17 Stephen Gilbert, "Poems", volume of collected typescripts (Special Collections, Queen's University Belfast, uncatalogued), p. 49.

18 Autobiographical fragment, op. cit., p. 3.

19 Ibid., p. 5.

20 Autobiography, op. cit., vol. IV, p. 207.

21 Ibid.

22 Ibid., p. 2.

23 Ibid., p. 207. Gilbert's marriage in 1945 to Kathleen Stevenson, known affectionately as "Topsy", was clearly a source of considerable pride, as shown by descriptions of her in his autobiography: "Her beauty filled me with awe, with wonder, a desire to worship and adore . . ." (ibid., p. 63).

24 Letter from Gilbert to Forrest Reid dated 31 May 1932, courtesy of Tom Gilbert.

25 Charles Kingsley, *The Water-Babies: A Fairy Tale for a Land-Baby* (London: Macmillan, 1863), p. 249.

26 When Tom asks why the trout are so disliked, the salmon explains: "My dear, we do not even mention them, if we can help it; for I am sorry to say they are relations of ours who do us no credit. A great many years ago they were just like us: but they were so lazy, and cowardly, and greedy, that instead of going down to the sea every year to see the world and grow strong and fat, they chose to stay and poke

about in the little streams and eat worms and grubs: and they are very properly punished for it; for they have grown ugly and brown and spotted and small; and are actually so degraded in their tastes, that they will eat our children." Ibid., p. 128.

27 Arthur Johnston, "*The Water-Babies*: Kingsley's Debt to Darwin", *English* vol. XII, no. 72 (Autumn, 1959), pp. 215-219. See p. 218.

28 Kingsley, op. cit., p. 226.

29 Baldassar Castiglione, *Il Libro del Cortegiano* (Milan: Giovanni Silvestri, 1822), p. 457.

30 Kingsley, op. cit., p. 226.

31 Stephen Gilbert, *The Landslide* (Richmond: Valancourt, 2013), p. 42.

32 Autobiography, op. cit., vol. I, p. 35.

33 From 1922 until 1925 Gilbert was a boarder at The Leas in Hoylake, a seaside town near Merseyside in the North-West of England. From 1925 until 1930 he attended Loretto in Musselburgh, near Edinburgh. In his autobiography, Gilbert comments on his mother's intentions in sending him to public school: "All the sacrifices have been made so that I can be a minister. Mummy sees me as a minister who will speak properly, without any accent. All the other Presbyterian ministers speak with Ulster accents, or Scottish accents. But I shall speak like a gentleman. I am her gift to the Lord, another infant Samuel." Ibid., vol. I, p. 305.

34 Autobiography, op. cit., vol. IV, p. 201.

MONKEYFACE

To

TOPSY

with all my love

I

The cage or run was built on the sunny side of a large suburban house on the outskirts of Belfast. It was twelve feet high, eighteen feet long, nine feet wide; and very strongly made. From one of the bars across the top hung a trapeze; from another a pair of leather-covered rungs, each about seven inches in diameter. One of the windows of the house opened into the cage, but the sashes had been taken out and replaced by a square, sliding steel door. At the other end of the cage was a narrow barred gate, secured by a heavy bolt and padlock. Above this second door a piece of black board had been attached to the bars. Printed on it, in white letters, was a single word:

BIMBO

It was early on an April morning and so far only one patch of sunlight had reached the cage. In this patch the occupant was sitting. He was in a crouching position on a small, low, wooden platform, or stool, about two feet square.

The interest of a zoologist would at once have been aroused by the appearance of the specimen. At first glance he would have classified it roughly as one of the higher apes, and he would have recognized immediately that it was neither an orang-utang nor a gibbon. The calm expression and broad mouth would have reminded him of a chimpanzee, but the jaw was too narrow for a chimpanzee's. No; it couldn't be either a chimpanzee or a gorilla. The creature had a bridge to its nose, quite a definite chin, and the forehead rose up practically straight above the eyes. It was a good forehead. The facial angle was high, higher, surely, than had ever been found in any human race except perhaps the ancient Greeks. And then the top of the head. . . . The cranial index must also be very good. But the creature was an ape. It *must* be, with its puckered brown face and that black hair which covered its head so closely, and completely surrounded its cheeks and ears. The ears were large and stuck out like cherubs' wings. The hair which covered most of the animal's body was black also, but longer than that on the head. It was thickest on the legs and back, thinner on the chest and stomach. There, of course, it might develop later, for obviously the animal was young. Perhaps it was an indication that the creature was a quadruped, the hair growing thickest on the parts most commonly exposed. The hands were naked, and though more clumsy in appearance than those of a human being, were better formed than those of any ape. Could it be an example of that hitherto doubtful species the "Koola-Kamba"?

However, no scientist was present to engage the creature's attention. It meditated by itself, and though its lips moved slightly, the meditation was silent. Apparently it was also amusing. The brown eyes were bright, and every now and then the mouth would remain still for a few seconds in a broad grin.

Gradually the patch of sunlight extended till it filled the cage. The animal became restless. Once or twice it peered round as if expecting something. Then it moved from the stool and stood looking across the cage. It stood on all fours, with its two back feet palms downward on the ground. The hands were clenched; that is to say in front it stood upon its knuckles. The head was raised: the creature was looking at the trapeze. It was clear now that the arms were considerably longer than the legs: for the back sloped downwards from the head to the tail, which rose straight into the air and curved over at the top.

For perhaps fifteen seconds Bimbo remained in this position: at the end of that time he took two slow steps forward with his back legs, and raised himself upright. His hands left the ground and he spread out his arms and lifted them slightly above his head to keep his balance. For a moment he was again stationary; then he waddled awkwardly towards the trapeze. The instant he grasped this his awkwardness ceased. He swung himself up and the most violent acrobatics began. During the next five minutes he was as much in the air as at any point in the cage. Suddenly this activity ended. Bimbo returned to his stool and sat there in the same attitude as before; but he was listening.

A shabby looking man in shirt-sleeves and leggings came round the corner of the house. He was unshaven, and his face, though cheerful, was hollow and rather dissolute looking. His teeth were bad. He was tall, lanky, and slightly stooped. He carried a brush, and a bucket containing a small coal shovel. He smiled at Bimbo and, putting down the bucket, unlocked and opened the gate.

"Good mornin' ye young blackamoor", he called to Bimbo, and added sympathetically, "Poor wee feller."

It was his daily greeting, and hitherto for several years it had been received in silence. Now, unexpectedly, when he had picked up his bucket, brush and shovel, and was entering the cage, there came a reply.

"Gugmawm yungbackma. Poufufla."

The man swore. The bucket and shovel fell with a clatter and at the same time Bimbo sprang with a grin of delight to the man's shoulder and folded one arm affectionately round his neck. To this at least the man was accustomed and he recovered himself. "What was that ye were sayin'?" he demanded, picking up again the things he had dropped.

"Zat yawasayan?" Bimbo repeated.

"Holy Jesus!" the man exclaimed. "What's come over ye this mornin'? Turned into a bloody parrot have ye?"

But this was too difficult and Bimbo did not repeat it.

As usual he helped to tidy up his cage. He enjoyed working and he liked this man better than anyone else. When the cage was finished—it was never very untidy—the man went away. Presently he returned bringing Bimbo's breakfast. This was a bowl of porridge, with a wooden spoon sticking into it, a mug of milk, and an orange. All these Bimbo ate most politely—just like a human being: he had very good manners.

When he had finished he sat quite still in the sun with his eyes half shut, and reflected on his little joke. He had played similar jokes before, sometimes with birds and once or twice with a dog. Always the victims were surprised and startled, and one of the dogs had been annoyed. It was amusing, but it required a lot of practice in private to make it successful. If the victim heard him practising the surprise was lost, and by the time the imitation was correct the hearer was accustomed to it.

But the man hadn't heard him practising: he had practised in secret. There was another man who had quite a different cry, but

Bimbo didn't like him and didn't see him often: so he had never tried to imitate him.

This morning, however, shortly after Bimbo had finished his breakfast the other man appeared outside the cage. He had a smooth face, with a large, soft, brown moustache. His eyes also were brown and rather lifeless. He was very clean. "Well, Dolan," he said, "can you make him do it again?"

Dolan scratched his head. "Ah don't know as ah can, Sir. Ah'll do me best. Here, Bimbo, say to the master what ye was sayin' to me."

There was no response.

"Perhaps," the better-dressed man suggested, "he'd repeat it after you."

Dolan looked uncomfortable. "It sounds a bit foolish, Sir, when you come to think of it."

"Never mind." This was said in a slightly patronizing tone.

Dolan made an effort. "Good mornin' ye young blackamoor," he repeated woodenly. "Poor wee feller."

Bimbo understood. He was pleased. "Gugmawm yungbackma. Poo oofla." He thought he'd got it rather better this time.

"Extraordinary," the well-dressed man exclaimed. "Most remarkable." Yet he didn't really sound interested and added almost immediately: "I must catch my train—and don't forget what I told you to do, Dolan. You haven't time to spend all morning fooling round with that monkey, remember."

Dolan made no answer, but he watched his employer hurrying down the drive towards the gate. His expression was unfriendly. "Mister Browne," he said, "Mister Browne, solicitor. I'd like to see the mug as'd take his troubles to you for sympathy." Mr. Browne, however, was out of earshot and Dolan turned to Bimbo. "I'd sooner take them to you, me old sparrin' partner." He opened the cage and went in. Bimbo jumped to his shoulder again and began to lick his ear, which certainly seemed to be in need of some such attention.

2

Mr. Browne was hardly out of sight when a woman's head and shoulders appeared from an upstairs window above the cage.

"Is it talkin' he is this mornin'?" she demanded.

"Who told *you* he was talkin'?" Dolan asked, looking up.

"Sure wasn't I in the room here?" Mrs. O'Neill answered. "And haven't I ears in me head? How'd I help hearin'?"

"You'd think the master might ha' stayed a wee while," Dolan remarked a little regretfully. "It isn't every morning ye'd hear an ape beginnin' to talk."

"Och him!" Mrs. O'Neill shrugged her shoulders contemptuously. "Sure he'd catch that same train if it was the day of judgment itself. If it'd been the owld master now, God rest him, he'd have been in the quair state of excitement. *He* was the boy for the animals."

"I heered tell it was the owld master as found Bimbo and brought him home," Dolan said, "but I never knew the rights of it."

"Sure, wasn't I in the house at the time?" Mrs. O'Neill responded. "Aye, and well I remember it, too. It was him indeed poor man. He was worth two of thon fellow any day. There was nothin' cowld about *him*. But he must be off again to South Americy; and when nothin's heard of a man for five years he's dead I say—unless he married one of them belly-donnas and is keepin' quiet about it."

Dolan took out a plug of tobacco and cut a piece from it. "Boy's a-dear," he murmured politely, "if that was the way of it he'd be best to keep his mouth shut, so he would."

Bimbo listened to the noises they made without understanding or particular interest. Sometimes, sitting in a corner, or swinging on the trapeze, he, too, made noises in his throat and mouth. These noises, though they varied, had no coherent meaning. They expressed his moods. When the sun shone he was happy and would croon or chuckle to himself. But on cold wet days, when he wasn't allowed out into the cage, he would sit moping in his room and utter low, throaty grumblings.

This was a sunny day and he felt happy. He sprang backwards and forwards about the cage—from the rings to the trapeze, from the trapeze to the bars—letting out an occasional yell from sheer good spirits. At times he meditated. For a long period he had lived in this cage; yet vaguely he could remember a different kind of existence. It was like another life, or a dream. Sometimes, crouching half-asleep in the sun, he would dream part of that dream again. There was a great forest where other creatures like himself, only larger, swung in the trees, or at times ran swiftly along the ground through long tunnels in the undergrowth. But he couldn't remember running himself. Always he seemed to have been a spectator, a warm and comfortable spectator, at whom every few minutes a large brown face had peered closely and lovingly. Then one day, when he was lying in a little hollow at the foot of a tree, he had seen a new creature—a creature dressed in white, who walked stiffly and erect. This creature had found him and lifted him up. He was accustomed to being lifted and at first had only gazed at the stranger in curiosity, but when the night came he had been very unhappy. He had wanted something that was missing. It was the kind brown face, the warm arms which had encircled him, and pressed him close: but they had been missing ever since.

Bimbo understood names. He knew his own name. Some people had several names. Mrs. O'Neill was sometimes called Cook. The man who had brought him here was the man who had found him in the forest; but he had disappeared long ago. He had been called "Theo" and "Dock" and "Doctor Browne" and "Sir". Mr. Browne was called "Sir", too. Dolan had only one name which was simpler.

Bimbo did not speak again until the evening. Then, unexpectedly, Mr. Browne visited the cage. He was wearing a dust coat and he carried a tin of golden syrup and a wooden spoon. Bimbo's eyes glistened when he saw the tin. Golden syrup was his favourite food. He stretched out his hand for it, but Mr. Browne wouldn't give it to him. "Not till you've earned it," he said.

Bimbo was disappointed. He looked imploringly at Mr. Browne and reached out again for the tin. Mr. Browne put the tin and the spoon outside the cage and bolted the door. "Now," he began. "Good morning you young blackamoor. Poor little fellow."

Bimbo didn't answer. His whole attention was still concentrated on the golden syrup. He squeezed his hand between the bars, and succeeded in grasping the tin, but it was too big to pull through. He drew back his hand and considered the problem. He saw that he could not get the syrup unless Mr. Browne should give it to him. He must please Mr. Browne. He looked at the man and realized that there was something he wanted.

"Good morning you young blackamoor," Mr. Browne repeated. "Poor little fellow." This time he made some attempt to reproduce the accent of Dolan.

Bimbo realized what was required: he gave his imitation and it was even more successful than before. A stranger, without having heard Mr. Browne, might quite likely have understood what he was trying to say. Mr. Browne opened the door and picked up the tin of golden syrup. Bimbo was filled with excitement. His mouth watered. Mentally he ran his tongue round the inside of the tin. Mr. Browne, however, did not give it to him. Instead he dipped in the spoon, lifted it out, let it drain somewhat, twisted it round, and only then offered it to Bimbo. Bimbo considered this miserly conduct. Nevertheless he accepted the reward.

He spent a considerable time licking the spoon, licking his face, licking every particle of hair on which a drop of syrup might have fallen. Mr. Browne was impatient: he made several grabs at the spoon, but Bimbo kept possession of it until it had been licked clean more than once. As soon as Mr. Browne got it back he returned both it and the tin to their position outside the cage.

"Up Ulster," Mr. Browne now enunciated clearly. "No Surrender."

But Bimbo had at last realized the name for golden syrup. He didn't wish to waste time on idle chatter. "Goo' mawm y-yun backma," he said, rather plaintively. "Pawlilil fella."

Mr. Browne frowned.

Bimbo frowned, too. He turned round on his stool, so that his back was to Mr. Browne, and sat very still with his hands covering his face and his knees drawn up to his chin: but every now and then he opened his fingers a little and peered out to make sure that the golden syrup was still there.

"Up Ulster," Mr. Browne said again. "Up Ulster! Up Ulster! Up Ulster!"

Bimbo began to despise him. He was like the dog next door who went on barking the same bark for hours on end when he had nothing better to do. That was the dog who had been so annoyed when Bimbo had imitated him. Bimbo decided to annoy Mr. Browne in the same way. But Mr. Browne was inside the cage: the dog had been quite safely outside.

Bimbo sprang to the trapeze. "Pulsa," he mimicked, swinging backwards and forwards. "Pulsa! Pulsa! Pulsa!" and he grinned derisively at Mr. Browne.

The result surprised him. A pleased expression came over Mr. Browne's face. "Good," he exclaimed. He turned round, unbolted the door and began to push it open: it opened outwards.

Bimbo began to laugh. It was a quick, excited laugh; and he swung the trapeze to and fro faster and faster, in a sort of delirium. Suddenly he let go, and shooting through the air passed just above Mr. Browne's head, and grasped the bars of the gate with all four paws. The gate was snatched from Mr. Browne's hands and flew back with a clang. Mr. Browne stumbled, staggered a step and fell forwards, saving himself however with his hands. Bimbo rebounded from the gate, landed on the ground, sprang to the golden syrup, seized it. . . . Half a minute later he was sitting at the top of a beech tree, which grew beside the house. He settled himself comfortably with his tail curled round one of the branches and looked down at Mr. Browne. Mr. Browne was dusting the knees of his trousers with his hands and looking up at Bimbo rather ruefully. Bimbo laughed loudly at him to make sure he heard. Then he prised the lid off the tin, licked it clean and threw it at Mr. Browne. It hit him on the cheek and bounced off on to the ground. Mr. Browne took out a handkerchief, moistened it with the tip of his tongue, and began to rub his face with the wet spot.

Bimbo gazed into the tin of syrup. Its clear, smooth, golden depth fascinated him. Very cautiously he poked a finger into it. When he drew his finger out a long streamer of syrup was attached; but immediately the syrup began to slide back into the tin, so that the streamer grew thinner and thinner. . . . Bimbo licked his finger and tasted the delightful, sweet taste he liked so much. The streamer attached itself to his chin. It was only a thread now. It broke and subsided making a little whorl on the top of the golden surface. The whorl, too, melted, vanishing away in gradually diminishing concentric rings. Bimbo slowly licked himself clean. Then he regarded the tin once more. A surge of greedy desire took possession of him. He forced four fingers into the tin and snatching them out quickly pushed his whole hand into his mouth.

It was half an hour before he was satisfied that the tin was completely empty. The tin looked rather unhappy now, he thought; besides it was a good deal battered: perhaps he had treated it rather roughly. He felt sorry for it, almost as if it had been alive, and he had robbed it of a precious possession. He also felt sorry for himself. There was an odd, mournful sensation in the pit of his stomach.

He had intended to stay in the garden, to defy Mr. Browne, to let Dolan chase him in the morning. Now he longed for his comfortable box-bed in the room in the house. He looked down and saw that the door of the cage had been left open. Another tin of golden syrup had been placed inside the cage near the steel door. The sight of this for a moment repelled him. He flung away the first tin and heard a thin rattle as it landed on the drive beside the house. He shivered and a cloying feeling of sickness welled up inside him. He climbed slowly down the tree and walked unsteadily on all fours to the door of the cage. When he reached the second tin of syrup he hesitated. Suddenly he picked it up and turned with an effort, intending to throw it out through the door of the cage. He was too late. Mr. Browne was at the door and it shut with a clang. Bimbo dropped the tin and went through the sliding iron door to his room. His bed was a large square box against the ceiling, reached by a rope which hung down beside the entrance. He climbed the rope, crawled through the doorway and curled up in the straw. He felt very sick. He didn't want anything, except to be left alone. He didn't want freedom. He didn't care.

3

In spite of this inauspicious beginning, Bimbo very soon learned to say a certain number of words, phrases and sentences. They had no meaning for him. He only knew that if he repeated them correctly he would be rewarded: but for at least a week golden syrup failed to attract him: the sight of a tin made him retire to his sleeping box and close his eyes. At the end of that time the thought of it ceased to disgust him, and gradually his old craving for it began to return.

He had a good memory: his vocabulary increased rapidly and at the same time his pronunciation improved a little: it was not good yet: he reproduced rather the sound of a sentence, and the accent of the speaker than the words themselves.

Bimbo always knew the time. He measured it not by minutes, seconds and hours, but by the regular happenings of his daily life—chiefly the comings and goings of Dolan. He was therefore surprised one evening when going-home time came and Dolan showed no signs of departing. Coming-in-the-morning time had often varied considerably, but going-home time had hitherto been as regular as could be.

Bimbo went to the edge of the cage and looked at Dolan. After such a breach of routine anything might happen. Dolan, it is true, was not actually working, but there was nothing unusual in that. He often didn't work for hours at a stretch. Now, however, he turned the wheelbarrow upside down, sat on it and lit a pipe. There was something definite about this which was unnatural.

Bimbo waited. So uneventful was his life that he had patience enough to wait for hours if there was the slightest prospect of any unusual occurrence. He wondered if Dolan had forgotten to go home. Perhaps he was dreaming and hadn't noticed the afternoon slipping away. That sometimes happened to Bimbo himself, though as soon as he thought again he always knew exactly what time it was. He considered banging on the bars to attract Dolan's attention, but instead he kept particularly quiet. He was afraid of doing anything which might interfere with whatever was going to happen. He sat down in the sunniest part of the cage and watched Dolan. Dolan continued to smoke peacefully with slow, gentle, economical puffs. He was never a quick smoker. At the end of half an hour he took his pipe out of his mouth, spat for the seventh time, and stood up. He felt in his pocket and brought out a small wad of brown paper, which he pushed into the bowl of his pipe.

Then he put the pipe into his pocket, and walked round the corner of the house. Bimbo knew he hadn't gone home for he could see part of the drive down which Dolan would have to pass.

During the next hour and a half only one thought occupied Bimbo's mind. What *was* Dolan doing? When Dolan returned it was clear that he had been doing something—a good deal in fact. He was wearing a neat, though rather shiny, blue serge suit, a collar, a knitted woollen tie, brown shoes, and a bowler hat. He had evidently both washed and shaved. He came over to the cage and peered in at Bimbo rather sheepishly. Bimbo sniffed through the bars. He smelt soap, but though that smell was strong, it was clearly only superficial. From beneath this foreign scent came the old familiar smell of Dolan's body. Bimbo felt reassured.

"We're givin' a party," Dolan whispered, and he nodded in the direction of the drive. "Here's the first o' them."

The nod made Bimbo look. He saw a man and a woman approaching the house. It occurred to him, as it had occurred to him once or twice before, that perhaps *all* sounds had a meaning. He understood Bimbo, Mister Browne, Cook, Dolan. . . . Perhaps everything had a particular sound, or several sounds of its own. He considered this for a little. Suddenly an idea came to him. His face lit up for a moment: then he frowned and thought hard again.

"Dolan!" he called.

Dolan looked round. He was surprised, yet getting accustomed to surprises. "What yer want *now*?" he demanded, in a rough, but not unfriendly voice.

Bimbo picked up the enamel bowl in which he received most of his meals. "Gub?" he inquired. "Gub?"

Dolan stared at him for an instant. "Sure didn't ah give ye yer grub?" he said. "You won't get any more till breakfast. Don't you know that? Don't ye be gettin' too greedy now."

Bimbo gave a little sigh. The experiment had failed. He wondered how he could make Dolan understand what he wanted.

Dolan meanwhile was showing signs of impatience. "Here's more o' them," he announced, with a peculiar effect of irony. "Ut's them Miss Suttons as keep the school." But Bimbo had already noticed these three ladies coming up the drive together. One of them impressed him particularly. She was neither young nor quite old enough to be described as middle-aged, but something in her expression seemed to set a chord vibrating in Bimbo's stomach. He experienced an odd feeling of joy mixed with sadness. The strange thing was that she wasn't really near enough for him to see her face clearly—and in a minute she was out of sight round the corner of the house. Yet he knew why her appearance had given him that unexpected sensation. Something about her had reminded him of the face he remembered dimly, that face which had been so much part of his life in the forest long ago.

When she first came in sight he had been standing upright close to Dolan, supporting himself partly by his legs, partly by the grip of his hands on the bars. Now he dropped on to all fours and went slowly across the cage to the corner where his stool was. On this he crouched. He felt homesick, and at the same time hopeful and vaguely excited. When would she come? He knew she had come specially for *him*.

Another hour dragged by and a few more visitors came. Then there was a sound of voices. Dolan stood up, smoothed his jacket, tugged down his waistcoat, and brushed the knees of his trousers with the back of his hand. Bimbo heard Mr. Browne's voice—and the whole chattering party flowed round the corner of the house.

Bimbo was not accustomed to more than two or three people at a time. The first sight of Mr. Browne, with his guests, frightened him a little. He saw them as one creature—an exaggerated Mr. Browne—a fat, many-legged insect-like body—creeping towards him. He felt an inclination to run inside, climb the rope, and bury himself in the straw of his sleeping box. But he didn't run. He remembered that he was protected by the bars of his cage, that Dolan was close beside him. He looked at the visitors again, saw that they were separate individuals, and that Mr. Browne was really quite thin. The lady who had impressed him before was hanging back a little from the others. He was able to study her more particularly now. She was a big, brown-eyed, sallow-faced woman, with a rather weary air, as if she found it a trouble to drag herself about. Bimbo caught her eye for an instant. She seemed sympathetic and a little sad. Suddenly her expression altered: she looked startled, almost horrified. Deliberately she turned away.

"Here he is," Mr. Browne was saying. "It's the warmest side of the house. My brother, poor chap, insisted on having him here. Dolan, I think you'd better go in first. Seeing so many people at once may upset him, and he's more accustomed to you."

"Yes, Sir."

Dolan opened the door and entered the cage, but Bimbo didn't look at him. His eyes were still fixed on the sallow-faced lady. He would make her look again. After a moment she did look, and this time she gave him a rather troubled smile.

"He seems to have picked you out, Martha," an older lady said. "You'd better go to the front and let him see you better."

There was a laugh, and the sallow-faced lady came forward with a sort of hesitating deliberation. Mr. Browne, however, had noticed nothing. "Make him speak," he ordered Dolan. "Anything will do to start him. I've got the golden syrup."

But Bimbo spoke of his own accord. He again picked up the bowl. "Gub?" he asked.

"Gub?" Mr. Browne inquired. "Now what can he mean by that?"

"I think he's tryin' to say 'grub', sir," Dolan replied. "He seems hungry the night."

"All the better." Mr. Browne gave a rather hard smile. "He'll be more anxious to talk and get his reward. Say something to him, your old greeting will do very well."

But words seemed to have forsaken Dolan. He moved about uneasily and at last he managed only a faint "Good mornin'."

Bimbo paid no attention. He touched the bowl and looked at his new friend inquiringly. "Gub," he said, with great emphasis.

"Yes, Gub," Mr. Browne took him up, "but you'll have to earn it first. Up Ulster."

Bimbo gave a last, pleading look at the sallow-faced woman, but she seemed puzzled or undecided. "I don't believe. . . ." she began; then frowned and stopped.

Bimbo put down the bowl slowly. "Pulsta," he repeated sulkily.

"That's better," Mr. Browne commented, with guarded approval. "Not an inch!"

"Tinince," Bimbo muttered languidly.

The guests expressed surprise and applauded. Mr. Browne entered the cage and administered a spoonful of golden syrup.

"He doesn't seem quite himself the night," Dolan whispered.

"He'll *have* to be himself," Mr. Browne answered in an undertone, adding deliberately and aloud, "What we have, we hold."

"Vodvavole," Bimbo gabbled perfunctorily, without making the slightest effort to be exact.

"This is *very* bad," Mr. Browne said. "He'll have to do better than that. We're not going to have any sulking here. WHAT WE HAVE. . . ."

An oldish man in spectacles interrupted him. "I think it's very good," he declared. "Most amazing, really, when you come to think of it. Almost a proof of the theory of evolution—the missing link you might. . . ."

"Not good at all," Mr. Browne retorted. "He can do far better than this. Come on, or you'll get no more." So far he had kept the tin behind him. Now, while Bimbo still sucked the spoon, he raised it cautiously above his head, "WHAT WE. . . ." he was beginning for the third time, when he received a most unpleasant surprise. Bimbo sprang at him, hit his knuckles a sharp rap with the spoon, grabbed the tin, and retreated, growling, into a corner of the cage by himself.

Mr. Browne said something. It wasn't clear exactly what he said, because at the same moment he put his fingers to his mouth and began to suck them.

A young man laughed. "Hardly your round," he called out cheerfully. "You'd better go to your corner, the way he has, and let your seconds do some repairs."

For a moment Mr. Browne glared. Then he smiled faintly at his visitors. "I'm afraid we haven't had sufficient rehearsals," he remarked. "Dolan! Get hold of that spoon, and the tin before he can open it."

"I don't know as it'll be that easy," Dolan answered uncomfortably. "He mightn't be wantin' to give it up."

"Whether he wants to or not, take it *from* him," Mr. Browne ordered.

Dolan hesitated and suddenly the sallow-faced lady spoke. "I don't know, but—I hope you won't think it very presumptuous of me—but I think I know what he wants. If you'll let me. . . ." and without waiting for anyone's permission she unbolted the door and went into the cage.

"Be careful, Miss Martha," the young man called warningly. "He may be dangerous. You never can tell. These apes and monkeys, they're very uncertain you know, and a bite. . . ."

But Miss Martha paid no attention. She crossed the cage and squatted down in front of Bimbo. Bimbo stopped growling and looked at her. His bad temper vanished. Perhaps things were going to turn out right after all.

Miss Martha pointed to the tin which he he held clutched in his arms. "Tin," she said emphatically.

Bimbo held up the tin. "Ting?" he questioned.

Miss Martha smiled at him. "Tin," she repeated.

Bimbo felt pleased, but not quite certain. He looked round quickly, and once more picked up the enamel bowl. "Gub?"

Miss Martha shook her head and gave a little frown. "Bowl," she told him.

"Bo'?"

Miss Martha smiled again. "Bowl," she answered.

Bimbo put his finger in his mouth and considered. He held up the spoon and looked at her inquiringly.

"Spoon," she told him.

"Poon?" he repeated.

"Spoon," she agreed.

Bimbo was delighted. Now he understood. He would only have to listen and watch and soon he would find out the meaning of every noise—the dripping of rain, the barking of dogs, the songs of birds. But a doubt crossed his mind, perhaps she was just imitating him or making noises at random. He would test her. He leaped across the cage and clutched Mr. Browne by the arm. Again he looked at her and waited.

"Mr. Browne," she said, after a little pause.

That proved it at any rate: now he was certain. "Miss Bowng, Sah, Zimmassa."

She nodded her head. "Mr. Browne, Sir, The Master."

One question remained. He pointed at *her*. She hesitated a moment. "Miss Martha," she told him, and at the same instant stood up.

"Meessimafa," he called, and sprang right on to her shoulder. He pressed his nose for a moment against her cheek. With another spring he was on the trapeze. From there he went to the rings and began to swing himself backwards and forwards.

Mr. Browne picked up the tin of syrup and the spoon. "That seems to be all," he remarked drily. "I can't say the entertainment went exactly as I expected. Still. . . ."

"Still it was very good," a tall man in black took him up, "and I must say, Miss Sutton—Miss Martha—is to be congratulated on *her* part."

Miss Martha looked slightly embarrassed. She turned to Dolan. "Have you never tried to teach him the names of things? He could learn to talk properly, you know. I believe he'd learn very quickly."

Dolan put up his hand as if to touch his cap, but instead he scratched his head. "No, Ma'am. Can't say we have. It was all 'No Surrender' and 'To. . . .'" He looked at the man in black, stopped, and grinned. "We was makin' a loyalist of him first. Ah was gettin' him primed for *The Twalth.*"

"Well," Mr. Browne said, holding open the door of the cage for Miss Martha, "it's getting rather chilly. I vote we go inside."

He led the way and his visitors followed. Only Miss Martha lingered by the cage. "I'll be back," she whispered to Bimbo, and somehow he understood.

4

On the morning after the party Miss Martha returned alone. Bimbo had been expecting her, but the moment he saw her on the drive his excitement became extreme. He expressed his delight by leaping from side to side of the cage and hanging upside down from the roofbars. Finally, when she actually came in, he hurled himself from the trapeze to her shoulder with such force that she nearly overbalanced. Dolan, who was following her, reproved Bimbo. "Get down out o' that, ye young rascal," he shouted.

"It's all right," Miss Martha said. "I'm not made of china," and she returned Bimbo's hug and stroked him.

"He doesn't know any better," Dolan apologized.

"I hope he's soon going to know all sorts of things," Miss Martha responded. "At any rate I'm going to see how much I can teach him. We'll find out first if he remembers what he learned last night."

The syrup tin, the wooden spoon and the enamel bowl still remained in the cage. Miss Martha put Bimbo down and began by calling out the names she had told him. After a moment Bimbo realized what she wanted. In turn he picked up the tin, the spoon and the bowl, and handed them to her. Next she named everything else she could see. When she repeated the names Bimbo was able to pick out the objects she mentioned. He made no mistakes. It didn't even occur to him that he should. His memory was perfect. This part of the lesson presented no difficulty whatever.

Presently Miss Martha turned to Dolan. "Look here, Dolan," she began, "we've mastered nouns: the next thing is verbs."

"Verbs, ma'am?" Dolan said, with a puzzled expression. "How d'you mean, ma'am?"

Miss Martha did not trouble to explain. "When I say 'go'," she told him, "I want you to walk slowly away from me across the cage. When I say 'stop' you must stop, and so on. Do everything I tell you and nothing more, and do it slowly."

Dolan sighed. "Yes, ma'am."

"Dolan!"

Dolan was startled. "Yes, ma'am?"

"Go."

Dolan began a funereal march towards the opposite side of the cage.

"Stop!" Miss Martha called peremptorily.

Dolan came to a shuffling standstill. "You gave it on the wrong foot, Miss," he objected. "An' could you not say 'Halt!'—I'm more used to it that way. It's the trainin', ye see."

"No," Miss Martha answered firmly. "I could not. I'm not teaching you drill."

"No, ma'am," Dolan agreed a little derisively. "Ye is not. I don't suppose ye knows how."

"Turn," Miss Martha ordered.

Dolan about-turned in military fashion and winked at Bimbo. Bimbo understood winking, but this wink he thought it better to ignore.

"Come," Miss Martha commanded. . . .

"Now, Bimbo," she said, a moment later, "it's *your* turn."

Bimbo looked at her interrogatively.

"Bimbo!"

Bimbo hesitated and stood up.

"Go."

Again he hesitated. Then he began a slow march, as like Dolan's as he could make it. But he found it a little difficult to keep his balance with his hands by his sides instead of on the ground in front of him. Little by little he raised his arms till they were held above his head. He did this partly to help his balance, partly from a subconscious expectation that he would find branches there to give him support.

After this Miss Martha came to see him two or three times a week, and he progressed rapidly—in one direction at least. He began to understand what he heard. It was much more difficult to make people understand what he himself said. He learned most, not directly from Miss Martha, but as any ordinary child learns—by listening to what people said and watching what they did. As, however, he had fewer opportunities of hearing conversation than ordinary children his learning was deliberate and concentrated, rather than unconscious and haphazard. Very often, of course, he found that people talked without doing anything. This puzzled him at first, but gradually he came to comprehend the idea of abstract conversation, though he didn't know always what such conversation actually meant.

At this time he was very happy. On the whole he had been contented enough before, but it seemed as if he had been living in a dream, when the most enchanting reality was waiting for him to open his eyes, to reach out and take possession of it.

One sunny afternoon Miss Martha suddenly decided that she would give Bimbo his lesson in the garden. "There's no sense in keeping him cooped up in this horrid cage all the time," she told Dolan. "D'you think you could find us some chairs and we'll sit on the lawn."

Dolan hesitated. "I doubt the Master won't like it," he said.

"Nonsense," Miss Martha answered. "Why shouldn't he like it?"

"He'd be sayin' Bimbo'd escape."

"Nonsense," Miss Martha repeated, resting her hand for an instant on Bimbo's head. "You won't run away, will you, pet?"

Bimbo had very little idea what she meant by running away. Nevertheless, he guessed from her tone and the form of the sentence the sort of answer she required, and responded at once, "No, Bimbo 'on't 'un 'ay."

Dolan went to see Cook and presently reappeared with a deckchair for Miss Martha and a kitchen chair for Bimbo. He carried them on to the lawn and settled down to weed a nearby flowerbed, while Miss Martha gave Bimbo his lesson. There Mr. Browne found them when he returned from the office rather earlier than usual. It was obvious at once that he disapproved, but instead of complaining to Miss Martha, he tackled Dolan.

He had not got very far when Miss Martha interrupted him. "You needn't blame Dolan," she said. "It's my fault. He told me you wouldn't be pleased, but it's all nonsense to say Bimbo'll try to escape. If he'd wanted to he could have been away hours ago."

"It's the principle of the thing I'm thinking of," Mr. Browne replied rather crossly.

"It's the principle *I'm* thinking of, too," Miss Martha returned. "There's no reason at all why he shouldn't be allowed out the whole time. It would do him no end of good and he'd be far happier."

For a long time they argued, while Bimbo and Dolan continued their previous occupations. Bimbo's occupation was merely to sit on a chair with his feet dangling down in front of him. Nevertheless he found it required considerable effort. Miss Martha had told him that this was the correct way to sit, the human way. Only tailors sat with their legs tucked in below them. Bimbo found the tailors' way the most natural, and he had a constant inclination to adopt it. So he didn't pay much attention to what Mr. Browne and Miss Martha were saying, though he noticed from the very beginning that Miss Martha was getting the best of the argument. Dolan probably did pay attention, though he pretended to be engrossed in his weeding.

In the end Miss Martha gained a complete victory. Bimbo was to be allowed out all day whether she was there or not. Mr. Browne gave in grumblingly, making only one proviso. "In that case he can clean his *own* cage and bring his *own* food from the kitchen. It'll be one less excuse for Dolan."

Bimbo didn't understand what this meant, and when Mr. Browne and Miss Martha had gone he questioned Dolan about it. Dolan's reply was not very helpful. He said that Mr. Browne was a slave-driver and it was the last straw which broke the camel's back.

Bimbo realized that a slave-driver was Mr. Browne, though he thought it odd that he should have so many names, but he didn't know what a camel was, unless of course it was a new name for Dolan.

"Wots kammel?" he asked Dolan.

"It's an animal with a hump on its back," Dolan told him. "I've got the hump, too," he added, "but only sometimes."

This didn't make Mr. Browne's meaning any clearer: so the next time Miss Martha came Bimbo asked *her* for an explanation; but she was even less satisfactory than Dolan, for she told him not to worry about it, and that it didn't matter. Instead she began to show him some picture books she had brought with her. They had pictures not only of camels, but of all sorts of animals and trees, and of people in foreign lands. Bimbo had never seen a book of any kind before and for the next week he spent all his time turning over the pages and gazing at them in wonderment. There was one book which interested him particularly. It showed monkeys dressed up in clothes, riding bicycles, driving about in traps, and sliding down water-shoots—monkeys wearing spectacles and reading books, monkeys sitting at tables and eating meals, monkey babies in perambulators. . . .

It was a comic picture-book, but Bimbo didn't know this. He asked Miss Martha where the country was where these monkeys lived.

"There's no such place," she said bluntly. "I don't know that it wasn't a mistake to show you all this."

Bimbo was puzzled. "'Ere were 'ey?" he asked. He knew how the words should sound, but it was terribly difficult to reproduce them correctly. "Hair were 'ey?" was the best he could manage, and this only at the third attempt.

Fortunately Miss Martha was very clever at understanding. "They never were anywhere," she answered. "So don't worry any more about it. I'll explain it all some day. Now go and find Dolan. I want to speak to him." Dolan never seemed to mind leaving what he was doing. He came slowly, but readily.

"Is there such a thing as a blackboard and a piece of chalk about the place?" Miss Martha demanded.

"I'll ask Cook, ma'am," Dolan said, beginning, very gradually, to move away.

"You needn't," Miss Martha told him. "I'm sure there isn't. Why would there be? Do you think Mr. Browne would object if I sent you round to the school to get one?"

It was a hot day and Dolan moved into the shade to consider. "I don't know," he answered finally. "Ye'd never tell what he wouldn't object to."

"I know, then," Miss Martha decided. "You pass the school on your way here."

"I do sometimes," Dolan conceded reluctantly.

"You pass it every day," Miss Martha told him. "You can call in to-morrow morning and I'll have a blackboard and easel ready for you. That'll save a lot of trouble."

Dolan seemed doubtful about this. He scratched his head two or three times, but Miss Martha looked at him sternly and informed him he could go back to his work.

So the next morning the blackboard was there and Bimbo was taught the alphabet. Miss Martha came again in the afternoon, and before she went away Bimbo was able to point at the different letters when she named them. He was able also to repeat the alphabet in a fashion though he stumbled over the pronunciation of G, H, J, Q, R, U, W, X, and Y. His own attempts to draw the letters with the chalk were clumsy; and however much he tried there was never room for more than four letters on the blackboard at once—and it was a big blackboard.

"Now," Miss Martha said, "it'll be no time till you're able to read and then, I hope, you can come to school."

This was the second time she had mentioned the word "School" and Bimbo asked her what it meant. She explained and added that her sister, Miss Sutton, kept a school. "There are a whole lot of us," she said, "and we all teach in it. I'm hoping to arrange that you can come next term."

"I teaks?" Bimbo asked, for he felt that he would like to help Miss Martha.

"I'm afraid you don't know enough yet," she told him.

"Ssoon I weel," Bimbo replied.

"I hope so. I'm going to leave two or three reading books with you when I go on my holidays, and I hope you'll be able to read them all through when I get back."

Bimbo felt confident that he would.

5

On the afternoon of the 24th of August Bimbo was sitting on a high branch of the chestnut tree near the gate when he saw Miss Martha coming along the road below him. She was walking very fast, with long energetic strides like a man's. It was a warm day, and she looked hot, excited and pleased.

"Mees Marfa!" Bimbo called. She glanced up and waved, and immediately he came hurtling down the tree, and tore along to the gate to wait for her; for he was still forbidden to leave the garden.

"I've done it," she exclaimed, as soon as she reached him. "I've wangled it. I've persuaded him. You're to be allowed to come."

"Oo?" Bimbo said, and then suddenly guessing, "To skoole?"

"Yes, to school," she told him. "Mr. Browne's agreed. I was with him in his office half the morning, but you'll have to be very good, remember—very, very good indeed."

"Oh yess, Meess Marfa!" Bimbo replied promptly. He felt overcome with joy and clutched her hand. In this way they walked up the drive together towards the house.

Bimbo had never spoken to any children; yet he had made up for himself a curious, muddled picture of what school must be like. It was based partly on what Miss Martha had told him, partly on the occasional glimpses he had of boys and girls passing along the road outside, and partly on Dolan's stories of his own life at school.

As his hope of going to school had diminished, his imaginary school had been more and more idealized—and now the dream was going to become real. Once or twice he gave Miss Martha's hand a little squeeze. When they had almost reached the house he tugged her to one side and led the way down a narrow path towards the kitchen garden.

"Where are we going?" she asked.

"We go tell Dolan," he answered.

School was to begin on the 3rd of September, and Miss Martha spent the few days that remained of the holidays in buying clothes for Bimbo.

His shoes had to be specially made, and they did not arrive until the last day. Both Miss Martha and Dolan were present when he tried them on. After watching Bimbo walk up and down in them, Dolan turned to Miss Martha. "Must be costin' ye a fair bit, Miss," he remarked, in a tone which was familiar, though not disrespectful.

"Not a penny," she returned cheerfully. "I'm making *him* pay for everything." She glanced in the direction of the house, and though Mr. Browne was out, it was quite obvious to whom she referred.

"You're a good 'un, then," Dolan told her. "It's more'n I could do."

Mr. Browne was never present during Miss Martha's visits. His interest in Bimbo seemed to get less and less. But the day before school began, when Bimbo had been shut up in his cage for the night, he came and stared through the bars. He remained only a few minutes: he frowned, but did not speak. Finally he shook his head disapprovingly and turned away.

Next morning Dolan arrived a little earlier than usual. He at once unlocked the cage and handed Bimbo a small, flat, square, brown paper parcel. "That's a wee present for ye," he said. "It'll help ye in puttin' on yerself." And he went away to open the lights in the greenhouse, and water some plants in a shady border before the sun could get at them.

Bimbo loved parcels and this present from Dolan added to his excitement. He felt inclined to tear off the paper and string immediately, but he remembered that there was still an hour and a half to wait before it would be time to start for school. So instead he carried it carefully inside and put it down on the floor. He found it difficult to undo the string, for his fingers were clumsy, but eventually he succeeded and folding back the paper lifted out the present. At first it puzzled him: it was just a flat, wooden square, but when he turned it over he found that it was a little glass window, through which another Bimbo stared out at him. For a moment he thought that the other Bimbo must be looking up at him through a hole in the floor, but when he pushed the mirror aside there was nothing underneath. Then he understood. He had seen his own reflection before—in a spoon, in the tin plate which was sometimes used for his dinner, in a rain puddle on the drive—but never so clearly as this. For half an hour he played with the mirror, making faces at it, looking into it at the sun and the garden.

When Dolan returned to take him to school Bimbo did not know how to thank him. Miss Martha had taught him to say "Please" and "Thank you", but they did not seem sufficient. He said both words several times, touched the mirror and Dolan, and said, "Nice window, nice Dolan."

Dolan's face showed only the faintest sign of pleasure. "Are ye not dressed yet?" he asked gruffly. "Did ye look at yerself in the wee glass at all. Yer jersey's on back to front. Take it off and put it on right."

Bimbo obeyed and they set off together.

It was one of those bright, clear, autumn mornings which seem like spring mornings, except that the foliage on the trees is dark, and heavy, and tired. For some distance Bimbo and Dolan walked without speaking. The road was empty and Bimbo had no more questions to ask about school. He was absorbed completely in contemplating the school he had created in his own imagination, filled with an inward excitement, which grew with every step they took. Almost unconsciously he began to lean forward, his hands coming nearer and nearer to the ground.

Dolan's voice startled him unpleasantly. "What are ye doin'?" Dolan demanded sharply. "Ye've got to walk straight now, remember. Yer crawlin' days is over."

Bimbo pulled himself up guiltily, and fixed his attention on the external world. Almost immediately he heard a rattle and jingle of cans, the beat of a horse's hooves: the milk cart swept into view in front of them.

Dolan and the milkman were old acquaintances, but the milkman had never seen Bimbo before, though Bimbo had seen *him.* Now he pulled hard on the reins, and as the horse slowed down, he, and the two little milkboys, stared at Bimbo with frank, friendly curiosity.

"Good morning, Billy," the milkman called cheerfully, leaning over the side of the cart. He had a whip in one hand and the reins in the other.

Dolan scowled at him. "Mornin', Jack," he replied shortly. Bimbo lifted his new school-cap, as Miss Martha had said he should do when he met friends.

The milkman gave Dolan a peculiar smile. "Changed yer job, have ye?" he asked. "Workin' for Bertram Mills now, are ye?"

"Looks like it, doesn't it?" Dolan answered sourly, and the milkboys laughed. The milkman whipped up his horse and drove on.

To Bimbo the whole incident was completely inexplicable. Presently, however, a possible solution occurred to him. "Ol' woon' toublin'?" he inquired sympathetically.

"No."

"Tummick?"

"Ah tell ye there's nothin' the matter with me," Dolan told him gruffly. He began to walk more slowly than ever, till Bimbo could control his impatience no longer.

He took Dolan's hand and attempted to tug him gently forward, but it was no good. So he decided to try persuasion. "Run?" he suggested. "'E run?"

"Quit yer hurry," Dolan retorted. "Yer in plenty of time an' ye'll get yer fill of school soon enough."

"Skoole fah?" Bimbo asked.

Dolan shook his head. "No," he said, "but it's a brave wee step all the same."

This was hardly satisfactory, and Bimbo was meditating a further question when fortunately for Dolan they came to the end of Beechwood—which was the name of the road where Bimbo and Mr. Browne lived—and turned to the right. They were now on Belmore Road.

A lady and a small boy in a dark blue jersey were walking along the opposite footpath. The boy had fair hair, bleached by the sun, blue eyes, and a smooth, round, rather inquisitive face. "Is that the monkey-boy, Mammy?" Bimbo heard him ask. He noticed, too, that on the boy's back was a new schoolbag. Bimbo also had a schoolbag, though there was nothing in it yet, except a pair of slippers, which, like the shoes, had been specially made for him.

"Yes, dear," the mother whispered. "Hush!"

Dolan touched his forehead. "Mornin', ma'am," he said sheepishly. Bimbo again lifted his cap politely. The fair-haired boy wasn't wearing a cap, but he gave Bimbo a little, curious, friendly smile. Bimbo grinned.

"Ooee go 'it' 'em, talk?" Bimbo suggested, but Dolan shook his head silently and kept to his own side of the road.

Soon they reached a cross-roads where there was a grey stone church. Here they encountered other children in charge of mothers, nurses and governesses. One little girl asked, "Mummy, has he got a tail?"

But Bimbo didn't hear the answer. Perhaps the mother didn't know, for the tail was curled away inside Bimbo's trousers. It had been rather a problem: he had to remember to keep it still, because when he didn't it was inclined to escape and stick out. If it did escape Bimbo didn't think it would be easy to get it back again without undressing.

In another minute they came to a wooden gate: to it was screwed a brass plate with these words:

MISS SUTTON'S SCHOOL
AND KINDERGARTEN
FOR BOYS AND GIRLS

Beyond the gate was a short path leading to quite an ordinary looking house. The front door was open and Miss Martha was standing in the hall with one of her sisters.

"Mees Marfa!" Bimbo called at once, and immediately she came out and ran down the steps to meet him.

"Oh, there you are," she exclaimed. "You're in very good time. Good morning, Dolan."

"Good mornin', Miss," Dolan responded, with a sigh of relief. "Ah suppose ah could be off now."

When he had gone Miss Martha took Bimbo through the hall, which was packed with boys and girls, mothers, governesses and nurses. . . . They all stopped talking to stare at Bimbo. "Are *they* new, too?" he whispered to Miss Martha.

"Yes," she answered. "This is their first day." She lowered her voice. "Take off your cap. You always should as soon as you come into a house."

She led the way into a large bright room, where the remains of breakfast were still on the table. "Now," she told him, "you'll have to keep quiet and amuse yourself for a little. We're hardly ready for you yet," and she gave him a picture book to look at till it should be time for his first class to begin. He listened to the noises from the hall, the opening and shutting of doors, the chatter of the grown-ups, the shy voices of the new children, footsteps going to and fro. . . . Once Miss Martha came in for a book. She remained only for a moment. As she went out she said, "It's always like this on the first day—perfectly frightful, but I'll be back."

Presently Bimbo noticed that sounds were coming from outside as well as from the hall. They were cheerful sounds. He crossed to the window and looked from behind the curtains. Just below him was a path along which boys and girls were walking in twos and threes. Most of them looked happy or, at least, much happier than the new children in the hall.

A big, fat, jolly-looking girl attracted Bimbo's attention. She seemed to be telling a story to two friends who walked one on either side of her. "So I just pushed her right into the middle of it," the fat girl was saying.

"Oh, Francie, you *didn't*!" exclaimed one of the others.

"Yes I did," Francie retorted, "just like that," and she pushed her friend into a flower-bed.

Bimbo smiled. That was the sort of thing he expected to happen at school. He watched to see if there would be any more fun, but there wasn't. The children seemed a dull, orderly, well-behaved lot. They followed each other sedately and disappeared in turn through a door on the left.

Very soon the path was empty. A bell began to ring and Bimbo supposed that there was no one else to come. He was about to go back to his picture book, when he heard the sound of running footsteps. A boy with a schoolbag below his arm dashed past the window. He had dark blue eyes, black wavy hair, a freckled face and a snub nose. He rushed in, banging the door after him. Bimbo had seen him in Beechwood several times—twice on foot and once on a bicycle.

When he had gone the house became completely silent. Then, in the distance, there was a great shuffling of many feet. Suddenly there was the sound of music and singing. This lasted a few minutes, and again there was silence.

Bimbo wondered what they were all doing and he was glad when doors began to open and shut, and the whole clamour of people moving about recommenced. Miss Martha came back. "Now, Bimbo," she began, "come with me. First of all I'll show you where to put your cap." She conducted him along a passage, through a conservatory, and into another building with a corrugated iron roof. They passed the door Bimbo had seen from the window and went up two steps. "This is the boys' changing room," Miss Martha said. "You've got your slippers, haven't you?"

"'Ess," Bimbo answered and looked round. It was a small room with a skylight, but no other windows. On one side were a great many square pigeon-holes, painted green with a number over each. On the other sides were rows of black iron coat-pegs also numbered in white. Besides the door by which Bimbo had been brought in there were two others. From each of them came the subdued sound of voices.

"What you've got to remember now," Miss Martha told him, "is your number—sixty-three. Put your shoes in the pigeon-hole with sixty-three *over* it—not under it, remember—and hang your cap on peg sixty-three. Now sit down on that bench and put on your slippers."

Bimbo obeyed. As he was changing the fair-haired boy he had seen on the road came in by the door leading from the house. Miss Martha looked at him rather sternly. "Where have *you* been?" she demanded, in a tone of voice Bimbo hadn't heard before.

"Please, I got lost," the fair-haired boy replied. "I think I went with the wrong people." He looked a little frightened.

"But you were told you were in transition. Why didn't you stay with *them*?"

"I thought everyone was going out. I didn't want to be left behind."

Miss Martha accepted this explanation. "Oh, well," she said, "you can just come in with us. This is Bimbo, Bimbo Browne. Bimbo, this is Michael Barton."

Bimbo looked at Michael. He remembered that they hadn't yet spoken. "Goo' mornin'," he said.

"We met on the road," Michael informed Miss Martha, a little less timidly.

"You know each other then?"

"No."

"Oh, well, you do now," Miss Martha remarked. "Are you ready, Bimbo?"

"'Ess, Mees Marfa."

"Come along then. Miss Price will want to begin." She opened the door and Michael and Bimbo followed her. As soon as he was inside Bimbo looked round eagerly. They were in a large room lit by windows on two sides and by skylights. There was a class at each end of the room. In the one on the right were very small children indeed. They sat on low chairs in a half-circle round a mistress, who was teaching them the alphabet. They had got as far as B, but they all stopped and turned to stare. The mistress stopped, too. Bimbo thought she looked kind. So he smiled at her and said, "B for Bimbo."

In the class on the left the boys and girls were slightly bigger—about the same age as Michael probably. What they had been doing was not clear, but they also stopped to stare. However, they didn't stare for very long. The mistress in charge of them gave her desk a most frightful rap with her ruler, and frowned angrily.

"Manners! Manners!" she snapped. "Don't you know it's rude to stare?—and it's rude to me to turn away when I'm speaking to you."

Most of her class at once fixed their eyes on her attentively and fearfully, but two or three seemed quite unconcerned. One of these was the boy who had arrived late. He even put out his tongue slightly when the mistress's back was turned. Bimbo was pleased. He thought the mistress looked horrid. He put his own tongue out a little, experimentally—in sympathy.

Then it occurred to him to look at Michael. Somehow he didn't expect to see *his* tongue out, and it wasn't. On the contrary he had turned quite pale. He was gazing at the mistress with his eyes wide open and a circle of white showing all round.

But the mistress's expression had now changed. Her class subdued, she turned towards Miss Martha and smiled at her emphatically. She was blonde with a full, smooth, oval face, and large rather liquid, grey eyes. She had a prominent bosom, which was thrust out before her as she stepped away from the blackboard to greet Miss Martha. It reminded Bimbo of a picture in one of Miss Martha's books, of the figure-head of a ship thrusting through the waves.

"I'm sorry, Miss Price, if we've kept you back," Miss Martha said. "This is Bimbo, and here's Michael Barton who got lost."

Miss Price looked at Bimbo and smiled again. "Isn't he a little dear?" she exclaimed. Yet Miss Martha didn't seem altogether pleased.

Bimbo, without quite knowing why, wasn't pleased either. So he scowled at Miss Price.

"Bimbo!" Miss Martha called sharply.

"'Ess, Mees Marfa."

But instead of replying she pointed to the back of the class. I suppose they'd better sit there," she suggested. The desks were arranged to form three sides of a square, the fourth side being occupied by the blackboard. Boys sat on the right, girls on the left. The desk at the back had two girls at the left-hand end: the other half was empty.

Michael was about to sit down at the end nearest to the other boys, when Miss Martha stopped him. "No, Michael," she said. "You can sit next to the girls very well: it won't do you a pick of harm."

Michael blushed and Bimbo wondered what Miss Martha meant. Did Michael really think that the girls would do him harm? Bimbo took the seat which had been denied to Michael, and after watching him for a moment Miss Martha gave him a reassuring smile and left the room. To Bimbo's surprise Michael edged along the bench till they were sitting close together. Evidently he intended to keep as far from the girls as possible. The girls looked sideways and giggled surreptitiously.

The lesson was arithmetic—addition and subtraction. Bimbo

knew the figures up to nine, and he could count things to ten times ten which Miss Martha said was a hundred.

Miss Price began with one and one. Then one and two, and one and three, and so on until nine was reached. Next she did one and two, and two and two, and two and three, and suddenly, as a surprise, two and seven which turned out to make nine, just as Bimbo had thought it would. It was quite interesting and much easier than learning to read. Soon Miss Price had the blackboard covered with figures and Bimbo had to watch carefully to make sure he wasn't looking at the wrong sum. She wrote neatly and firmly with the chalk and he liked watching her. When she picked up the duster and began to rub it all off again he was quite sorry. It seemed such a waste.

"Now," Miss Price said, "you're going to do some sums for me," and she wrote on the board a four and a three, and drew a little line underneath like this:

4
3
—

"What do four and three make?" she asked. "Meta Hemingway, you. . . ."

"Seffen," Bimbo said.

Everyone looked at him and Miss Price dropped her chalk. "Quite right," she told him; but she seemed a little disconcerted. She frowned and added, "You mustn't answer out of turn. If you know, put up your hand, and if I want you to answer I'll call out your name. Do you understand?"

"'Ess, Mees Price," Bimbo responded. He was pleased to be getting on so well. He looked round the rest of the class and grinned. He wondered how many of them had known the right answer.

Miss Price went on with her questions. Presently she passed to subtraction and each time she asked a question Bimbo put up his hand. But he soon noticed that Miss Price only asked questions from the children who hadn't put up their hands. So he decided to play a little trick on her.

Miss Price put a big nine on the blackboard, with a five underneath and a line below as before. "Five from nine," she demanded, "leaves. . . . ?"

All the girls put up their hands, and a sharp-faced boy with spectacles and two others: but Bimbo didn't. Instead he frowned and looked puzzled. Miss Price's eyes travelled slowly round the class. Bimbo saw her smile ever so slightly when she noticed his hand wasn't up. He looked at her sadly.

"Well, Bimbo," she said, "I suppose you know as usual."

"'Ess, Meess Price," Bimbo answered truthfully.

"Tell us then, please. We're all waiting to hear."

"Four, Meess Price."

Miss Price looked disappointed and Bimbo was glad. "If you knew, why didn't you put up your hand?"

Bimbo considered a moment and decided to explain: yet it was difficult to think of the right words. Eventually they came out rather slowly. "'And up, no ask. No 'and, ask."

Miss Price flushed slightly. "What's the good of my asking if you know?" she snapped.

Bimbo thought again. It seemed to him that Miss Price was rather stupid. He decided to point it out to her. "Not know, can't tell," he explained. "Bimbo know, can tell."

Miss Price looked baffled, but after a moment's hesitation she turned and wrote again on the board. "Five from four," she said. "What's the answer to that?"

This was a masterpiece. Not even Meta Hemingway stirred. Miss Price looked round the class triumphantly, but when her eyes lit on Michael Barton she paused and stared particularly hard. She stared for quite a long time and one by one the other boys and girls looked in the same direction. Bimbo looked, too, and understood. Michael's eyes were wide open and quite still. He wasn't looking at Miss Price. He was staring straight past her at nothing at all.

Miss Price moved away from the blackboard stealthily in a half-circle. She was like a huge, malevolent cat. The class watched her with their mouths half open like so many fledgeling birds. Bimbo had a feeling that if he made the slightest movement she would pounce upon him. He made no movement and she stopped right in front of him looking at Michael. Michael didn't move either: he didn't seem to see her. Slowly she raised her ruler and suddenly, with a flash, brought it cracking down on the desk. The whole class jumped. Michael jumped highest of all. His eyes filled with tears and his face turned pink. But Bimbo was relieved: it was as if, with that bang, Miss Price had broken her own spell.

"Five from four, Michael Barton," she hissed.

Michael remained silent. Bimbo could see that he was trying not to cry, and he felt sorry for him.

"Were you not paying attention, Michael Barton?"

She swivelled round suddenly. "Hugo, if I have to speak to you again, you go straight to Miss Sutton." It was the late-comer, the dark-haired boy whom Bimbo had noticed before. He, at any rate, was unsubdued and Bimbo admired him for it.

He wouldn't be subdued either, he determined—not at least by anyone he disliked, and certainly he disliked Miss Price. He thought rapidly and whispered. "Say, 'Not go'."

Miss Price turned back slowly and comfortably, as if she had been pretending to forget her mouse for a little. "Well, Michael Barton?"

"Please, Miss Price, it won't go."

"Who prompted you?"

Michael blushed again and Bimbo wondered if he would tell.

"Was it *you*, Meta Hemingway?"

"No, Miss Price, I didn't say anything."

Miss Price glared. "Don't tell *me* lies, Meta Hemingway."

"It wasn't her," Michael mumbled.

"It wasn't she," Miss Price corrected. "Who was it, then?"

Bimbo decided to confess—not in any spirit of repentance, but just to show that he wasn't afraid. "'As I," he said.

"You?" Miss Price stared at him for a moment and Bimbo returned her stare as defiantly as he could. Miss Price marched back to the blackboard. "Well, you're wrong in any case," she told him. "You're left owing one."

6

The next class was reading. Miss Price took a pile of thin grey-backed books from the cupboard in her desk and distributed them. They were all the same, and Bimbo recognized the book at once. He knew it by heart: it was one of those Miss Martha had lent him.

He was pleased and thought: now I'll be able to show how clever I am.

"Open your books at the first page," Miss Price said, "with the picture of the pussy cat climbing the tree." All the books were opened and Miss Price looked round to make sure that every child had found the right place. Bimbo had, and he gazed at the first sentence, repeating it slowly under his breath. Miss Price's voice made him glance up with a start. "That's not the place I told you," she called sharply, and strode across the room to where Bimbo was sitting. Bimbo was surprised, but in a moment he realized that she was speaking to Michael, not to him. "That pussy's not climbing a tree," she went on. "That pussy's drinking milk."

"I thought p'raps she was going to climb the tree," Michael said softly. "There's a tree outside the window in the picture."

Miss Price snatched up Michael's book, rustled the pages, and slammed it down again in front of him. Then she returned to the blackboard.

"'Z after 'at puss d'ink milk," Bimbo whispered. "Come down t'ee after."

Miss Price frowned. "Silence!" she ordered. After a pause she continued. "We'll each read a sentence in turn round the class. I'll read the first. Pay attention everyone. 'The cat ran up the tree'."

Bimbo nudged Michael. "Eezee," he remarked. Michael reddened slightly, but pretended not to notice and went on staring at his book. Miss Price threw another fierce glance in their direction, and Hugo looked up for a moment and smiled. Bimbo grinned at him.

"Now, Helen, you read the next sentence," Miss Price said to the girl nearest to her.

"'Nan,'" Helen began slowly. "'Nan saw the cat and came out.'"

"Good," Miss Price commented. "Next—you, Mildred Taylor."

"'Nan had a can.'"

Very slowly indeed the story unfolded. Nan put the milk into a pan and induced the cat to come down the tree and into the house to drink it. In the house were her brother Jack and a sister, Ann.

The girls nearest to Miss Price read easily, but one or two of the others stumbled over their sentences. After the girls came Michael.

To Bimbo's surprise he read quite fluently and correctly, "'Jack spilled the ink.'"

Next it was Bimbo's turn. He already knew his sentence without looking at the book. "'Zee eenk fell on zee vloor,'" he said smilingly.

"Look at your book," Miss Price told him, "and read it properly."

Bimbo did look and there it was.

"Zee," he began again.

"The," Miss Price corrected.

Bimbo heard the difference, but to sound it was beyond his powers and he decided to skip it. "'. . . . eenk fell on zee vloor,'" he mumbled hurriedly.

But Miss Price had no intention of letting him off easily. He had to go over the sentence at least ten times, and when she read out the marks he was lowest of all—two out of ten.

A handbell began to ring and the lesson was over. It was playtime and many of the children rushed out shouting. Others, who were probably new, stood about uncertainly. Miss Martha came to the door. "See that none of them go out in their slippers," she warned Miss Price, and raising her voice for everyone to hear she called, "All who are taking milk and biscuits come with me." At the same time she beckoned to Bimbo. "You're one of the milkites," she told him.

"Meelikites?" Bimbo repeated uncertainly.

"Yes: there's a glass of milk for you in the conservatory."

In the conservatory there was a faint smell of earth and of geraniums. On a trestle table at the far end were thirty or forty tumblers of milk. Miss Martha handed one to Bimbo and gave him two arrowroot biscuits as well: but the older boys and girls helped themselves. Bimbo watched them, and *they* all watched him. He took a sip and licked the milk from his lips. Then he put one arrowroot biscuit into each cheek, and drank up the rest of the milk. Suddenly he caught sight of himself in a small mirror hanging from one of the posts which supported the roof. He was almost surprised to find that it worked in exactly the same way as the mirror Dolan had given him. He knew that what he saw was just himself, but he wondered now how he could be both inside the mirror looking out and outside looking in. It seemed strange and mysterious, as if there were another world going on by itself if he could only get there. The reflection showed a line of cream, like a pale moustache, clinging to his upper lip. He looked at the other children, and found that most of them had also cream marks on their lips. But on *their* faces the cream looked whiter. He put out his tongue and licked carefully round his mouth. Three boys and two girls immediately did the same.

"Now," Miss Martha said, "out you go and get some fresh air, but don't forget to put your shoes on first." Obediently they all went to the changing room. Bimbo couldn't tie his shoe-laces, though he had managed them all right in the morning. However Miss Martha did them for him and he followed the others into the playground. Only Michael remained inside, for he hadn't finished his milk.

The playground was rather larger than a tennis court. There was grass at the edges, but in the centre it had been worn away, leaving bare earth of a reddish brown colour. On three sides were privet hedges and on the fourth—the side farthest from the school—a row of five tall trees, with a low, black, spiked, wooden paling behind them. Bimbo immediately picked out the tallest as the one he would most like to climb. It was a beech, with a smooth, silver trunk. He thought of climbing it straight away, but he decided to wait till he had made friends with the children.

As soon as he came out, every boy and girl began to stare. Those who had not taken milk had clearly been awaiting his arrival. When he moved in any direction some of them retreated backwards before him, while others closed in behind him. By the time he had gone five yards he was completely surrounded.

For a moment he was frightened. The fact that there was no break in the circle confused him and almost drove him into a panic. But when he caught sight of Miss Martha he was a little comforted. She was standing at the door, looking out rather anxiously. He smiled to reassure her, and she smiled back and went away. All the same he didn't feel much assurance: if they wouldn't come any nearer than that, it didn't give him much chance to make friends. Still, they couldn't just stand and stare at him for ever. So he decided to wait, and to stare back, and to try to look friendly.

Presently Michael appeared and tiptoed shyly towards the edge of the circle. He was in his slippers and seemed worried. He was followed almost immediately by Miss Price. "Why haven't you got your shoes on?" she demanded.

"Please, Miss Price, I've forgotten my number."

"Stupid boy," she told him. "D'you expect *me* to remember it for you? Come in at once."

Michael followed her sheepishly. A few minutes later he reappeared, but during his absence no one had moved. Bimbo was still the centre of a staring circle. He noticed Michael standing at the edge of the circle and felt interested in him. Probably he, too, was feeling rather lonely: it would be a good idea if they could make friends. Bimbo took two steps towards Michael, but Michael, like the other children, shrank away from him. So Bimbo stopped. He could hear them whispering. He knew that they were talking about him, but he could not make out what they were saying until two boys began to argue and raised their voices.

"I tell you he's a monkey."

"He's not then. Mammy says he's a monkey-boy."

"Sure every monkey's a monkey boy at first. . . ."

"Unless it's a monkey-girl," Hugo suggested.

"Unless it's yer gran'mother," the other boy retorted angrily.

"And anyhow," Hugo went on, "Mammy says it's quite different and she says I'm to be very nice to him."

"So'm I," another boy said, and there was quite a chorus. It turned out that everyone was going to be nice to Bimbo.

"I'm to be kind to him," Michael piped up when everyone else had finished. "I promised Mammy I would."

Bimbo waited for them to start, but instead some of them began to tease Michael, while the rest continued to stare silently.

"D'you think he's got a tail?" The voice came from behind, but Bimbo guessed whose it was. He turned round quickly and caught Hugo's eye. Hugo smiled in the same way as he had done in class. He evidently wanted to make friends, but neither of them knew what to do. After a moment they both looked away rather awkwardly.

The boy beside Hugo hadn't noticed this exchange of glances and he replied thoughtfully, "I don't know. P'raps it's tucked up inside his trousers."

"I don't believe he has one," Hugo said. "He's just like you and me."

"I'd rather be like him than as fat as Francie," the other boy replied, in a voice that could have been heard all over the playground.

The fat girl looked at him. He was just out of her reach and she made no movement. "You be quiet, Herbie Stewart," she told him. "Don't make yourself sound nastier than you look."

"I don't look as nasty as you, you big fat lump-ye," Herbie retorted, moving a little further away.

The fat girl smiled good-humouredly and looked at Bimbo. "I wonder what age he is, the poor lamb," she said. Nobody had the slightest idea, but the question made Hugo think of arithmetic.

"I say, Francie," he inquired suddenly. "What's five from four?"

"You can't take five from four, silly."

"That's what *he* said," Hugo informed her. "Miss Price said it was wrong."

They both looked towards Bimbo and he knew that they wanted him to join in. They were speaking *at* him rather than about him. He drew closer. "Me right?" he asked.

"Yes," Francie answered decisively. "She was just being horrid. She's a horrid old thing."

"We f'iends?" Bimbo ventured.

"Of course we're friends," she agreed, but she wasn't looking at him. She was watching Herbie who had come closer again and was listening to the conversation. She made a sudden grab and caught his jersey. "Who's nasty now?" she demanded threateningly, as she shifted her grip to the back of his collar. "Who's a nasty, fat lump?"

She began to shake him—and she knew how to do it, too: she rattled him backwards and forwards almost casually, smiling a little at his pleas for mercy. His sentences came out in short gasps. "Oh please, Francie! I didn't mean. . . . I'm. . . ."

She stopped. They looked at each other till, with a jerk and a twist, Herbert slipped out of his jersey and escaped.

Francie was left holding it at arm's length and for a moment she stared at it; then she threw it to him. "There," she told him in a grown-up kind of voice, "put it on again. Don't be running about half-naked."

Bimbo noticed that some of the children were getting tired of watching him. He heard the word "Tig" several times and wondered what it meant. Suddenly they all scattered across the playground running from a small boy with red hair, of whom they seemed all at once to have become afraid. Only Hugo and Francie remained standing beside Bimbo, and he was pleased to see that they at least were not frightened. The red-haired boy dashed up to Hugo and touched his arm. "You're It, Hugo," he called, and darted away.

Hugo looked at Francie, but she said, "Oh, don't give it me, Hugo. You know I can't run."

"What about *him* then?" Hugo asked.

"Och no," Francie replied. "You're gettin' lazy. Away you go after Herbie or some of them."

So Hugo chased Herbert. Presently he overtook him and touched him on the shoulder. "You're It," he called. After that it was Herbert who did the chasing.

Now Bimbo understood. It was a game. He had never seen a game played before and he longed to join in. Whenever the boy or girl who was "It" for the moment passed near him he made a little spring away, but no one paid any attention: no one even tried to catch him.

He noticed that they nearly all chased Hugo and presently the thin, sad-looking girl whom Francie had pushed into the flower-bed succeeded in catching him. She was able to run faster than any of the others. Hugo paused and looked round. He smiled at Bimbo and came towards him. Bimbo knew that Hugo was going to try to make him "It". He gave a little chuckle to himself and began to run: but he couldn't run very fast and Hugo caught him easily. "You're *It*," he said, and added, "You've got to catch someone."

"I'll cats *you*," Bimbo answered.

"Try," Hugo retorted. "You couldn't."

Bimbo did try, but he hadn't a chance. Not only could he not catch Hugo: he couldn't catch anyone. He realized that he wasn't a good runner. All the children seemed to have longer legs than he had. He couldn't even catch Francie. Though she giggled all the time, she was able to elude him. Quite soon he began to feel a little down-hearted. He had wanted to join in the game and now he couldn't play properly. Presently, however, an idea came to him. If he chased Michael and kept after him for long enough Michael was sure to do something silly, and be caught. So Bimbo chased Michael. He went round and round the playground after him, like a stoat after a rabbit. At first Michael kept well ahead. Indeed he had to stop at intervals, so as not to overtake Bimbo from behind. Every time this happened all the children laughed. Bimbo didn't care: he knew he was going to catch Michael; and when other children were quite near he paid no attention to them.

Michael began to look weary. It wasn't that he was puffed: it was just that he seemed to be tired of being the only one pursued. Then Bimbo had another idea. He began to chase Michael towards the trees. Three times he did this and the third time what he had expected happened. Michael tripped over a root and fell. Bimbo was on him with one spring. "Oorit," he said.

Bimbo was hot. He had never realized what a handicap his clothes would be, and he decided to take them off so that he could run better. But seeing Miss Martha at one of the windows of the house he changed his mind.

Bimbo expected that Michael would immediately try to catch him. Instead Michael went after a little girl with pigtails. The little girl ran quite fast at first, but as she wasted most of her breath by shrieking Michael caught her very soon.

She, in turn, caught the fat girl, Francie: indeed Francie made very little attempt to run away. When she was caught she sighed and said, "Oh well: there's only one thing I *can* do," and she came at a slow, ambling run towards Bimbo.

Bimbo had expected that some lazy child would try to catch him, but he was determined not to be caught again: so he had remained under the trees. As Francie approached he stood beside the beech in a crouching position.

"Run, Monkeyface, run," Hugo called, but Bimbo paid no attention. He watched Francie carefully. When she got near she slowed down. Bimbo saw that she expected him to dodge round the tree in one direction or the other. He remained motionless as a statue.

Francie halted in front of him rather uneasily. "What are you going to do?" she asked.

Bimbo made no reply.

The fat girl hesitated. "Hugo," she said, "I don't like to."

"Go on," Hugo told her. "Don't be a silly."

"But he looks so funny," she explained. She blushed and added hurriedly to Bimbo. "I don't mean that, but you're looking at me in such a funny way."

Bimbo smiled to reassure her.

"He won't bite you," Hugo called.

Gingerly Francie put out her hand, and then, when she had almost touched him, Bimbo sprang. It was a good spring, he shot up ten feet—right into the tree. He heard a little gasp of surprise from all the children and Francie's voice floated up to him. "You're It," she said.

"Oh no he's not," Hugo declared. "You never touched him."

"I almost did," Francie answered, "and it's not fair going up a tree."

Bimbo pulled himself into a comfortable position on a thick branch, put one arm round the trunk, and looked at them. From all over the playground they were running towards the foot of his tree. They gathered round Francie and stared up. Bimbo was filled with pride. He broke off a twig and threw it down at them. "Can't cats," he taunted them. "Can't cats Bimbo."

"Are you goin' after him, Fatty?" Herbert inquired rudely, and from a safe distance he sang:

"Fatty, fatty Francie
Isn't as thin as Nancy."

Francie turned to Hugo who was standing beside her. "There," she said, "you're It. You can catch him if you like."

Hugo looked at Bimbo and the tree, and hesitated. "I will, then," he replied after a moment. "Just see if I don't."

The lowest branch was well out of his reach, but another boy gave him a back and he managed to pull himself up to it. He was still some distance below Bimbo and on the opposite side of the trunk. All the same Bimbo thought it wise to move. Almost unconsciously he kicked off his shoes and they fell on the upturned face of the pale, sharp-looking boy and knocked off his spectacles. Next he peeled off his stockings: this made him feel more comfortable.

It was an easy tree to climb and seeing Hugo so close below him Bimbo went up higher. Hugo followed more slowly, but each time he came near, Bimbo sprang up a few feet further and waited for him. Looking down through the leaves at Hugo's face Bimbo saw that it was dogged and determined. He came on slowly, but steadily. At last Bimbo was among the small branches at the top of the tree and he knew that he could go no higher. The children on the ground were quite hidden from him, but in a moment he saw Hugo again, looking eager and triumphant.

From far below came Francie's voice, "Stop, Hugo, stop. The branches'll break and you'll fall."

Next he heard Meta Hemingway: "Hugo's very good at climbing trees. I don't know anyone who's as good."

I'm better, Bimbo thought, and he peered intently at Hugo without moving. Hugo pulled himself up a little higher and a branch cracked. He was within reach of Bimbo at last and very slowly he stretched out his hand. "You're. . . ." he began, but before Hugo could touch him Bimbo let go with both hands and dived past him through the tree. He checked himself slightly with his feet, curled his tail round a branch, and grasped a lower branch with his hands. For a moment he remained like that, his feet upmost, then, as he let his legs and body swing down, there was a crackling of small twigs. Hugo was two or three feet above his head now, and Bimbo, twining himself round the stem of the tree, looked up at him. Hugo was startled: he was holding on tightly with both hands.

"Cats me?" Bimbo taunted, and dropped again. He came down almost as if he were falling, but pulled himself up fifteen or twenty feet above the ground. There he hung from a thick branch. His head was downwards and he swung slightly to and fro as he looked at the children. They stared back in silent amazement.

Suddenly a little girl screamed, "Look! He *has* got a tail. It's come out from under his trousers."

Bimbo pulled himself into a sitting position, curled his tail round the bough and waited for Hugo. But there was no movement from the top of the tree. He's very slow, Bimbo thought to himself.

Francie was the first to get uneasy. "Are you all right, Hugo?" she called, and after a pause, "What's happened to you, Hugo?"

Bimbo listened carefully. Perhaps Hugo was coming stealthily to surprise him; but there was no sound, and no movement of the branches. Only the leaves stirred slightly in the breeze.

"Go an' help him, can't you?" Francie exclaimed suddenly. "Don't just sit there grinning at yourself."

Bimbo was startled. Why would Hugo want help? he wondered. He looked at Francie inquiringly. He was astonished to find that she and all the girls were gazing at him with expressions of hatred on their faces.

"*You* don't care if he falls and breaks his neck," Francie continued, almost sobbing now. "Poor Hugo. Oh, do go and help him."

Of course Bimbo would help. "'Es," he said. He liked the idea of helping Hugo. He started to climb again, quickly and expertly.

He found Hugo exactly where he had left him. His face was pale. He was still clutching the same branches. He hadn't moved at all.

"'Elp?" Bimbo inquired, rather nervously, for he felt at once Hugo's fear. He looked round, but could see nothing. He looked in the same direction as Hugo and saw only the roof of the school.

"No," Hugo said sharply. "I'm all right. Leave me alone, can't you." As he spoke he pulled his left foot from its hold and began to move it slowly downwards. Bimbo moved, too, to get out of his way. A moment later he looked up again and saw that Hugo's right foot was resting on a thin branch, which was hardly more than a twig. Bimbo made a warning exclamation, but he could not think of words to explain the danger. Hugo let go with one hand and began to feel for a new grip. As he did so the branch bent and broke. His left foot was still dangling in the air. He made a grab with his free hand but caught nothing. The jerk broke the branch to which he was holding with his other hand: he fell.

Bimbo himself was supported by branches which were no more than strong enough to bear his weight. Nevertheless, he shot out his right hand and caught Hugo's jersey. As he did so the branch which he was grasping with his left hand gave way. He clung by his feet for a moment longer and then let go, but he still held Hugo by the jersey. He was partly falling now, partly diving towards a stronger branch some ten feet below. As soon as his hand touched it he grasped it with all his strength, but that was not quite enough to stop them. They continued to drop, and as Bimbo's hand was dragged from its hold on the first branch, his feet grasped another.

He was holding Hugo close to him now, and again, but more slowly, he turned heels over head. As he did so the children on the ground came into view through a gap in the leaves—a queer huddle of white faces.

The rest was easy. Hugo's arms were clasped round Bimbo's body, but he made no other attempt to help himself. Even after they reached the ground he still clung to Bimbo. When eventually he let go he could hardly stand. His face was scratched and pale. He went shakily over to the paling, leaned over it, and was sick into the next garden.

For a minute he remained like this; but soon he pulled himself together and came back to Bimbo. All the other children stood round and stared at them both with their mouths open. "Thank you very much for saving my life," Hugo said.

These words and the sight of Hugo's scratched face quite overwhelmed Bimbo. He put his arms round Hugo and kissed him. Hugo received the embrace stiffly and Bimbo noticed that Herbert and some of the other children looked strangely shocked.

"It's quite all right," Francie said. "That's the way they say thank you in his country."

The tension among the children immediately relaxed. They had looked disapproving: now they all smiled.

"Three cheers for Monkeyface," Hugo called, still rather shakily.

As they were cheering Miss Martha came out ringing the bell. Bimbo sat down to put on his shoes and stockings again, and this time it was Francie who tied the laces.

The next lesson was history and Miss Price immediately noticed Hugo's face. "You've been fighting," she said severely.

7

In the changing room, when school was over, Hugo sat down beside Bimbo to put on his shoes. "You live in Beechwood, too," he said, "don't you?" Bimbo admitted that he did, and Hugo went on, "I know the way home by myself: we'd better go together."

Bimbo agreed gladly. He had hoped that something like this

would happen, and at playtime he had decided that he liked Hugo best of all the boys in the school, though in the beginning he had thought that Michael was going to be his friend. This was partly because Michael was the first boy he had met—and because he looked nice; partly because he felt a natural sympathy with him in his dreaminess and his mistakes. But Hugo was obviously superior to Michael; and he seemed to be friends with everyone in the school.

Bimbo fumbled with his laces, but his fingers were big and awkward and again he had no success. It was because he was in a hurry and knew Hugo was waiting. Before long he gave it up. "Please tie laces," he said.

Hugo knelt down and did so. "You're a baby, aren't you," he remarked good-naturedly.

For part of the way home they were followed by other children who wanted to walk with them. Every now and then Hugo stopped to shoo them away. Two or three followed as far as the railway station, but after that they were left to themselves.

Hugo did most of the talking: he talked about school: he liked school. Even Miss Price he found rather fun. "It's great to see her making them jump," he declared. "Did you see her scarin' that wee new fellow that sits beside you?"

After that he described past deeds of Miss Price who, it seemed, was now no more than a shadow of her former, fearful self. But when they reached Beechwood, and were not far from Mr. Browne's house, he broke off and pointed to a wrought iron gate on the opposite side of the road. "That's where I live," he said.

Bimbo looked and saw only a dark avenue overhung with trees. So he asked, "You lib in zee tooees?"

"No, you silly: in a house. It's the biggest house in Belmore, too. You come round this afternoon and I'll show it to you."

Bimbo, however, was afraid that Mr. Browne might not approve. He explained, with some difficulty, that it was only as a special concession that he had been allowed to go to school, and that Miss Martha had advised him to be careful not to offend Mr. Browne in any way.

"All right," Hugo said. "I'll come to your place. I'll be round after dinner."

They reached the Brownes' gate and Bimbo climbed over. Hugo remained outside. "Good-bye," he said. "See you this afternoon."

"Goo'-bye," Bimbo replied. He had been walking upright all morning and his back was aching with the effort. He was longing to get down on to all fours again, but he knew that Hugo was peering through the gate watching him. Dolan had impressed on him that he must always walk upright in public. So now he jumped into the shrubbery beside the drive. There behind a rhododendron bush, and with a feeling of luxury, he leaned forward and rested his hands on the ground. He felt satisfied with himself. He thought he had done well. He had followed all Miss Martha's instructions, and all Dolan's instructions to the letter: besides he had succeeded in his own particular object; he had made a friend.

When he was rested he looked out through the bushes. He saw that Hugo had gone. So he stepped out from the shrubbery, straightened himself up, and walked on. There was a bend in the drive and when he came round this he saw Dolan hoeing the gravel in front of the house. Dolan immediately stopped working, and leaning on the hoe waited for Bimbo.

"So you wasn't kep' in?" Dolan inquired jocularly.

"No."

"Mebbe they made ye head boy instead?"

"'Ot's 'at?" Bimbo demanded.

"Head o' the school," Dolan returned.

"No. Mees Sutton head," Bimbo told him. Dolan spat on his hands but it was some time before he started hoeing again.

Bimbo went to the kitchen and got a bowl of bread and milk and two bananas. It was his dinner and he carried it to the cage, where he could eat it alone: recently he had begun to dislike being watched at his meals. When he had finished he returned the bowl and spoon, and put the banana skins in the kitchen fire.

Next he took off his clothes, folded them carefully, and put them away in the black tin trunk where all his things were kept. Miss Martha had said he was not to wear his clothes in the garden, and besides he was more comfortable without them. He stretched, swung on the trapeze and on the rings; and went into the garden to look out for Hugo.

He watched from the chestnut tree near the gate, but it was a long time before Hugo appeared. He was followed by a number of other boys from Miss Sutton's. There were Albert and Jackie and Herbert. . . . Bimbo didn't know the names of the others: but he had noticed Albert and Jackie particularly. They were the two biggest boys in the school, and they seemed to be great friends. He thought Hugo must have asked them all to come and play and he felt pleased. But very soon he realized that Hugo and the other boys were quarrelling. Hugo's face was painted with broad, orange-yellow streaks, and he looked very cross. Bimbo didn't know if he was cross because of the yellow streaks, or if he had painted his face yellow because he was cross.

When Hugo reached the gate he came in quickly himself and tried to shut the others out. But Albert and Jackie said they were coming in, too. Bimbo decided that they must be enemies of Hugo's. Uttering a low growl he raced down the tree to Hugo's side and seized the gate. Everyone else, including Hugo, immediately let go, and stepped back, looking startled. The gate banged, but Bimbo still held it. He growled again at the boys outside and glared at them, though really he felt more triumphant than angry. The enemies withdrew to the opposite footpath. They looked uneasy. Bimbo knew that if he climbed over the gate they would probably run away. Instead he turned to Hugo. "We f'en's," he said. "Dey bad."

But he uttered the last word uncertainly. Probably it was all only a game, like tig. Hugo didn't enlighten him: in fact there was an appreciable pause before he spoke at all. Then he asked, "Where's your clothes?"

"In z'ouse," Bimbo replied at once, but the question impressed him a great deal. He realized for the first time that he had only seen parts of the other boys, of Miss Sutton, of Mr. Browne—of all the human beings he had seen at all. This, then, was the real difference between people and animals. People covered parts of themselves, and walked on their hind legs. Bimbo, having had a little experience of being a human being, knew it was nicer to be an animal. "Oo be animal," he told Hugo.

Hugo hesitated: but presently he got down on his hands and knees. He looked clumsy, and followed very slowly when Bimbo ran back into the shrubbery.

There they regarded each other uncertainly for a moment and Hugo asked, "What'll we do?"

Bimbo knew what *he* wanted to do. "Kime tooees," he responded promptly.

Hugo looked completely crestfallen. "I can't," he answered. "I promised Mummy I wouldn't. She wouldn't let me come till I did."

For a moment Bimbo was disappointed: he had wanted to show off. He thought for a moment. "Come," he said, and trotted away on all fours through the shrubbery. Hugo followed, but on hands and knees he was painfully slow and inefficient. After a yard or two he stood up and ran in human fashion, on two feet only, though he had to bend nearly double to avoid overhanging branches. Very soon they came to the grey stone wall which divided Mr. Browne's garden from the one next door. Bimbo climbed to the top and dropped down on to a soft bed of pine-needles on the other side. He landed neatly, but Hugo, coming after, fell forward on his hands.

Hugo was excited. Bimbo felt excited himself though he knew where they were going: it was to a secret place that he had never shown even to Dolan. The wall was behind them: otherwise they were closely surrounded by thick bushes on every side. Bimbo saw Hugo look round in a rather disappointed fashion. "Is this all?" he asked.

"No," Bimbo answered. Close to the ground between the wall and the bushes was a small gap overhung by a flowering currant. Bimbo squeezed through this gap into a darkness that was almost complete. "Come arter," he told Hugo. Hugo came. Bimbo knew he was frightened, and he was pleased: it made him feel brave and bold: it made the adventure more exciting.

They crawled on slowly, pushing aside trailers of briar, and avoiding hard, dead sticks of bramble which stuck up here and there through the leaves. The tunnel was narrow, but in places where there were gaps in the bushes overhead patches of sunlight filtered down. They shone on a carpet made of beech-leaves, and pine-needles and the husks of hazel-nuts. There was layer upon layer of it, generation upon generation, slowly rotting away.

At the end the passage widened out a little and was blocked by a grey stone pillar about seven feet high. On one side the pillar was joined to the wall, but on the other was a hedge and it was possible to see out onto the road. Hugo crawled up beside Bimbo, and lying at full length he looked out. "Is this your secret den?" he asked.

" 'Ess," Bimbo answered, though he didn't really understand.

"It's a very good one," Hugo said, "and a secret passage, too. It's like a real smuggler's den. I won't tell anyone about it. We can come here and hide—and no one'll know where we are." For a few moments they both lay silent, and Bimbo felt that they were isolated from everything outside, in a sort of happy unity. From the leaves came an earthy musty smell, faintly damp. It was cosy and warm. High above them a breeze stirred in the tree-tops and a few more beech leaves came slowly fluttering down. If they were to lie there long enough, Bimbo thought, the leaves would come down and come down, till at last there would be no sign of either of them.

Presently he again noticed the orange streaks on Hugo's face. He leaned forward and touched one of them lightly with the forefinger of his right hand. "Ot's 'at?" he inquired, and taking his finger away he put it to his nose and inhaled a slightly disagreeable, bitter smell.

"Iodine," Hugo responded with a sort of glum pride. "She put it on the scratches: it stung like anything, too."

Bimbo had never heard of iodine and his mind shifted back to the subject of clothes. He plucked Hugo's jersey. "A' time?" he asked. "Not put off?"

"I take it off at night," Hugo told him.

"Take off now," Bimbo said.

But Hugo shook his head very firmly. "No," he said.

" 'y?" Bimbo demanded.

Instead of answering Hugo put his finger to his lips. "Listen," he whispered. "Ssh."

It was Herbert and the other boys. They were coming slowly along the footpath, talking about Hugo and Bimbo.

"Where do *you* think they've gone?"

"What d'you think they're doin'?"

"Wait till *I* get him," Herbert boasted. "*I'll* show him."

At this Hugo stiffened, and Bimbo was afraid he would shout out. So he touched him. Hugo looked up and smiled. The voices faded away and at last Hugo spoke. "I'll ask him to-morrow what's he going to show me. Him!"

Gradually they began to talk. In his first short contact with the outside world Bimbo had seen and heard many things he did not understand. Lamp-posts, motor-cars, trains—they were all unfamiliar to him. He asked Hugo about them, and Hugo did his best to explain. Two words he was unable to explain—Mummy and Daddy. It appeared that every child in the school had a Mummy and a Daddy. Bimbo had neither. He gathered that they were two people who were specially good to the particular child to whom they belonged. He suggested that Dolan and Miss Martha might be his Mummy and Daddy, but Hugo said they were not.

All afternoon they stayed there, sometimes talking, sometimes dreaming. They were warm and comfortable—snug, like field-mice in a nest.

8

In a few days Bimbo became accustomed to school, but he didn't enjoy it as much as he had hoped: at times he didn't enjoy it at all. He had expected to be one of a crowd, to feel himself a member of a community: instead he felt a new kind of loneliness, a loneliness that in a way was more intense than any he had experienced before. There *was* a community of feeling among the children, but very soon Bimbo came to realize that he was outside it: they didn't regard him as one of themselves.

At first they made some effort to include him in their games, but it was useless. Whenever he was chased Bimbo went straight to the nearest tree and climbed it. It was his only means of escape: on the ground all of them, even the fat girl, could catch him easily. Once he was in a tree no one could catch him—and no one tried.

So he got into the habit of sitting on a favourite branch in one of the trees beside the playground, and watching the others. Occasionally Hugo came and sat beside him, but he found it dull, and as a rule he did not stay long. Bimbo didn't find it dull. It was much more interesting than his life in the cage. At the same time it made him realize that he was a creature apart. He resented being unable to do what the others were doing, and he began to imagine himself suddenly astonishing them by doing all the things they did—and doing them better than anyone. If only his legs had been longer, or the other children had been more ape-like, what fun they might have had together.

One day, however, Hugo spent the whole of playtime on the branch beside Bimbo. He had been chased by the two bigger boys, Albert and Jackie, and they would not let him come down: yet evidently they were afraid to climb up after him because of Bimbo. Instead they stood beneath the tree and shouted at him.

"D'you like bein' one o' the monkeys?" Albert asked.

"I'd rather be a monkey than a pig like you," Hugo retorted.

Albert flushed. "Don't you be givin' off guff," he said threateningly.

"You ought to be in the zoo, so y'ought," Jackie shouted. "Both of you. That's where you'd look nacherl, sittin' up on a branch catchin' fleas off other."

Everyone laughed at this and Bimbo laughed too. He liked it when people laughed: he liked laughing himself, and did so whenever there was the slightest excuse. He was surprised to feel Hugo catch his arm sharply, and demand, almost passionately, "What are you laughin' at? It's not funny."

Bimbo was surprised. "'S not?" he asked. "Why dey laugh?"

"They're tryin' to be funny, that's all," Hugo answered, and Bimbo felt that it was a very serious matter. For a moment he had been in sympathy with the crowd: now he was in sympathy with Hugo. He scowled at the others, and particularly at Albert and Jackie. These two were whispering together, and some of the other boys had gathered round them. Presently Albert glanced at Bimbo and grinned. Then he listened while Jackie whispered something further. Suddenly he looked up again and shouted, "Who's your father, Monkeyface?"

"Dono," Bimbo replied, and immediately he received a dig from Hugo's elbow, which almost knocked him off the branch.

"Don't answer," Hugo told him. Bimbo didn't see why he shouldn't answer. It wasn't as if Hugo had been able to tell him anything about his father. Perhaps some of the others would know more.

"'Ot is 'father'?" he asked them.

"Will I tell you what *yours* is?" Albert suggested.

"Say 'No'," Hugo whispered. "He's only making fun of you."

But Bimbo couldn't say "No": he was too curious. Instead he said "'Ess, pleess tell."

"He's a monkey in the zoo," Albert answered.

Jackie took this up at once. "Bimbo's father's a monkey in the zoo," he shrieked, "a monkey in the zoo, a monkey in the zoo." He began to sing it and the words made a sort of tune:

> *"Bimbo's got a father*
> *Who's a monkey in the zoo,*
> *A monkey in the zoo,*
> *A monkey in the zoo. . . ."*

Bimbo thought this was very clever of Jackie, and in spite of Hugo he wondered if it might be true. Anything might be true. Jackie might somehow have got to know.

Albert and Herbert and a number of other boys joined in the singing. "That's what they were whispering about," Hugo said. "I bet it was all made up beforehand."

Bimbo looked at Jackie thoughtfully. Jackie was scratching himself in imitation of a monkey, and absent-mindedly Bimbo did the same. "Did 'oo see'm in zoo?" he inquired.

"Of course I saw him," Jackie answered.

"Oh *can't* you keep quiet?" Hugo muttered.

"Sowwy," Bimbo said, but almost in the same breath he put another question to Jackie. "Wot 'e doing?"

Jackie hesitated. "Doin'? He was eatin' monkey-nuts of course. What d'you think?"

"Did say anything?" Bimbo asked.

"Oh, yes; he said a whole lot."

At this Bimbo's curiosity quite overcame his doubts. "Wot 'e say?" he demanded eagerly.

"*I* don't know," Jackie replied. "It was all in Monkey language. I couldn't understand. It was like this. . . ."

He began to gabble a rigmarole of meaningless sounds. Bimbo listened to him for a moment. Then he noticed Michael. Michael's face was scarlet and he was shaking with suppressed laughter. When he caught Bimbo's eye he looked at Jackie for an instant and burst out laughing aloud.

"They're makin' a cod of you," Hugo growled angrily.

Bimbo realized that they were. He was no longer inquisitive. He felt he would have to do something to please Hugo. He plucked some of the few remaining green leaves from the tree and began to chew them slowly. They had a dry rather bitter taste. The pulp he placed in his cheeks. Suddenly, he spat it out, spraying Albert and Jackie with a slimy, green froth.

The two victims let out yells of rage and disgust. Bimbo expected Hugo to be pleased. "Good?" he questioned.

"Oh, yes," Hugo answered, "if Miss Martha didn't see you." Yet he didn't *sound* pleased, and Bimbo noticed that the other children were moving away from him with expressions of loathing.

"Not glad?" Bimbo said doubtfully.

"Oh, yes," Hugo responded, "but it's a sort of dirty."

Michael stared at Bimbo from a safe distance. "Oh, look!" he exclaimed. "His teeth have all turned green."

Jackie and Albert went inside to wash, and the other children began a game of leap-frog at the far side of the playground. Taking advantage of the absence of his enemies, Hugo joined in, and Bimbo was left alone. He felt deserted and melancholy. He wished he had not gone on asking Jackie questions after Hugo had advised him to stop. He even wished he hadn't spat over them—and there, now, was Miss Martha looking very cross indeed, and coming straight towards him.

He tried to smile at her, but she wouldn't let him. "You've been naughty, Bimbo," she said. "Come into the house."

So he *felt* naughty and couldn't smile. He dropped down the tree, and went across the playground after her on all-fours. Everyone was staring at him, but he was so miserable that for the first time since he had come to school he failed to make the necessary effort to walk upright. He could even feel his tail hanging down, limp and dejected between his legs.

Miss Martha brought him into the dining-room and looked at him. "Get up on to a chair," she ordered, and sat down herself.

"I'm sowwy, Miss Marfa," Bimbo said.

She looked at him doubtfully. "Do you know what you're sorry for?" she asked.

"'Noying you, Miss Marfa."

"That's all very well," she responded, "but do you know *why* I'm annoyed?"

Bimbo thought he knew, but he didn't know the word spit. He considered for a moment and said, "Because did like dis to Dackie, Albet," and he pretended to spit, though this time he didn't actually do it.

"Yes," Miss Martha answered. "It was a horrid, dirty thing to do. I never told you not to, because I never thought of your doing it. I've tried to interfere with you as little as possible. If I gave you a long list of things not to do you'd either obey and be miserable, or disobey and hide what you were doing. I would rather let you find out as much as possible for yourself. That's why I was pleased to see that you'd made friends with Hugo. He's not a good boy, but. . . ."

However, here Bimbo felt it necessary to correct her, and he interrupted, "Oogo iss good, Miss Marfa. 'Ess, he iss good."

"Oh, I know," she agreed at once. "What I mean is he's not too good. He's sensible and he's full of life, and," she added plainly, "I like him. Anyhow I thought if you behaved in more or less the way he behaves you'd be all right, but I see now that's not enough."

She paused and Bimbo put in, "'Ess, Miss Marfa," to show that he was listening carefully.

"I didn't mean to tell you," she went on, "but at the beginning of this term I spoke to the parents of every child in the school and asked if they objected to your coming. Only a few did, but it happens that the mothers of the two boys on whom you spat were among that few. They said you mightn't have nice habits. I told them you were as good as gold. In the end I talked them round. They promised not to take their children away till they'd at least seen what you were like."

"You not want 'em go 'way?" Bimbo exclaimed in surprise. "You like Dackie, like Albet?"

To this she made no direct reply, and Bimbo guessed that she didn't *really* like them. He couldn't understand in that case why they should be at the school at all, till it occurred to him that they might be favourites of one of the other mistresses. "You see," Miss Martha went on, "you're in a rather peculiar position, and I see now that in some ways you'll have to be very careful. You're a great deal stronger than other boys and you must be careful not to hurt them. So it would be better if you didn't have fights. I don't want to lay down any hard and fast rules, but if you're thinking of doing anything that other boys don't do, ask Hugo about it first. If he's even doubtful about it, you'd be better not to do it, unless you're absolutely certain that you ought. And don't spit on anyone any more."

"No, Miss Marfa."

But Miss Martha was looking at the clock. "Gracious!" she exclaimed. "It's two minutes after time and no one's rung the bell."

9

After school Hugo and Bimbo started for home together as usual; but when they were going through Miss Sutton's gate two men stepped in front of them. "Here, Sonny," one of them said to Hugo, "is this the monkey that talks?"

Hugo scowled. "Bimbo's not a monkey," he answered. "Miss Martha says he's an ape-boy."

"Does the ape-boy talk then?"

Both these questions were put by the shorter of the two men, who had a wheedling, ingratiating voice. He was fat, with a puffy face, and he smiled almost continuously, showing some very bad teeth. When he was talking his cigarette remained glued to his upper lip and waggled up and down.

His companion, who was tall and thin, didn't ask questions, but walked away backwards holding what appeared to be a box in the air in front of his face. Suddenly he stopped and looked at Bimbo round the box, which was small and black. He had grey, staring eyes and hollow white cheeks. After a moment there was a click; whereupon the thin man immediately began to work at the box, holding it pressed against his stomach. He took out a flat piece of polished wood and replaced it by another piece of polished wood, apparently identical.

Bimbo knew that these operations had something to do with *him*, and he was wondering what the meaning of them was when the fat man addressed him directly. "H'are ye, Bimbo?" he inquired, with an attempt at heartiness which made him cough.

"How dooy do?" Bimbo responded politely, but he was much more interested in the tall man who continued to behave in an unusual manner. He had now moved to one side and was again holding up the box and peeping out at Bimbo from behind it.

The fat man noticed where Bimbo was looking and called immediately, "That's right, Bimbo. Just you watch the dicky-bird."

"Bi'd intah box?" Bimbo exclaimed in surprise.

"Aye," the fat man assured him. "You watch for't comin' out."

Bimbo watched, but though there was another click and the tall man went through the same movements as before, there was no sign of a bird. Bimbo began to feel angry. *He* knew what it was like to be shut up, though never, even comparatively, had he been in so small a cage. "Letta ooe bi'd out!" he demanded fiercely, glaring at the black box.

The tall man looked at him in surprise and then drew back hastily. But he was too slow and Bimbo would have had the box if Hugo hadn't suddenly thrown his arms around him. "Don't be silly," Hugo whispered. "There isn't any bird. They just say that to make you look."

Bimbo was shocked. " 'S 'e tellin' lies?" he asked.

"I s'pose so," Hugo was beginning in a puzzled voice, when the culprit himself interrupted.

"Here, Bimbo," he said, producing a notebook and pencil, "you just answer a few questions. Now tell me, do you go to school every day?"

" 'Ess."

"D'you like school?"

" 'Ess."

"Who taught you to talk?"

"Dolan, Meest' B'own, Miss Marfa."

By this time some of the children had gathered round and were gazing at the two men inquisitively. The fat man gazed back, and at last, very doubtfully, sought their assistance. "Who *are* all these people?" he inquired. "Who's Miss Marvel?"

"It's not Miss Marvel," Meta Hemingway corrected him at once. "It's Miss Martha—only *he* can't say it properly. Miss Martha's Miss Sutton's sister—the fattest one."

"One of the school marms, Joe," the tall man joined in helpfully. "Same as the name on the gate."

"An' who's this Dolan fellow?" the fat man went on. "I get Browne all right, but what's Dolan got to do with it?"

But before anyone had time to explain Miss Martha's voice broke in upon them sharply. "Bimbo, Hugo, Meta, children all of you, what are you doing? Come back into school at once."

They obeyed; but Bimbo wondered—and he thought that the others wondered, too—why she should bring them in by the front door, which in the ordinary way they were not allowed to use. In the hall the children looked at each other with odd, guilty looks, as if they had been caught doing something wrong, but had not yet been told of what exactly their offence consisted. Bimbo knew that they hadn't committed any offence.

Meanwhile the two men had followed the children as far as the step where they stood looking in at Bimbo with a sort of sheepish persistence. Miss Martha appeared to be about to shut the door in their faces. "You can't treat the Press like that, not nowadays," the fat one protested, trying to edge forward a little into the hall.

This was the sort of statement Miss Martha delighted to disprove. "Can't I?" she returned vigorously, and for a moment it appeared as if the fat man must be squelched quite literally by the closing door. He escaped, not by retreating, but by skipping forward boldly, and amazingly quickly, right into the hall. There he stood facing her, embarrassed, indignant, and quite out of breath.

"Look here, Miss," he began pantingly, but she flung the door wide open again, revealing his lugubrious, tall companion, who was hovering on the step like a sympathetic bird.

"Would you mind leaving my sister's house?" Miss Martha said —and had she given *him* such a look Bimbo would have climbed the nearest tree as quickly as possible.

The fat man, however, remained. "There's nothin' ah'm lookin' forward to more," he replied earnestly, with a sudden broadening of accent that was both convincing and slightly pathetic.

Miss Martha at any rate began to relent. "I suppose it's not altogether your fault," she conceded. "It's your employers and the public. After all I read the paper myself—even the Sunday papers. . . ."

"Sure we all do," the little man assured her, adapting himself at once to the new situation. "Besides they'll all have somethin' about it. We might as well get it right as not. What I want to know first is who owns him? Would *you* have an interest in him, for instance?"

"A very great interest," Miss Martha returned promptly. "I don't mind telling you that: but. . . ." She broke off and glanced at the attentive faces of the children who were gathered in a little group just behind her. "Perhaps we'd better go in here," she suggested, taking a step towards the dining-room door. "I don't want. . . ."

But whatever she did not want, the sentence remained unfinished. The last remarks Bimbo heard came indeed from the little fat man. "It was bound to happen," he said. "You couldn't expect to hide a story like this, not right under everyone's nose." Then the door closed.

In a few minutes the children were allowed to go home, but Bimbo was kept while a taxi was sent for, and Hugo stayed with him. They both enjoyed the journey home: for Bimbo it was a completely new experience.

Later on Mr. Browne told him that he must keep to his room for the rest of the day, without even going out into the cage, and the sliding steel door between the two was closed. That evening both the front doorbell and the telephone rang more frequently than usual. Bimbo knew that something was happening, but he went to bed without discovering what it was.

Not until Dolan arrived in the morning did he receive any explanation of the previous day's events. At half-past eight Dolan opened the steel door and announced that Bimbo could come out into the cage or go anywhere he liked, provided he kept in sight of the house. It was only as an afterthought that he added, "There was a piece about ye in the paper last night, Bimbo."

"Oh!" Bimbo cried, realizing at once the significance of the little fat man. "Wot paypa say?"

This question caused Dolan some reflection, but eventually he replied, "Nothin' ye don't know already."

"Beeg piece?" Bimbo inquired.

Dolan considered. "Aye," he decided, "a brave wee piece—an' they had yer 'photy', too, two o' them—one just yer face, an' one of the whole o' ye."

Shortly afterwards Mr. Browne came round the corner of the house. "Don't go to school till you're called for," he instructed Bimbo. "Mr. Clarke's going to pick you up here with his car and drop you at the school in passing. It's not out of his way. He takes Hugo on wet mornings—it'll save any unnecessary publicity. Remember to say thank you."

Yet in a few days it became clear that publicity could not be avoided. At first Bimbo rather liked it, liked seeing his photograph in the papers—for he soon learned to ask for copies to be sent to him—liked being asked how he was getting on at school, and what he was going to do when he was grown up. . . . But he got tired of it very quickly and tried to escape whenever he saw anyone who looked like either a photographer or a reporter.

This was not easy. After the London papers came the illustrated weeklies, foreign papers, zoological papers, monthlies, scientific quarterlies. . . . Men with cameras or with notebooks kept appearing in the Brownes' garden or in the playground at Miss Sutton's. The front doorbells in both houses went out of order. But worst of all were the people who came just to stare. Bimbo hated them. They were waiting for him outside Miss Sutton's the morning after his first encounter with the reporter: and for more than a week they continued to watch him arrive and depart in the Clarkes' big black car. Bimbo hated their gaping white faces, the shameless intensity of their joint curiosity.

Gradually, of course, the crowds diminished, the newspapers lost interest: but by that time Bimbo had developed a great dread of being stared at and an extreme shyness towards all strangers. At the end of a fortnight he was sent to school on foot as before, but he never knew at what corner he would encounter a party from the slums who would be waiting there for the precise purpose of seeing him. As a rule they would not see him for very long. Bimbo always bolted into the nearest garden and continued his journey by special ways of his own. Sometimes they pursued him; sometimes they threw stones at him: yet he was never either caught or hit.

The publicity about Bimbo had one other result: every day for a period the postman had an enormous number of letters for Mr. Browne. Bimbo asked Dolan what so many people could be writing about. "The most o' them's offers," Dolan replied. "That's what they are. They don't stop at hundreds neether. Leastways that's the talk that's goin' round."

"Offahs?" Bimbo repeated, mystified.

"Aye, offers for *you*—offers from showmen. They want *The Talkin' Ape*—hit o' the century, better'n the fattest woman or the wee-est horse."

"Oo mean Mistah B'owne might sell me?" Bimbo asked in horror.

"No, he won't sell ye," Dolan responded reassuringly. "What'd the likes o' him want with more money?—sure hasn't he all he needs? Not that he's too free when it comes to handin' it out," he added reflectively. "He's near, that's the truth of it."

10

One afternoon, when most of the excitement was over, Hugo and Bimbo were lying in the secret hiding-place on the far side of the garden wall. Bimbo liked going there: it was warm and cosy among the pine needles and dead leaves; and no one was likely to find them. Yet this afternoon, when they had just settled down, they heard a rustling in the undergrowth. Someone was approaching through the passage behind them.

Albert and Jackie had gone along the road a few minutes before, and Hugo immediately sprang to his feet. "They must have found a way in," he exclaimed. "What'll we do?" He stood with his back to the wall, looking round anxiously.

Bimbo knew it wasn't Albert or Jackie. He peered into the tunnel, and saw, far away through the darkness, two tiny orange lights. They were eyes, but not human eyes. " 'S'nanimal," Bimbo said. He sniffed, but there was no wind and he could not catch any fresh scent.

Hugo looked surprised and slightly alarmed. "What kind of animal?" he asked.

"Beeg an'mal," Bimbo answered. "Line, tiger p'raps. Like picter book." But he didn't really believe this. He thought it would be nice if it *were* a lion or a tiger. He liked to pretend it was, and it was fun to frighten Hugo.

"It couldn't be," Hugo said. "They're all shut up in cages in the zoo. I've seen them."

"One has p'raps 'scaped," Bimbo suggested.

But Hugo refused to be deceived any longer. "It's only a dog," he declared. "I can see it."

Bimbo gave in grudgingly. " 'S ve'y beeg dog," he asserted. "Nearly's big's line."

"If it isn't anyone's," Hugo decided, "I'm goin' to have it for *my* dog."

"P'raps it's just its own dog," Bimbo said, "an' live all 'lone."

As he spoke, the dog, which was even larger than he had expected, forced its way into the den. It looked at them both for a moment: then it bowled Bimbo over with its nose and began to lick him.

Bimbo had never really met a dog before; yet at once a sort of wave of greeting seemed to pass between them. Bimbo found that it was nice being licked, that he liked the feeling of the warm pink tongue: sometimes he shut his eyes and laughed: sometimes he looked up into the dog's eyes, big, brown eyes, surrounded by soft, wrinkly fur. The dog had a black muzzle and a brown face, with a white patch on the forehead. His coat was brown and white. His ears were short and cocked up as if he were always listening. Presently he decided that Bimbo's face and chest had been washed enough: so with a huge round paw he turned him over and began to lick his shoulders and neck.

"He's the *biggest* dog I've ever *seen*," Hugo announced emphatically, "and he thinks *you* need a wash. I wonder what kind he is."

Instead of answering Bimbo rolled on to his back, and reaching up a long, hairy arm he caught Hugo's jersey. " 'Snice bein' licked," he said softly, and he pulled Hugo down on top of him.

"But *I* don't want to be licked," Hugo objected. The dog, however, didn't pay attention to this. He licked Hugo as thoroughly as he had licked Bimbo, and Hugo, after all, didn't really seem to mind.

The dog was well kept, and on his collar was a small brass plate with his name—Leo IV—neatly engraved on it. Nevertheless, Hugo decided that he was a stray. "I'm going to ask Mummy if I can keep him," he announced. "You come, too. She's never seen you either."

"Mus' 'tay," Bimbo answered. "Not 'lowed on road, 'cept go school."

Hugo looked at him. "Why not?" he asked. "I'd come if I was you. Sure nobody'd know."

Bimbo wasn't even tempted. He was afraid that if he broke any of Mr. Browne's rules he might lose his freedom. He had explained this to Hugo before and he reminded him of it.

But Hugo didn't seem very satisfied. "Why don't you *ask* him?" he urged. "He can't mind that."

Bimbo felt doubtful, but he didn't think Mr. Browne would punish him just for asking a question. "All 'ight," he agreed. "Go ask now." It was nearly five o'clock, and Mr. Browne usually arrived home about half-past four. They were almost certain to find him in his study, taking his afternoon tea.

So they went back along the secret passage, and over the wall into the garden. But when they reached the lawn, and saw the house in front of them, Bimbo was frightened. He he had never been in any part of the house except his own room and the kitchen, though he had peered into all the ground floor rooms at different times; the thought of what he had seen there did not encourage him now. The rooms were gloomy, and in all of them were dead animals or pieces of dead animals. Mr. Browne's study was particularly gruesome, with a huge moose's head decorating one wall, and a stuffed eagle another. Bimbo knew these creatures had not died natural deaths. They had been shot at one time or another by various members of the Browne family. Perhaps they once had been kept as he was kept: perhaps they had had to obey rules like the rules Mr. Browne had made for him: perhaps they had broken these rules. . . .

"Like me to come with you?" Hugo asked. "We should bring Leo, too. I expect he'd like to see Leo."

"Oo come," Bimbo said, "not Leo. *He* not like Leo."

So Leo was left on the lawn where he settled down with his

head between his paws and his big eyes watching them steadfastly. Hugo led the way towards the house. At the porch he paused. "You go first now," he said. "I don't know the way."

"I not know, too," Bimbo replied.

Hugo stared at him. "Sure you told me he was in the study."

"Ess: in study."

Hugo looked puzzled, but he opened the door and went in. Bimbo followed him and they both gazed round curiously. They were in a dim, panelled hall, rather large for a suburban house. The floor was uncarpeted, but smooth and well polished. Its only covering was a tiger skin complete with head and tail. The mouth was open, as if in a fierce snarl, and yellow glass eyes glared up at them. This was what Bimbo saw first, and he didn't like it; but as he looked round he felt the hair on his spine slowly rising and a cold shiver passed up his back. Suspended round the walls, gazing sadly down, were the heads of several kinds of deer. There was also the head of some other horned animal, which Bimbo did not recognize. It had not been shown in the picture books Miss Martha had lent him. It seemed to Bimbo a most ghoulish spot, and he was startled to hear Hugo speak quite cheerfully.

"Big-game hunters," Hugo said. "Bang! Bang! Got him—a man-eater, too."

Bimbo was shocked, much more shocked than if he had discovered Mr. Browne in the middle of a cannibal feast. He looked at Hugo, and was half surprised to see that his appearance had not altered. He still looked pleasant and kind, and even cheerful, with his black curly hair falling over his forehead. It was a lesson to Bimbo not to trust looks. "Ood oo keel an'mals?" he asked, in a low, threatening voice.

"I was only pretending," Hugo said in surprise, "—just for fun."

But Bimbo was not satisfied. He was beginning to learn of the customary human behaviour towards animals. He had recently discovered that men killed animals as an amusement. He had realized it gradually, from scraps of information picked up here and there. The knowledge had crept into his mind with a slow, chilling effect. But he had never associated Hugo with such behaviour, and now he caught him suddenly by the shoulder. "Say oo'll nevah, nevah, nevah, s'oot an'mal. P'omise." Hugo looked at him doubtfully for a moment. Bimbo shook him. "P'omeess," he said angrily, and saw a look almost of fear come over Hugo's face. It gave him an odd feeling of satisfaction. The dead animals he associated with himself, and Hugo had associated *him*self with the hunter. Now the hunter was in fear of the hunted.

"I promise," Hugo said.

"Promise oo'll nevah. . . ." Bimbo prompted.

"I promise I'll never shoot anything," Hugo said, but as Bimbo's grip relaxed, he added, "unless there's another war, of course: then I'll shoot the enemy."

But strangely enough Bimbo didn't mind about that so much, and anyhow at that moment something else attracted his attention. It had been there all along, of course: it was strange he hadn't noticed it before. Among the smells in the hall he suddenly picked out Miss Martha's. It was *it* all right, quite clear and fairly fresh, though overlaid by the thick heavy odour of cook and cut into by the thin sharp smell of Minnie, the housemaid.

He gave an extra sniff to make certain. "Miss Marfa here," he announced.

Hugo was now sufficiently accustomed to Bimbo to know how he had obtained this information. He smiled and scratched Bimbo's back. "She'll be with Mr. Browne," he responded. "If you find her you'll find him."

Mr. Browne's smell was there, too, of course, but it was a peculiar smell, like a blend of furniture polish and soap. Miss Martha's smell on the other hand was quite distinctive—a warm pleasant smell that brought Miss Martha to his eyes quite as clearly as if she were standing there. He dropped to his knees to take it in more strongly. It led the way straight down a passage six or seven yards long. Bimbo followed it, and Hugo followed Bimbo. At the end of the passage was a heavy oaken door which was closed. Bimbo put his nose to the bottom of the door and sniffed. "S'e in dere," he whispered. "'E dere, too."

He could hear voices from inside—Miss Martha's warm and quick; Mr. Browne's slow, cold and deliberate. They were talking about *him*, he realized immediately. He hoped he would hear something interesting.

"I can't see how it will do any good whatever," Mr. Browne was saying. "However, as I've reason to believe that my brother would have liked him to have every opportunity of development, I won't stand in your way."

"I don't think you'll be disappointed," Miss Martha answered warmly. "In fact he's already showing signs. . . ."

"It's not a case of being disappointed," Mr. Browne interrupted, "—or pleased. Suppose even that he took an honours degree at one of the universities, what's to become of him? Is anyone going to employ him? It would have been far better if he had never opened his mouth. I often wish. . . ."

But what he often wished Bimbo, to his intense annoyance, did not hear. Hugo gave him a sharp punch in the ribs and hissed, "You *can't* listen: it's eavesdropping."

Bimbo didn't know the word. It was obvious he *could* listen and he had every intention of doing so. He gave a low growl to warn Hugo to keep quiet, and pressed his ear against the keyhole. Miss Martha was speaking now. "I'm very glad he's come," she said, "and if he does do well I'm sure something will be found for him. I'm sure the state would take over his support if the worst came to the worst. But I thought your brother had maybe. . . ."

She paused deliberately, as if she expected Mr. Browne to finish his sentence for her. But Mr. Browne didn't get a chance: Hugo chose that moment to rap loudly on the door. Bimbo glared at him for an instant, and then grinned. It suddenly dawned on him that Hugo was only pretending: but what was funny was that he didn't really know he was pretending. Hugo had wanted to hear very nearly as much as Bimbo, but he pretended that he didn't, and that to listen was wrong. It seemed to Bimbo that he had stumbled on the key to all human behaviour. He would have liked to sit down and think about it, but Mr. Browne called, "Come in," and he had to put the subject aside for consideration later.

They went in, Hugo leading. Mr. Browne looked at them with a mixture of surprise and annoyance, but Miss Martha smiled. "Good afternoon, children," she greeted them.

"What's the meaning of this?" Mr. Browne inquired coldly.

"Please, Mr. Browne," Hugo replied, "Bimbo wants to know if he can go out of the garden yet and across to our garden."

"He used to be able to speak for himself," Mr. Browne said, with a thin little smile, which, in some extraordinary way, was both unattractive and pathetic. "If school has the effect of reducing him to silence again. . . . Why, I congratulate you, Miss Sutton."

Bimbo didn't quite understand what was meant, but he knew that Mr. Browne was being unkind to Miss Martha because *he* had not spoken. He felt that if he spoke well she would be vindicated. He thought for a moment and then made this speech:

"Please 'low go outside garden. Bimbo'll be ve'y careful and come back again. Bimbo'll nevah leave Oogo."

Mr. Browne looked at him rather sourly. "I don't care if you leave him or not," he answered, "—or where you go for that matter. You'd better ask Miss Sutton here. She seems to have assumed control of you."

Miss Martha flushed a little, but she answered quietly, "I think if you don't go too far away, it should be quite all right."

"Thank you very much," Hugo said politely, and seizing Bimbo's arm he pulled him out of the room. "Mummy always says 'Run away quickly before I change my mind'," he told Bimbo. "So I do the same with everyone."

On the lawn they found Leo waiting for them. He got up in a friendly, leisurely fashion, wagging his tail slowly. "Come on," Hugo called, and they all three set off together down the drive.

A slight breeze was blowing up towards them from the gate. Bimbo sniffed: Leo wrinkled his nose. But Hugo didn't notice anything and he began to whistle.

"I smell Albert an' Dackie," Bimbo announced. "They hide for you."

Next moment they heard voices and Jackie's head came into sight. For a moment he peered through the bars of the gate without speaking: then he said, "Look, Albert, he's got the whole zoo with him."

Albert came into sight. He gave one glance and shouted, "Run, men—every man for himself."

Bimbo did not know how much of this was real, how much pretence. But they all—for there were five or six of them—jumped to their feet and ran at full speed down the road. Hugo gave a yell of excitement, and he and Bimbo and Leo went after them.

Bimbo's running had improved: by going on all fours he was

very nearly able to keep up with the other two. But when they reached Belmore Road he stopped. "Miss Marfa say not go too far," he called after Hugo.

Hugo looked at him over his shoulder. "This isn't very far," he answered. Nevertheless he turned back.

II

Hugo and Bimbo met the next morning at the same time as usual and set off for school together. Bimbo was on the look-out, and ready to hide at the first sign of sightseers, but they didn't meet any. They had not gone very far, however, and were still in Beechpark when Bimbo sniffed and said, "I smell Leo." It was a warm, friendly hairy scent, but at first he couldn't make out from which direction it was coming.

"Leo!" Hugo shouted. There was a short, gruff bark in reply, and the next instant Leo emerged from a gateway on the right. He came towards them slowly, wagging his tail. They waited for him. When he reached them he stood on his hind legs and licked Bimbo's face and neck. They both patted him and scratched behind his ears.

"Why does he go to you first?" Hugo asked rather enviously.

" 'Cos I'm an'mal," Bimbo answered. "Lick oo a'tah."

Sure enough Leo presently did endeavour to put his paws on Hugo's shoulders, but he was too heavy and Hugo collapsed beneath his weight. He fell on his back and there he had to stay till Leo allowed him to get up. It was quite five minutes before they went on again.

Leo came with them, and when they reached Belmore Road he showed no sign of turning back. "Leo come skoole, too," Bimbo remarked cheerfully. "He sit 'side Bimbo."

But Hugo was shocked. "Oh he *can't* come to school," he exclaimed. "He wouldn't be allowed."

"He come," Bimbo replied briefly.

Hugo stopped. "Go home, sir!" he said. Leo and Bimbo looked at him, and Leo wagged his tail.

Hugo stamped his foot. "Go home, sir!" he repeated, but it

was no good, and after a further delay they all went on together. Hugo looked cross, but Bimbo was amused, and he thought out plans for smuggling Leo into school: to Hugo he pretended that no secrecy would be necessary, that it was quite natural for dogs to go to school—he liked to think it was. He imagined Leo sitting beside him and doing sums with his paws: probably he wouldn't be very good—Bimbo would have to help him. Miss Price would get cross, but she wouldn't dare to hit his knuckles with her ruler, because if she did Leo would bite her. The idea pleased Bimbo, and partly on that account, partly to tease Hugo, he said, "Bags I Leo sit 'side Bimbo."

Hugo looked at him and sighed. "You don't know anything yet," he declared contemptuously.

They walked the rest of the way in silence and reached the school gate without meeting any other children.

"All in skoole," Bimbo remarked. "We late."

"We're *not* late," Hugo snapped. "I looked at the time before I came out. We're early, that's what it is."

Bimbo put his nose close to the ground. "All in skoole," he repeated.

But Hugo was determined not to believe him. "We'll leave Leo here," he said, "so as Jackie an' Albert'll be afraid to come in. You. . . ."

"Dackie n'Albert alleddy in: all in," Bimbo insisted.

"Oh, you an' your smellin'," Hugo retorted. "You stay here, Leo. On guard."

"Leo come in," Bimbo said."Leo do lessons with Bimbo."

"He'll stay here," Hugo returned angrily, "an' do as he's bid."

"Leo come in wit' Bimbo."

"Leo'll stay here." Leo got up, stretched himself, gave a huge yawn and set off for home. Hugo tried to stop him: first he caught Leo's collar, but he wasn't strong enough to hold him. Then he ordered him to come back, but Leo went steadily on his way, without paying any attention.

After this there was nothing more to delay them: so they went through the school gate, and round the house to the changing room. Hugo still maintained that they were early though Bimbo didn't think he believed it any more. Bimbo himself had no doubts on the matter. At the gate and on the path there was a perfect medley of fresh, human smells. Some of them were particularly distinct and Bimbo could recognize them clearly—Jackie, Miss Price, Herbert, William, Meta Hemingway. . . . They might almost have been standing in front of him. It was curious that humans should have such a poor sense of smell, though, of course, they had other defects, too. As for their accomplishments, soon he would be able to do all that human boys could do—and there were a number of things besides smelling which he could do better than any of them. He was stronger than they were, better at climbing, better at jumping. . . .

When they reached the changing room it was empty: but on almost every peg hung a coat; in almost every pigeonhole was a pair of shoes. "Oh, well," Hugo said ruefully, "we'll be kept in after school—that's all they can do."

From the big classroom came the sound of the Lord's Prayer. Bimbo tried to understand what it was that made it seem so different when heard from the wrong side of the door; but he couldn't. The prayer finished: there was a shuffling of feet, a burst of talking, and the door opened. Immediately the sounds were multiplied, till it seemed to Bimbo as if something huge were about to burst forth and overwhelm him. He looked up and saw Miss Sutton gazing down at him sternly. He was amazed to find that since yesterday she had grown several inches. She was like a female Moses descending from the mountain. Bimbo had been reading the Old Testament with interest, and he half expected her to fling her Bible and hymn book to the floor in wrath. But she did nothing of the kind, and she spoke quite quietly. "Why are you late?" she asked.

"I don't know," Hugo answered sheepishly.

This seemed foolish to Bimbo: so he said, "We met Leo. Leo knock down 'Oogo. 'Oogo and Bimbo late."

"Who's Leo?"

Hugo plucked up his courage again and Bimbo was glad to let him speak. "Leo's a dog, a big dog, nearly as big as an elephant. He. . . ."

But here he was interrupted by Miss Martha, who was standing beside her sister. "Do you mean the dog that was with you yesterday afternoon?" she inquired sharply.

"Yes, Miss Martha."

"A Newfoundland," Miss Martha informed her sister, "and as quiet as a lamb. *He* certainly didn't prevent them from coming to school."

At this, Miss Sutton, who was looking more and more forbidding, frowned. "You shouldn't make things worse by telling stories," she said sternly. "You're ten minutes late. Miss Price will keep you in for twenty minutes after school. Now run on to your class. Don't delay any longer."

The Misses Sutton did not teach in the junior classes at all. Miss Martha took the second form, Miss Agatha the third, Miss Mary the fourth, Miss Letitia the fifth and Miss Sutton herself the sixth. Miss Belinda gave music lessons in the drawing-room. The whole six of them had been standing together in the doorway. Now they moved on, and a mass of boys and girls who had been penned in behind them, waiting to go to the different classrooms, swarmed out. As soon as the crowd had thinned sufficiently, Bimbo and Hugo forced their way in and took their seats at their own desks. There they had to undergo a fresh catechism from Miss Price. She said they had disgraced her class, and when she heard that she was to keep them in, she grew more angry than ever. "You're selfish little pigs," she told them. "You don't care how much of *my* time you waste, loafing about the roads up to goodness knows what."

Bimbo resented this: they had already been scolded by Miss Sutton; their punishment had been decided. Surely there was no need for Miss Price to say anything. He wished he could pull her hair really hard.

At playtime it was wet and Bimbo joined in a game called Policemen and Robbers. At first it was quite fun, but presently all the smaller children were imprisoned in the big classroom, which was supposed to be the police station, and they couldn't get out. Bimbo didn't mind. He had allowed himself to be shut in when Hugo was caught, and now, seeing the blackboard with no one in charge, he felt a desire to write on it. Hugo watched him, and suddenly he said, "Draw Miss Price having a fit."

But Bimbo didn't know what a fit was. So he gave the chalk to Hugo. "You draw," he said.

"Oh, no, Hugo, *don't*," Michael burst out unexpectedly. "She'd be awfully angry if she saw it."

"Don't be a wee silly," Hugo answered. "She won't see it," and he began to draw.

At first Bimbo saw nothing, but a mass of lines: then he saw a contorted face which gradually began to have a certain resemblance to Miss Price. It was peculiar, because you could hardly have called it a picture of anyone: yet in some way it did have Miss Price's expression. All the prisoners gathered round to look. "It's like her, isn't it?" Hugo said, and he wrote slowly below it:

Pore Miss Price she had a fitt
Hear you see her having it.

"That's portry!" Michael exclaimed.

All the other children gazed at Hugo in admiration. Bimbo too, was astonished. He hadn't known that Hugo had these powers. The door opened and Albert looked in to see why his prisoners were so quiet. He came over and stared at the blackboard. "It's the very spittin' image of her," he pronounced. "You leave it up, and she *will* have a fit."

However, when the bell went Hugo thought it safer to turn the board round. So Miss Price began the lesson without noticing that anything was wrong. It was arithmetic, and immediately she began to use the board. Her method was to put up sums like this:

7)649152

—and make the children work them out in turn. But it was one of those mornings when the whole class seemed dull, and Miss Price got cross. "Next, next, next," she kept calling. Some of the children just gazed at her glumly, and most of the others gave wrong answers. They were all wondering what would happen when she turned over the board. Bimbo was wondering too. Nevertheless, he concentrated on the sums and gave the right answer to every question.

Miss Price noticed this: but her manner of doing so was insulting. "Why you're letting Bimbo beat you!" she exclaimed. "You should be ashamed of yourselves." And a moment later she told

Meta Hemingway to write out her nine times tables twice and hand them in before prayers the next morning. That startled everyone a bit, because Meta was usually a favourite; for a time things went better. Miss Price put up more and more sums: as she didn't rub them out the blackboard got fuller and fuller. Presently everyone knew she must turn it over soon, and Bimbo could feel the suspense. It was awful. He and Miss Price had to do most of the questions between them. Yet Hugo, strangely enough, didn't *look* nervous. When Miss Price's back was turned, he even winked. Michael was the most worried-looking person there, which was strange, considering he was perfectly innocent: all the same it was like him.

"I can't think what's wrong with you," Miss Price exclaimed. "You get stupider and stupider. You're the stupidest children I ever taught. Why. . . ."

At the word "wrong" she had picked up the blackboard. At the word "why" she stopped. For a moment she didn't move. Then she fixed the board firmly in its new position, and stepped back to look at it. Bimbo saw a bright red blush creep round to the back of her neck. She turned, and her face was scarlet from the roots of her hair to as far down as he could see.

For a while she glared at them without speaking. "You're no better than gutter-snipes," she said. "I suppose you think this is funny. Well, I'm going to leave it there for Miss Sutton to see, and you'll hear to-morrow what *she* thinks of it. Meantime I'll keep the whole class in for half an hour: perhaps the joke won't seem so funny after school."

Bimbo had expected that Miss Price would demand the name of the culprit so that she could punish him, but he realized very soon that what she had done was sufficient. For the other children began to scowl angrily at Hugo, till presently a thin little smile showed on Miss Price's face.

Hugo looked uneasy and Bimbo wondered what he would do. At first he glared back at the others, but soon he put his hands to his forehead, and stared at the desk.

"Put your hands down, and look up," Miss Price told him sharply.

Hugo obeyed reluctantly, and showed a lugubrious face. "Please, Miss Price, it was me," he said. "I did it."

"I already knew that," Miss Price answered coldly. "You will now go to Miss Sutton, in the sixth classroom, and tell her what you've done. Don't leave anything out. I shall be talking to her myself after school."

Hugo got up, looking very miserable indeed, and left the room. He was away at least twenty minutes, and when he returned it was obvious he had been crying. "Not so funny now," Miss Price remarked, but Hugo went to his seat without answering.

Bimbo longed to go and sit beside him, and sympathize with him. Two or three weeks ago he would have, but now he knew better. He knew he couldn't say anything till after school, and then only in private. He wondered if Miss Sutton had caned Hugo. When she was stern she looked quite capable of it.

Shortly before it was time for school to end Meta Hemingway put up her hand. "Please, Miss Price, do we still have to stay in, now Hugo's owned up?"

"Certainly you do," Miss Price replied. "All of you saw what he did. If any one of you can tell me on your honour that you tried to prevent him I'll let *that one* go home."

Bimbo considered this offer, but it was of no use to *him*. He was to be kept in in any case for being late, and besides he would want to wait for Hugo. He looked round to see if any of the children would put up their hands and say, "Please, Miss Price, *I* tried to stop him." Of course, the only person who was really entitled to say that was Michael, but Michael looked miserable and ashamed, and soon it became clear that no one was going to speak.

For some reason, Bimbo realized, Michael was afraid, and he decided to speak for him. He raised his hand. "Please, Miss Price, Michael did."

She looked at him sharply and disbelievingly. "Michael did what?" she demanded.

"Michael try preven'm," Bimbo answered. "Michael say, 'Oh, no, 'Oogo, don't! See be awf'y ang'y if see saw't'."

Miss Price turned to Michael and glared at him. "Is this true?" she demanded.

Michael appeared to be about to cry, but he mumbled something which was taken for "Yes".

At any rate it made Miss Price angrier than ever. "For heaven's sake *go* home then," she snapped, "and do at least have the courage of your convictions."

Very sheepishly Michael gathered up his books and departed. He looked far more guilty than any of those whom he left behind. They remained for the full half-hour, sitting quite still, with their arms folded in front of them. That was Miss Price's rule for children who were kept in, and it was far worse than having to do lines or sums.

When at last she told them that the half-hour was over, Hugo and Bimbo got up with the rest, but Miss Price stopped them. "Oh, no," she said, "you and I have a further penance before us."

"But, Miss Price," Hugo objected. "You don't *need* to keep us. Miss Sutton only *said* twenty minutes and we've been half an hour."

Miss Price smiled rather grimly. "Don't try to bamboozle me," she said. "Sit down again and don't let me hear a squeak from either of you till I tell you it's time to go home."

Nevertheless, Bimbo knew that she had forgiven Hugo.

12

Since coming to school Bimbo had been too busy receiving new impressions and adjusting himself to quite a changed way of life to think much of how he was getting on. About the middle of November, however, he did think of it. He knew that he had an extremely good memory—indeed it was nearly perfect—and so far he had had no trouble in understanding what he was taught. At the same time he was clumsy with his fingers, with the result that his writing was exceedingly bad. He imagined that this, and the difficulty he sometimes had in pronouncing certain words, caused him to seem very backward. So he decided to make a definite effort to speak more clearly and to conduct himself generally more like an ordinary small boy.

Of course he made mistakes, and usually they were pointed out to him. Yet often, though he realized that he was behaving differently from anyone else, he preferred to go on in his own way. He knew that the other children watched him in the hope that he would do something extraordinary. At times it pleased him to be watched, and he would do unexpected tricks to amuse them. At other times he would feel that his peculiarities were an injustice—an injustice for which the other children were, in some undefined manner, responsible. Then he would think, "I will stay as I am: their laughter does not harm me."

Miss Price didn't like him: so he did nothing to please her. He even took extra care in preparing his lessons for her, so that she could not have the satisfaction of giving him too many bad marks. Nevertheless, she could still find fault with him, and she did, at the slightest excuse.

Every few weeks she delivered to her class what she called "Little Talks on Good Manners and Etiquette." Bimbo hated them, especially when they were caused by some action of his own—such as spitting at a fly to give it a fright. That had been particularly annoying: it wasn't as if his spit had been wet or messy: it had been practically bone dry—just a bit of oat husk from his porridge, which he'd happened to find in his mouth. But the fuss she'd made—it must have lasted half an hour—and the way, at the end, she'd asked the other children to forgive him and reminded them that they must make allowances for him. . . . Somehow that always came in—and Bimbo didn't want allowances, didn't want to be different: he wanted to be the same, as much as he possibly could.

Miss Price had a favourite boy in the class, as well as a favourite girl: the favourite boy was called William, and Bimbo neither cared for him particularly, nor objected to him. He used to stare at him sometimes, and wonder how he had managed to gain Miss Price's favour. Possibly it was because he always knew the correct answer when she asked her questions about etiquette and good manners.

"Now tell me, William," she began one day, "who walks on the outside, the lady or the gentleman?"

"The gentleman, Miss Price." Even Bimbo had observed this interesting fact, and he felt slightly disappointed that she had not asked William something a little more difficult.

The next question came to Bimbo himself—most unjustly, really, because he didn't sit near William.

"Bimbo, will you tell us please who comes first. Is it gentlemen first, or ladies first?"

Bimbo considered this from several points of view. He didn't mind at all keeping the whole class waiting. The problem was a complicated one. It should have been given to William: it was worthy of him. However, it had come to Bimbo, and he didn't intend to answer it carelessly. The answer to the last question had been "Gentlemen", and therefore it was almost natural to say "Gentlemen" again. But Miss Price had probably thought of this, was perhaps even counting on it. Bimbo decided to answer "Ladies", and then, with the word on the tip of his tongue, he stopped. Perhaps the question had a scriptural significance. If so there was no doubt about it. Adam had arrived in the Garden of Eden a long time before Eve. It was only last week that Miss Sutton herself had read them the story of the creation—and Adam was certainly a man. He decided to risk it.

"Gentlemen, Miss Price. Gentlemen first."

In a moment he knew he was wrong. She gave a little, lingering smile. "I forgot," she said. "Of course, we must make allowances. William, perhaps you can tell him."

"Ladies first," William answered gallantly, and received a smile of approval from Miss Price.

As a rule Bimbo was not inclined to argue, but on this occasion he felt that the question was ambiguous, and the correct answer dependent on what you assumed it to mean. "Adam came before Eve," he said. "Miss Sutton told us. Ladies not first that time."

His tone was anything but deferential, and Miss Price reddened.

"Don't be impertinent," she snapped. "William's quite right."

Bimbo had noticed that if he smiled when Miss Price reproved him it irritated her. So now he said nothing: he just smiled, and watched her.

Hugo, however, felt that Bimbo had been treated unjustly and decided to come to his rescue. "Bimbo's right," he declared. "It depends what you mean." It was brave of him, but Bimbo wished that he had not diverted Miss Price's attention: it lessened the effect of his smile.

That it was having an effect he could see from her face, and when she spoke to Hugo she seemed to have lost her temper completely. "Silence!" she screamed. "Speak when you're spoken to, not otherwise," and she banged her ruler down on the desk. As usual she startled the whole class: but Bimbo wasn't startled. He had known what was going to happen and he continued to smile.

Miss Price turned away from him towards the blackboard. For a moment she seemed uncertain what to do: then she said, "Now that we've improved our manners a little I think we may go on with arithmetic."

She began to write up a sum on the board, and doing so appeared to restore her self-confidence. Bimbo waited for her. He knew she would have to turn round presently, and when she did he had the most dazzling smile ready for her. At first she tried to meet his glance with a resolute frown, but it was too much for her, and she looked away. Still he kept his eyes fixed on her, and still he smiled, watching her grow more and more uncomfortable. He was waiting in the hope that she would tell him to stop smiling: he wanted to say he was so happy he couldn't help it. What would she do then?

But suddenly his attention was distracted: his smile vanished: he became intensely alert. Just above his right knee he felt a faint, tickling sensation. Immediately he became interested. Did he only imagine it, or had he—he hoped he had—a flea? He forgot all about Miss Price. His whole attention was focused on that one point. If the flea so much as trembled he would feel it. But he had often been disappointed before. Clothes, he had discovered, completely upset the sensitivity of his skin. Often when he had been quite sure of a flea there was nothing there at all. So he waited, determined not to begin the hunt till he was certain that a flea was there; and equally determined, if a flea was there, to catch it.

Very cautiously the flea shifted one of its hind legs. It was a big flea, and Bimbo knew that it was gathering its legs into position for a hop. This was the time to pounce. Keeping the palm of his hand hollow, he brought it down with a bang on his thigh. The flea was imprisoned: it evidently realized this, for the hop was not attempted. Instead it started to move through his fur on a cautious tour of investigation.

For a moment Bimbo felt an odd sort of sympathy with it. It occurred to him that the flea would enjoy itself if it could get onto Miss Price. And he imagined how annoyed Miss Price would be when it bit her. Yet in spite of these thoughts the fate of the flea was never for a moment in doubt. In anticipation he had already tasted it, and his behaviour was controlled by instinct rather than thought.

Without changing the position of his right hand he began to contract it so that the flea's prison became smaller and smaller. Presently he had it pinned exactly in one position. It lay quite still there in the hope of deceiving him, but he could feel its small, hard, husk-like body quite distinctly. It was time to bring his left hand into use. Raising the edge of his right hand slightly he partly uncovered the flea. Then he caught it quickly between his left finger and thumb, and plucked it out. For a moment he held it up to inspect it. As he did so it pressed its two hind legs against his finger and tried to pull itself out. Again he felt vaguely sympathetic with it, but he didn't let it escape. Instead he put it up to his mouth and bit it between his front teeth. The taste of a flea always interested him. It was peculiar that so small a creature should have so much taste: there was the hard outer husk, which he felt rather than tasted: there was the blood it had been drinking, which squirted out in a tiny fountain when he squeezed the body between his teeth: lastly it was slightly salty: and when it was gone there remained in his mouth an elusive musty odour like the smell of a crushed fly.

"Bimbo!" Miss Price called sharply.

Bimbo looked up. They were all staring at him, but at first he hardly noticed. "I have ate him," he said softly. "I have ate him up." The "up" was an afterthought. Yesterday Hugo had told Leo to "eat up" a biscuit. So evidently "eat up" was what people talked about; though surely "eating down" would have been more natural. The main thing, however, was to speak like other boys.

Only now it occurred to him to wonder why Miss Price had called to him. Why, too, were the other children staring at him so fixedly? Surely it wasn't all because he hadn't been paying attention. Well; it wasn't so easy to catch fleas and do arithmetic at the same time. He'd like to see *her* try.

"Yes, Miss Price," he answered suddenly, and as he did so he remembered his smile. He made it even broader than before.

And this time it certainly produced results. Miss Price had been looking shocked. For almost half a minute she must have been staring at him with her mouth open. Now she shut it with a snap. "You horrible, disgusting, dirty creature," she exclaimed, in a voice that was more than usually shrill. "Go out at once. Go and stand outside the door. Do you hear me?"

Bimbo realized with surprise that she must regard his conduct as very bad indeed: yet he wasn't quite sure if he was being punished for smiling, or for inattention. He got up slowly: he even thought of disobeying. And he might have disobeyed, had he not remembered what Miss Martha had said about his being in a peculiar position, and the need there was for him to be very careful: this perhaps was one of the occasions when he ought to be careful: so he went straight to the door and shut it quietly behind him.

At first he stood outside with a virtuous feeling that he was obeying Miss Price's instructions to the letter. He hoped Miss Martha might come along so that he could tell her how good he was being. However no one came, and at the end of five minutes he was tired of being virtuous. He bent down and tried to look through the keyhole: but a piece of paper had been stuffed into it, and he could see nothing. He decided to go out to the playground and look in from there. Then a fresh idea came to him and he thought no more about being careful.

He went to his pigeon-hole and got his shoes. He changed into them quickly, for by this time he had learned to tie his own laces without difficulty. His idea was simply to imitate Miss Price, and now he looked round for something to make him a little more like her. There was nothing he could use but the school caps. He took two—Hugo's and his own—and stuffed them into the front of his jersey to make it bulge out. But he wasn't satisfied: he wanted to get something which would suggest Miss Price at first glance. He'd have to get hold of her hat: it was familiar to every child in the school. He knew where it was kept. Each morning she hung it, with her coat, in a cupboard at the far end of the conservatory. It was a place where the children weren't supposed to go, but there was no one about and in a moment Bimbo was there and had opened the door. Sure enough the hat was on its peg: it was a most peculiar light blue object, square, almost flat, and transfixed by a large, silver hat-pin. Bimbo tried to put it on, but it just lay on the top of his head, and his hair wasn't long enough to give the pin a grip. Fortunately he had a piece of string in his pocket with which he was able to tie it on quite securely. Then he looked at himself in the small mirror which hung from one of the posts supporting the roof. His appearance pleased him, and attempting to adopt Miss Price's walk he went out to the playground.

With the exception of the cedar the trees were bare now. This suited Bimbo, for he wanted to be seen, not hidden by leaves. On the ground were some fallen branches. He picked one up and broke it till he had a piece about the same length as Miss Price's ruler. Next he crossed the playground and climbed a chestnut tree which grew close to the classroom window.

As soon as he was high enough he looked in. Miss M'Fadden, who taught the kindergarten, had her back to him; but the children in the kindergarten were staring at him with expressions of amazement on their pink, chubby faces.

However, it was in Miss Price's class that he was really interested. She herself was writing at the blackboard, and in spite of his absence she still seemed to be in a bad temper. From the intent manner in which her pupils were watching her he could tell that they were frightened. Suddenly she swung around and brought down her ruler with a crash on the desk in front of Hugo. Hugo snatched away his hands and sucked his fingers; but Bimbo wasn't sure whether he was really hurt, or only pretending.

Bimbo glanced again at the kindergarten children to make sure that they were watching him, and frowned till his eyebrows almost hid his eyes. He swished his stick through the air and brought it against a branch with a loud crack. Then he snatched his other hand to his mouth, as Hugo had done, and sucked his fingers. The kindergarten children nudged each other and began to point and laugh. Miss M'Fadden spun round: for a moment he thought a flicker of a smile passed over her face. If so she suppressed it quickly and putting on a cross expression signed to him to go away. But Bimbo liked Miss M'Fadden, and he immediately pointed at the hat and at Miss Price to show whom it was that he was imitating. There was no need for Miss M'Fadden to worry: he wasn't trying to annoy her.

Now Miss Price had seen him. Her ruler was motionless by her side and she was gazing at him—and of course her class gazed, too. Bimbo was delighted to have such an attentive audience. He decided to continue his performance. First he pretended to write on the blackboard, but every now and then he turned round as Miss Price did when she was asking questions. He made great play with his ruler. For a time the performance was extremely successful. From inside came roars of laughter, which reached their loudest when Bimbo rapped one of his imaginary pupils over the knuckles. Everyone seemed to be enjoying his exhibition, except Miss Price: even Miss M'Fadden didn't look as if she were really angry, though every time Bimbo's eye met hers she shook her head reprovingly. Nevertheless, she helped Miss Price to lower the blinds, and when that was done the electric light shone through them.

Bimbo was about to jump to the window-sill and hammer on the window when he caught sight of Miss Martha. Immediately he snatched Miss Price's hat from his head and would have thrown it into the next garden had Miss Martha not been too quick for him.

"Bimbo," she said, "come here at once and bring me that hat." If Bimbo had chosen to stay up the tree Miss Martha wouldn't even have attempted to catch him: she wouldn't have had a chance. Bimbo knew this and for just a moment he thought of climbing higher: but he didn't. He felt suddenly very guilty and wicked, and he found himself coming down the tree as meek and shamefaced as could be. He was filled with repentance: he wished he hadn't imitated Miss Price. He saw that Miss Martha wasn't friends with him at present. Maybe he'd be expelled from school and have to spend all day locked up in his cage again.

"Sorry, Miss Marfa," he said, with a mixture of remorse and apprehension, and he handed her Miss Price's hat.

She took no notice of his apology. "Come with me," she ordered. "I see I'm going to have to keep my eye on you. We'll have a little talk when this lesson's over."

She brought him into her own classroom and made him sit at a desk by himself. It was the class Albert was in and they all stared at him, for it was obvious that he was in disgrace. However, Miss Martha told them to go on with their work and immediately the staring stopped. It was wonderful how quiet she was—so different from Miss Price.

13

Presently the bell rang and Miss Martha dismissed her class. One or two went slowly as if they hoped to hear something if they lingered long enough; but the door was shut after the last of them before Miss Martha spoke a word. Then she went and stood in front of Bimbo with her hands on the desk. "Now, Bimbo," she said, "I want you to tell me what happened—exactly."

So he told her everything—how he had smiled to annoy Miss Price, how he had caught the flea, and of his pantomime outside the window. She listened carefully to the whole account; but when he began again to say that he was sorry she cut him short in a way which made him uncomfortable.

"You expect to be scolded, Bimbo," she said, "but I'm not going to let you off so easily as that. Instead I want you to hear what I've done since I first saw you. That night when I was at Mr. Browne's party, and we went round to your cage, I suddenly got the impression that you were very intelligent, and that I would like to help you. When I saw a little more of you my first impression was confirmed. I thought that maybe you were intended to do something—something very remarkable, I mean. I felt that whatever it was—this destiny of yours—it was up to me to try and prepare you for it. Now I may be quite wrong in this impression I have formed. I should warn you that I once had a precisely similar impression about another boy. It didn't lead to anything. As a matter of fact he went into the Navy and was drowned at the age of sixteen.

"Of course he was a much more ordinary boy than you are and it was a great deal easier to help him.

"I've told you already of some of the difficulties I had in getting you to school in the first place. There were others as well. Not only did I have to persuade parents; I had to gain the consent of my own sisters. None of them disliked you, but they were all very doubtful of the wisdom of bringing you here. Nevertheless, in the end we agreed that it was only right that you should be given a chance. At the same time, we like having you. For one thing it is very interesting, and I in particular like having you.

"So far we have managed to get over, or to get round, a great many obstacles. The possibility remains that new ones may arise with which we shall be unable to cope. At any time some of the parents may get together and decide that you are a harmful influence in the school. Even without deciding that, they might change their minds about allowing their children to associate with you. Alternatively if you annoy Miss Price too much *she* may find that she cannot put up with you any longer."

"Would she go 'way then?" Bimbo asked curiously.

Miss Martha gave him a sharp look. "I don't know what would happen," she said, rather crossly. "Good teachers aren't so easy to find. . . .

"In any case," she went on—and her voice had a quality in it which did not invite further interruption—"if you behave badly it doesn't help the school. We have to think of the good of the other children just as much as of your good—more perhaps. Besides, on the prosperity of the school depends the prosperity of my sisters as well as of myself. If troubles start in a school they can often have very great effect in a very short time. If my eldest sister decided that your presence was a real danger to the future of the school I think she would be perfectly justified in getting rid of you. Anyhow," she added smiling, "I don't suppose you want to ruin us."

Bimbo was horrified at such a suggestion. "Oh, no, Miss Marfa," he assured her earnestly.

"That's good," she said cheerfully. "I suppose you *have* taken it all in."

"Yes, Miss Marfa."

"All right, then. Now run along and get your milk. You can think about it this evening and in the meantime don't get me into any more trouble."

While Bimbo was drinking his milk he considered very carefully every word Miss Martha had said to him. He determined that he would behave politely to Miss Price no matter how nasty she should be, and that he would do nothing to displease Miss Martha. When he had finished his milk and was going out into the playground he reminded himself of what he had to do in the evening. He was to think over her talk again—just before he went to bed would be a good time. It had been wise of her to tell him that. With no one to disturb him he would be able to think better, and quietly to make good resolutions for the future. Now with the children gathering round and shouting, "Here he is," it was almost impossible to think at all. Realizing this he put Miss Martha quite out of his head for the time being and concentrated on what was going on about him.

"I told you he wouldn't be expelled," Hugo said triumphantly. "You aren't, are you?"

"No," Bimbo responded. He was pleased to find that he was again the centre of interest and began to consider how he could keep that interest.

Meta Hemingway looked disappointed. "I suppose Miss Martha got him off as usual. It's not fair so it's not." Suddenly another thought struck her and she brightened up. "You're not getting publicly flogged, are you?"

It was an interesting idea and as luck would have it Bimbo was saved the necessity of making an immediate reply.

"Talk sense," Albert told her. "Did you ever hear of anyone gettin' flogged?"

"I did in a story," Meta said, "—only he asked to be expelled instead. He was an awful coward."

There was a murmur of assent, rather doubtful on the part of the boys. When it died away Bimbo made an announcement, "I'm bin publy flogged," he informed them.

They stared at him with a curious mixture of expressions. Some of them believed him: Albert certainly didn't. "Where?" he asked suspiciously.

Bimbo knew about floggings. He had read the same school story as Meta. It had appeared in a boy's paper Hugo had lent to him, and Hugo had explained it. Bimbo's sympathies had been with the boy: he had thought him very wise not to accept a flogging. Now, however, he answered Albert's question. "'Ere," he said, touching the place with his hand.

Albert was indignant. "I don't mean where *on* you. D'you think I don't know that? Is it bein' done in a classroom, or the changin' room—if it's bein' done at all."

"Bin done in beeg classroom," Bimbo answered.

"When?"

"Tree o'clock dis arternoon."

Jackie and Albert continued to look at him suspiciously, but Bimbo, gazing back at them with an expression of candour, saw that they were more than half convinced. Most of the others were completely convinced, though he was rather doubtful about Hugo; Hugo, of course, wouldn't say anything.

All of a sudden a solution occurred to Jackie. "You don't think it's a floggin' if Miss Martha does it?" he inquired contemptuously. "It has to be a man."

"Of course it has," Albert agreed. "Who's goin' to do it? Can you tell us that?"

Bimbo hadn't thought of this, but he wasn't in the least put out. "A please-man," he informed them. "There's a please-man comin'."

"Listen him," Jackie exclaimed, "—a please-man! He means a policeman—there's a peeler comin' to beat the fleas off him."

"He'll be skitin' them all over the place," Albert said. "I bet he's hivin' with them this minute. Look out, boys, or they'll be hoppin' onto you."

It was the girls, however, who paid most attention to his warning. Those who were near Bimbo stepped back hastily. "Dirty thing," Meta called.

One of the boys who had been in Miss Martha's class turned and looked at her. "Fleas aren't dirty," he said reflectively.

"How do you know, James?" Meta asked. "I suppose you've got them, too."

"No," James answered, "but lots of people have." He was a quiet boy, with a serious manner. All Bimbo knew about him, was that he lived in the same direction as Michael, and that they often came to school together. His hair was brown, and curly, in a loose untidy sort of way. He had weak blue eyes and a rather pale freckled face. "Some people can't help having fleas," he went on. "It's only dirty when you don't catch them." And he began to tell them about an aunt of his, who was like that. Fleas simply couldn't resist her. Every time she travelled by tram she got a flea. If there was a flea at the very far end it would hop the whole length of the tram just to get a bite at her. When she came back from town she always had to undress right to the skin—and the flea would be caught and drowned.

Bimbo thought that James was a very sensible person, though his aunt seemed a bit impatient. After all it was better to let fleas wait for a while: they got juicier—though, of course, there was always the risk that you might lose them.

But on Hugo the story made a very different impression. "You've got fleas yourself, Meta," he shouted, "—only you're far dirtier because you can't catch them. Albert's got fleas, too. All of you've got fleas, only you can't catch them—lot o' butterfingers!"

The others paid no attention. They had started to play "Charlie across the water," and they refused to allow Bimbo or Hugo to join in. Hugo immediately tried to organize a game of tig for two, but somehow it wasn't very exciting. Bimbo was glad when Miss Martha came out ringing the bell and they all had to go in.

The next lesson passed very quietly. Bimbo was on his best behaviour and so apparently was Miss Price. She didn't bang her ruler: she didn't shout. The strange thing was it made everyone feel a little nervous. It was quite a relief when going home time came.

Hugo and Bimbo went together as usual: for the first little way neither of them spoke, but Bimbo knew that Hugo was nearly bursting with curiosity.

"Why did you tell them you were bein' flogged?" he demanded as soon as they were out of earshot of the other children.

"Want to play joke, Meta," Bimbo answered. "She come back t'see."

"I bet she doesn't," Hugo returned. "You don't think she believed you, do you?"

"Yes," Bimbo replied. "I'm comin' t'wats."

"There'll be nothin' to watch," Hugo assured him. Nevertheless at a quarter to three that afternoon he was standing with Leo and Bimbo on the road outside Miss Sutton's school. They crawled through a hole in the hedge and dodged from bush to bush round the garden trying to keep out of sight of the windows. It had been raining and each time Hugo knocked against a branch a spray of drops descended on their heads. Bimbo hated water and these unexpected shower-baths made the skin twitch right up his spine. He didn't see why Hugo needed to be so clumsy and he felt cross with him.

When they reached the playground they stopped. It was dismal looking—an expanse of smooth pink mud, with two large puddles in the centre. Bimbo hoped Meta would arrive soon. He glanced up at the trees: they were bare and black and dripping. He might have climbed one to see if she were coming; but he didn't want to get wet, and besides some of the Misses Sutton might have seen him from the house. Instead he decided to go back to look up and down the road.

"I'll come, too," Hugo answered at once.

Bimbo thought of the wet bushes. "Oo make beeg row," he objected. "Oo stay 'ere."

"Sure what's it matter," Hugo retorted. "She's not comin'. I told you all along. . . ."

But at that point Bimbo put his hand over Hugo's mouth: they both waited, intensely still: a moment later there was a definite crunch of footsteps on the gravel and they saw Meta walking boldly round the house towards the side door. As she approached, however, it was opened from within and Miss Martha came out. She stared at Meta. "What on earth are you doing here, child?" she demanded.

Meta stood on one leg. "Please, Miss Martha, nothing."

Miss Martha looked puzzled. "Why weren't you away home, then, long ago?"

At first Meta didn't answer this; but soon a self-righteous little smile appeared on her face. "Please, Miss Martha, I wanted to see Bimbo being flogged for being so naughty."

"What?" Miss Martha exclaimed. "You really thought you were going to see Bimbo flogged?"

"Yes, Miss Martha. He said he was going to be flogged—publicly."

Bimbo wasn't sure that he liked the way the conversation was going. He didn't want another talking-to from Miss Martha so soon after the last. She'd think he didn't pay any attention to her—and he did. Besides, this was something quite different. Of course she had told him not to tell lies—and until now he hadn't thought of this as a lie. It was difficult to know what a lie really was. Miss

Martha had defined it as saying something *had* happened which hadn't happened at all. She'd said it was wicked to tell lies, but the very next day she herself had announced that it was raining cats and dogs. Bimbo had rushed to the window to see this phenomenon, but nothing of the sort had been going on. Miss Martha, naturally, had been able to explain the matter. She'd said she had been using a figure of speech—and that that wasn't wicked at all.

Bimbo glanced at her now to see if she seemed very angry. She didn't: she was looking in an odd way at Meta. "He was only pulling your leg, Meta," she said, "and it seems to have been pulled rather too easily."

"He was telling lies," Meta answered. "Isn't he bad, Miss Martha?"

But this failed to get the reply she expected. "I shouldn't worry so much about other people being bad," Miss Martha told her. "A nice little girl wouldn't have wanted to see him flogged. Now run along home."

Bimbo enjoyed all this very much. Probably Miss Martha thought he'd been quite right to play a trick on Meta. All the same he didn't want to meet her just now and he wished she would return to the house, so that he and Hugo might go away. Meanwhile they crouched behind their bush, as quiet as mice. Bimbo knew he could stay like that for an indefinite period, but he could feel that Hugo was already getting fidgetty.

Miss Martha, however, showed no sign of going. She remained stock still—as if she were in a trance. It was a cold day, too, and in spite of his fur and clothes Bimbo was beginning to feel extremely chilly himself. Suddenly Miss Martha came to life again. She glanced rapidly round the playground, and then, while looking in quite the wrong direction, called, "Bimbo, come out!"

Bimbo was amazed. How on earth had she known? He immediately stood up and went to her, with Leo at his heels.

Miss Martha patted Leo. "So this is the ferocious monster who won't let you come to school in time," she remarked. "Is Hugo with you?"

A fortnight earlier Bimbo would have answered "Yes" without hesitation, but his recent reading of school stories had shown him that such an answer was not only improper, but unwise. So he cast his eyes discreetly towards the ground.

"Good heavens!" Miss Martha exclaimed. "Don't tell me this is schoolboy honour. Hugo, come out at once"—and this time she looked in the right direction.

"You've both been telling stories," she began.

"It was only me," Bimbo said.

"Very well, then: it's got to stop, and you're both going to promise me that you won't say a word to anyone, nor to Meta herself, about seeing her come here this afternoon."

They had to promise—there was nothing else to be done. It was a pity, for as Hugo said, what was the good of a joke if you weren't allowed to tell it.

14

Some weeks later, on a dull December afternoon a few days before Christmas, Bimbo sat by himself on the bare floor of his room. The sliding steel door was open and he looked out into the cage. He was not really cold, for the central heating was on: still, he was not warm enough to be comfortable. He could have got warm, as he very often did, by swinging on the rings and the trapeze, but he didn't feel like doing anything at all. He was lonely and unhappy. It was the day of Michael's Christmas party. Hugo was going, and James was going, and so were a good many other children from Miss Sutton's. Bimbo had thought *he* would be asked—Michael had said he would ask him—yet in the end no invitation had come.

Term was over, but in the last few days before it ended Bimbo had heard a great deal about parties. Several of the children at Miss Sutton's were giving Christmas parties, and some of them had promised to ask Bimbo: so far, however, he had only received one invitation: that was for Hugo's party on New Year's Eve. Bimbo knew the wording of the invitation by heart and it was just for the pleasure of looking at it again that he now decided to take it from its hiding-place. He sprang across the room and went up the rope to his bed-box in the corner. There was no artificial light either in the room or in the cage, and except on very bright days it was dark in the bed-box. But Bimbo didn't need light: the card was hidden under the straw and he knew its exact position. He pulled it out, put it in his mouth, and dropping down the rope took it to the window. Hugo had delivered it by hand because Bimbo had been afraid that if it came by post Mr. Browne might see it and forbid him to attend. The pasteboard had looked very stiff and white: it was no longer so stiff, and the writing had become a little smudged: nevertheless it was still quite easy to read.

Master Hugo Clarke
Requests the pleasure of the Company of
Master Bimbo Browne
at
A New Year's Eve Party
3 p.m., 31st December
Games
Beechwood House *R.S.V.P.*

3 p.m.—that meant three in the afternoon—and if Hugo's party were at three Michael's would probably begin at about the same time. In that case it would have started half an hour ago. Bimbo tried to imagine what exactly they would all be doing, but he couldn't. The talk he had heard about parties had failed to call up anything in the way of a picture. He knew that there would be games, and excitement, and nice things to eat; but he didn't know what the games would be or what the food would be like—or what really was the cause of the excitement. The more he thought about it the more curious he became. Of course he would find out at Hugo's on New Year's Eve, but he wanted to know at once—and suddenly he decided to go to the Bartons' and peep in through the windows.

As soon as he had made this decision Bimbo's unhappiness disappeared. He put the card away and opened the tin trunk where his clothes were kept. On top was an overcoat: it was a garment he disliked, but this afternoon it would be useful. He put it on, buttoned it up to his chin and pulled his schoolcap well down over his eyes. The mirror Dolan had given him was on the mantelpiece. He picked it up and peered into it. He was pleased with what he saw. Very little of his face was showing. In this light no one he encountered on the road was likely to notice that he was anything but an ordinary boy. Of course, most of the Belmore people were accustomed to seeing him: what he feared was that someone would tell Mr. Browne that he had been out after dusk prowling around the roads by himself—for Mr. Browne would certainly object.

Bimbo didn't know where Michael lived. He intended to go to the Clarkes' gate and follow Hugo's trail from there. The difficulty, as he knew very well, was that ordinary boys didn't go along the road on all fours sniffing for a scent. He would just have to be careful and do his sniffing when no one was about.

The first thing was to find out what Cook and Minnie were doing. If they saw him going out in his overcoat they might report him to Mr. Browne, for as a rule he only wore it to school. So he took it off, and went round to the back of the house to reconnoitre. He found them in the kitchen. Dolan was standing at the door talking to them. Evidently they had just finished tea.

Bimbo ran back, and rolling his coat and cap in a bundle, hurried out again through the cage. As he shut the door and was about to cross the drive Dolan came round the corner of the house. He stared at Bimbo in surprise. Then he wagged his head humorously. "He'll give ye ten shillin's for it," he said, "an' don't take a penny less neither. Boy's-a-dear ye're beginnin' young."

Bimbo didn't understand this speech, but he covered his mouth with his hand to indicate secrecy.

"Mum's the word," Dolan replied. "Mum it is," and he winked.

Bimbo winked back and scurried across the lawn to the shrubbery. There he put on his overcoat again and pulled down his cap as before. He went out through the secret passage and it was not until he reached the road that it occurred to him that Hugo might have been taken to the party in a car. He hoped not, for though car smells were strong, two or three different cars had often exactly the same smell.

He came to the Clarkes' gate without meeting anyone. Fortunately Hugo had gone on foot. His scent was clear and unmistakable, though rather more soapy than usual. After one sniff to discover the direction he had taken, Bimbo set off boldly, walking upright. It was dusk, but not yet dark. In Beechwood the lamps were still unlit.

The journey turned out to be less difficult than he had anticipated. Parts of the road were in deep shadow and as only a few people were about he was able to go for considerable distances on all fours. It was more comfortable and soon he began to pick up other scents, belonging to boys and girls from Miss Sutton's. They must all have been going to the party. He was able to guess, too, some time before he reached it, which was the right house; for there were lights in all the windows. Not till he was actually in the garden did he realize that the blinds were drawn. This was a disappointment. If he were to see anything at all he would have to get inside by some means or other. He went round to the back and found an uncurtained window on the first floor just above the yard: it was slightly open and only a faint light shone from within.

Bimbo sprang to the yard wall and from there to the window-sill. Very slowly he pushed down the upper sash and the next instant he was inside. He stood on tip-toes, ready at the slightest movement or sound to climb out again and make a hasty escape.

But there was no one in the room. The odd thing was that it had evidently been packed with people quite a short time before. It was full of smells. The whole party seemed to have been going on here—and then, for some reason, they had all gone away. Bimbo listened intently. They were downstairs now: he could hear a distant hubbub of shouts and laughter. Perhaps they went round all the rooms in turn. What had they done in here? he wondered.

He relaxed and began to examine his surroundings more closely. As he had seen from outside it was not quite dark: there was a pale, glimmering light from a gas mantle with the flame turned low. He could see the indistinct shapes of two arm-chairs, and a table pushed back into a corner; but what was most strange to find inside a house was a fir tree: its roots were in a square box close to the far wall. The box was covered with red paper and the tree had things growing on it, which Bimbo had never seen growing on any tree before. There were red and yellow paper lanterns, and coloured bits of glass, and small wax candles. Only one lantern was lit: it looked like the Moon and shed a faint yellow light over the blue-green fir leaves. The tree was a Christmas tree, Bimbo guessed suddenly. Very gently with one finger he touched the queer frosty-looking wool which hung in festoons from the branches. It was prickly and Bimbo drew back his finger; but now that he realized what the tree was he examined it thoroughly from top to bottom. He had been told that there were presents on Christmas trees, but there were none on this. They must have been pulled: indeed he might have known as much from the tissue paper and coloured wrapping paper which littered the floor. A draught rustling through it now caused an abandoned balloon to set off on a bobbing indeterminate journey across the floor. Bimbo wondered if perhaps there had been a present for him and if someone else had taken it. Of course it might have been put on one side for him, or got hidden by accident under one of the piles of crinkly paper.

He began a new search, but the crackling of the paper made him nervous and he stopped every few seconds to listen for other noises. It was in one of these pauses that he heard footsteps on the stairs. He became quite still and held his breath to hear better. Two people were coming and in a moment he recognized who they were. They were Michael and Hugo, and they were coming in here. Bimbo looked round hastily. There was no time to escape: the door was beginning to open: he dodged behind the Christmas tree and crouched down.

"Oh, come on," Hugo called. "What's keepin' you?"

"Nothing," Michael answered, after a moment's hesitation. "It's dark, isn't it?"

"It's not dark enough," Hugo returned. "Here, I'm going to put out the gas. There's plenty of light from that old Chinese lantern." His voice had a bullying tone which Bimbo had never heard before. The gas went out with a hiss and a phut and the room became very much darker.

"What do you want?" Michael asked, and Bimbo knew that he was trembling. "I don't like it in here."

"It's about Bimbo," Hugo replied. "Why's he not here? You said you'd ask him, didn't you?" Bimbo pricked up his ears. Hugo was quite right, though it was a pity he hadn't spoken to Michael a little sooner.

"Yes, I did say I'd ask him," Michael admitted apologetically, "and I tried to. I asked them lots and lots of times to let me have him, but they just said, 'No' every time. Daddy said he wouldn't hear of it."

"And that's all you did?" Hugo sounded contemptuous.

"What else could I do?"

"You should have said you wouldn't have a party unless they had Bimbo, too."

Peeping through the branches of the Christmas tree Bimbo could see both of them. Hugo was holding Michael's wrist and every now and then he twisted his arm slightly. It got a little extra twist now and Michael burst forth in a sort of whine. "It wouldn't have been any good. You see it's Marjorie's party, too—they'd just have sent out the invitations anyhow. I wasn't even allowed to help to write them, though I can write quite well now and they let Marjorie. . . ."

"Shut up," Hugo interrupted. "You make me sick. He's asked to my party, anyway, and Bertie's havin' him, too."

"Bertie!" Michael exclaimed. "I didn't think he'd be allowed to have him."

"He's not allowed. He doesn't know yet he's goin' to have him, but he will. I'll twist his arm till he promises."

"Oh," was all Michael responded, but there was light enough for Bimbo to see his expression. He was evidently rather shocked at Hugo's ruthless behaviour.

"It'll have to be kept secret, of course," Hugo went on deliberately. "Nobody'll know he's there except us—you an' James an' Bertie an' me. You an' James have got to help."

"Got to help," Michael repeated forlornly. "How d'you mean got to help?"

"You an' James have got to call for him. I'll meet you before you get there. I have to see about gettin' him in. But I may need you afterwards as well. If you hear me havin' hiccoughs, that's a secret sign. It means you've got to follow me—you an' James I mean. The others won't know. D'you understand?"

"Yes, but. . . ."

But Hugo had no more to say. He crossed to the door and opened it. Michael followed more slowly. As soon as they had gone, Bimbo tiptoed after them. Hugo was going downstairs a little in front of Michael. "Maybe I'll have a cold and won't be able to go to Bertie's party," Michael muttered, as if he were talking to himself.

Hugo heard him and stopped. "If you're not there," he said, "I'll break your arm for you—next term in the middle of the playground—and that's more than I'm going to do to Bertie."

They went out of sight round the corner of the staircase. A moment later Bimbo heard a grown-up voice he did not know. "Where have you been?" it demanded.

"I was leaving the room," Hugo answered quickly. "Michael was showing me the way."

When he had made sure that there was no one else about Bimbo crept as far as the bend of the stairs. From there he peered through the banisters into the hall. It was full of children and the noise was tremendous. They were streaming out of a door on the right and in through another which faced the bottom of the stairs. Bimbo could see part of a big table covered with a white cloth, two smaller tables and a sideboard: they were loaded with bowls and glasses which contained different coloured shining stuffs, with lumps of pure white snow on top. There were big plates of sandwiches, too, and plates of nuts and fruit, red shining apples, pale yellow-green apples, bananas, oranges, grapes, and tangerines in silver paper. . . . Bimbo would have enjoyed some of them. It was funny listening to the sound: it came to Bimbo in waves—up and down, up and down, and once, suddenly, there was a dead silence for no reason at all. Everyone had just happened to stop talking at the same instant. Bimbo wished he could make out what they were saying, but he only heard what everyone was saying and that was clamour.

To Bimbo it wasn't really a party, but a vision of a party. He thought it all looked beautiful—the bright dresses of the girls moving backwards and forwards: it was like seeing a flower-bed with all the flowers walking about. Presently they became quieter and he heard the same grown-up voice saying, "Take one each and cross your arms."

On the table were lots of tubes—yellow and blue and green and red—each about a foot long. Every child picked up one of these and some of the boys took two. Then they crossed their arms and made a chain, but instead of holding hands they held the ends of the coloured tubes and linked themselves together that way. Bimbo heard the grown-up again: "Are you ready? Well then, Ready, Steady—*Pull*," and with that there was a series of sharp cracks and the next moment all the coloured tubes, which seemed to be only paper after all, were broken and torn, and the children were staggering apart. It looked like an accident, but whatever had happened nobody seemed to have been hurt and everyone seemed to like it. There were fresh roars of laughter and shouts, and they all began to put on paper hats and caps which had appeared from Bimbo didn't know where.

And that was all Bimbo saw: for one of the maids came out of the kitchen and began to go up the stairs. Bimbo hurried back to the Christmas-tree room. He had stayed long enough, he decided. So he climbed out of the window and set off for home.

What he had seen interested him very much. He longed more than ever to go to a party. But what he thought about most was the conversation he had overheard between Hugo and Michael. He felt grateful to Hugo and wished he could think of something kind to do for him.

15

Hugo's party took place two days before Bertie's and Bimbo enjoyed it immensely: he enjoyed the games they played—particularly Blindman's Buff and Musical Chairs. He was very good at Blindman's Buff—better than anyone else. He didn't have to feel people and guess who they were: one sniff and he knew. He liked the supper, too, specially the jellies and fruit, but the most exciting thing of all was the visit of Father Christmas.

Bimbo knew Father Christmas had been asked, but Hugo hadn't been sure if he'd be able to come or not. So it was quite a surprise when just after supper the drawing-room door opened and there he was. The game of Hunt-the-Thimble stopped at once and everyone crowded round him. He had the queerest face Bimbo had ever seen: it was like a face on top of a face and its expression never altered. Bimbo couldn't make up his mind if it was really a nice face or not: but the presents were nice. He gave Bimbo a writing set—a red pencil, paper and envelopes, and twelve penny-halfpenny stamps—all packed in a cardboard box: he also gave him an unburstable rubber ball.

The writing pad was what pleased Bimbo most. He liked the idea of writing letters and the day after the party he wrote to Miss Martha. He told her all about it and how well he had got on at Blindman's Buff. He started his letter in the morning and just got it finished in time for Dolan to post on his way home in the evening. He didn't tell Miss Martha that he was going to Bertie's party. He hadn't actually received a written invitation, and he knew very well that Bertie's father and mother weren't expecting him. But he had enjoyed Hugo's party so much that he would have done nearly anything to get to another.

Bertie's party was later than either Michael's or Hugo's had been, and Hugo had arranged for Michael and James to be at Mr. Browne's gate at a quarter past four, a quarter of an hour before the party was due to begin. Bimbo was to be there at the same time, and he muffled himself up and pulled his cap well down over his face so that no one would be likely to recognize him in the darkness without looking very closely. Actually he reached the gate five minutes early: nevertheless he found the other two waiting for him. "Hullo," Bimbo said.

"Hullo," Michael answered.

"Are you comin'?" James asked.

Bimbo could see that they were uneasy, though there was no real reason why they should be: all they had to do was to take him to the house; there Hugo was waiting for them and they would be able to leave him and go on in. Yet apparently they didn't like doing even this, and for some time they walked along in a rather gloomy silence. They went towards Belmore village which was in the opposite direction to the station. Presently a lamplighter passed them. He was riding a bicycle and his brass-topped pole was over his shoulder. A few yards in front of them he stopped and got off his bicycle. Propping it against a lamp-post he pushed his pole through a little trapdoor in the bottom of the lamp. There was a flicker and the sound of a soft explosion: it was like the phut the gas had made when Hugo had turned it off in the Christmas-tree room at Michael's party: but this time exactly the opposite happened: the whole inside of the lamp became filled with yellow light and a circle of radiance dropped down on to the dark ground below. It shone out sideways, too, showing raindrops hanging on the thorns of the bare leafless hedge. The lamplighter rode on again zigzagging backwards and forwards across the road from lamp to lamp. Even after he had lost sight of him Bimbo could see the lights springing out one by one, ever more and more faintly.

Bimbo had not seen the lamps being lighted before. "I'd like to be man dat light up," he said. "Do 'oo t'ink dey'd 'low me?"

"You mean when you're grown-up?" Michael asked.

Bimbo had thought of no definite time, but he agreed, "'Es, wen I growd up."

Michael considered. "I'm sure they would," he decided. "You wouldn't need a pole or a ladder. You'd just climb the lamps with a box of matches. They'd. . . ."

"When we're grown up," James announced, "they won't need lamplighters. There's a new lamp that lights itself—at the right time every night, too: it's got a clock in it."

Michael wanted to know how it worked. "Is it an alarum clock?" he inquired. But James did not get time to answer, for going round a corner they found themselves face to face with Miss Martha.

"Oh, hullo!" she greeted them. "Where are you all off to, so bright and shining in your Sunday best?"

"Please, Miss Martha, we're going to a party," Michael answered, "at Bertie Screwfle's."

"That's nice," she commented. "Well, I hope you enjoy yourselves. Don't eat too much."

"No, Miss Martha," James and Michael chorused dutifully.

Bimbo, however, did not speak. He looked at Miss Martha's kind, smiling face and he felt ashamed. He knew she would disapprove of what he was doing, and that she would be disappointed in him and hurt, if she found out. Suddenly he made up his mind. "I'm not goin'," he declared. There was a pause while they all stared at him. Then he added, "Dey didn't ask Bimbo."

"I see," Miss Martha responded. "You're just walking with James and Michael for company?"

Bimbo hesitated, but he left the question unanswered. "I'll come back wid you now, Miss Marfa," he said at last.

She looked at him searchingly for a moment. "I was going to call at your house anyhow," she told him, "to thank you for your nice letter. I'm glad I didn't miss you."

Bimbo was glad, too, and turning about he walked back with her the way he had come.

"I haven't really had a chance before to talk about last term," Miss Martha began. "I was very pleased with how you got on—and for the last month you gave us no trouble at all."

With that Bimbo confessed. He didn't mention Hugo: only that he himself had been going to try to get into the Screwfles' and enjoy the party if he could.

Miss Martha didn't press him for details and she didn't scold him. "I'm very glad you changed your mind," was all she said, "and I hope you won't do anything like *that* again."

She came into his room with him and stayed for some time. She had brought several books, but he would not be able to read them till the morning. "I wish he'd let you have a light," she grumbled. "It's pure meanness—nothing else." But after that she stopped as if she regretted having spoken so freely, and a few minutes later she set off for home.

Bimbo was left alone in the darkness. He thought of Hugo and Michael and James at the party. Hugo would be cross with him for not coming: James and Michael would have told him what had happened. It would have been exciting getting into the Screwfles' house secretly: all the same he did not regret having abandoned the adventure.

Yet since he had begun to go to school and become accustomed to companions during the day, he had found it more and more tedious spending his evenings alone. He had various ways of occupying himself till it was late enough to go to sleep. Sometimes he told himself stories—usually stories out of books which he rearranged to suit himself. And nearly always he went over what he had done during the day. He would make a mental list of any words he did not understand, so that he could find out their meaning later. Tonight, however, there were none. He pretended instead that he was giving a party. He considered whom he would ask and what presents they would all get from the Christmas tree.

16

At Miss Sutton's the same little ceremony took place after prayers every Monday morning. The boys or girls in the different classes who had got the highest marks during the preceding week were called up in front of the whole school; and Miss Sutton herself pinned silver medals on their jerseys or gym tunics, as the case might be; usually it was gym tunics, for at Miss Sutton's the girls seemed to be cleverer than the boys. The medals were worn for a week and handed in the following Monday before prayers.

In Miss Price's class Meta Hemingway was nearly always the winner; if for some reason she wasn't, it was sure to be her friend Gertrude McArthur. Bimbo was never anywhere near them; but early in the Easter term he realized that it was only his low marks for writing, and the marks Miss Price deducted from him in every subject for untidiness, which kept him from being top. By taking great care, and doing his preparation very thoroughly, he could now get through his reading in class almost without mistakes. With his writing he was equally painstaking, and he knew it had improved considerably: unfortunately it did not please Miss Price, and she never gave him higher marks than four out of ten.

Bimbo didn't worry a great deal. He didn't mind much whether he was top of the class or bottom. The only subject he really cared about was reading, and not reading aloud, but visual reading: in that, though he alone might know it, his progress was entirely satisfactory. There was a sentence in the copy-book that he repeated to himself over and over again—"Reading is the key to knowledge."

One Monday morning, towards the end of February, Miss Price did not appear at prayers. It turned out that she was ill, and Miss Belinda took her class. She was a mild dreamy-looking woman; nevertheless she knew how to keep order. Lessons went on in practically the same way as usual, but Bimbo liked them better because they were quieter and Miss Belinda had a pleasant voice. The first day, too, she gave him seven for writing, and the next day eight—and for the rest of the week it was either eight or nine: nor did she deduct any marks from him for untidiness. Miss Price had been in the habit of making the children call out their marks at the end of each period, in order that she might enter them in her book. Miss Belinda just noted them down privately without telling anyone what they were. So Bimbo himself was the only person who guessed what was happening.

The next Monday morning at prayers Miss Price was in her place as usual. She looked quite well, but at the same time a little cross; and Bimbo guessed why; as he was coming in he had seen her talking to Miss Belinda.

After prayers Miss Sutton called out the names of the medal winners in the ordinary way, and one by one they went up—sixth form, fifth form, fourth form, third form, second form, first form —girls every one.

"Transition," Miss Sutton said, "Bimbo Browne."

There was a moment of astonished silence. Miss Price could not suppress a slight scowl. Meta, who had actually stood up, sat down again and put out her tongue at Bimbo. Then she sniffed very loudly and whispered something to Gertrude.

It was Hugo who began the clapping, and in a moment it became quite a storm. Every boy in the school joined in and clapped as hard as he could—and the nice girls like Francie clapped too. Bimbo enjoyed it. The medal winners were generally clapped a little, but never nearly so much as this. Bimbo walked slowly up the room, and Miss Sutton bent down and pinned the medal to his jersey. All the Misses Sutton smiled, but specially Miss Belinda and Miss Martha.

Even after Bimbo had got back to his seat the clapping went on, and Miss Sutton had to hold up her hand for silence before she could announce who had won the kindergarten medal.

But as soon as the rest of the school had gone and Miss Price had her class to herself she made a little announcement: "Gertrude McArthur is top of the class this week—top of. . . ."

"Bimbo is top," Hugo interrupted. "Gertrude didn't get the medal. I'll tell Miss Sutton on you."

Miss Price flushed all over her neck and face as she always did when she was angry. She took a step towards Hugo, with her ruler grasped tightly in her right hand. Her knuckles were white and shiny. For a moment it looked as if she would hit Hugo in the face. Bimbo curled himself up, ready to spring to his friend's assistance. However, Miss Price's eyes were fixed on Hugo and she didn't notice this. Hugo himself was prepared for her: he was sitting well back with his hands under the desk. But suddenly she stopped. "Hugo," she said, "you will write out twenty times 'I must never interrupt', and bring it to me before school tomorrow."

"Me, Miss Price!" Hugo exclaimed, in a most innocent injured voice.

"Yes, you," she snapped, "and all I was saying, was that Gertrude is top of the boys and girls."

"What about Bimbo?" Hugo demanded.

"Bimbo is something different."

There it ended, except that just for a moment, Bimbo smiled again at Miss Price. He meant to upset her and he did, for she turned away and didn't look in his direction for the rest of the lesson. But he only did it once, for he was afraid of giving her any real cause of complaint.

Next week Meta was top as usual, but on Monday afternoon Bimbo had a long talk with Miss Martha. She told him not to worry about marks any more, because they didn't matter. What did matter was that he should continue to do his best, and she would examine him herself from time to time and find out how he was getting on.

17

In the summer Bimbo had his final triumph over Miss Price. He was put up into the first form and got on so well that by the end of term he was second in the class. During the holidays which followed Hugo was at the sea-side, and Bimbo was left very much to himself. At Miss Martha's suggestion he filled in the time by working and as a result was given a double remove at the beginning of September. This brought him into the third form under Miss Agatha.

He had now become completely accustomed to the other children and enjoyed school thoroughly: but out of school he had a good deal less freedom than he would have liked. Among other things Miss Martha had made him promise not to go anywhere where there was a notice "Trespassers Prosecuted". For a considerable time this prevented him from playing in Belmore Wood, though Hugo and a good many other people paid no attention to the notices. Belmore Wood adjoined the bottom of the Clarkes' garden and Bimbo often gazed at the trees and longed to explore it. Miss Martha, however, was afraid that if Bimbo were caught trespassing there would be trouble, and she would not let him go into the wood without permission from the owner. As the owner lived in England she had to write to him, and it was not till late in the autumn that a reply was received. The owner, it appeared, was quite willing for Bimbo, or any children to whom Miss Martha might give permission, to play in the wood as much as they liked. What he did not want was that it should become a public playground for the inhabitants of Belmore Village. Miss Martha told Bimbo this news one morning after prayers, and he and Hugo arranged to visit the wood together that very afternoon. For a long time Hugo had been wanting to make a dug-out there, like the dug-outs the soldiers had used in the trenches. Bimbo wasn't interested in dug-outs, but he did want to climb the trees. Nevertheless, he agreed to help with the dug-out, and as soon as he had finished his midday meal he hurried across the road and into the Clarkes' garden. Hugo wasn't to be seen and guessing that he was still at his dinner Bimbo decided to wait for him. He made his way to the lawn and hid behind a clump of rhododendrons in a position where he could watch the hall-door. Before long he was joined by Leo. It was a cold, damp, November day with an even greyish white sky and no sign of the sun: they huddled close together to keep warm.

They had waited for almost an hour when Hugo appeared and looked round inquiringly. Bimbo gave a low, prolonged whistle and began to move towards him through the bushes. They met at the edge of the drive and went round the house to a stable-yard at the back where Hugo had hidden two spades. They collected these and going along a chilly stone passage came out on a narrow path. On their left and in front the ground fell away, and suddenly, down below them, Bimbo caught sight of the wood; a blue, autumnal haze hung over the trees. Bimbo trembled with a curious thrill, a mixture of excitement and sadness.

The path, which was ungravelled, had not an even downward slant, but was strengthened here and there by cross-pieces of wood which acted as steps or buttresses. On either side was a slope of rough grass among which were clumps of withered bluebell leaves.

At the foot of the garden they left the path and made their way through scattered trees towards a stream. If the trees had been a little closer together Bimbo could have leaped from one to another and kept his feet off the cold, squelchy ground. He didn't like water or mud, but Leo seemed to be enjoying himself. As they came nearer the stream the ground became wetter still and the grass grew in reedy tufts. They jumped from tuft to tuft till they reached a half rotten tree-trunk which had fallen across the stream. Hugo ran over this, taking short steps, and spreading out his arms slightly to keep his balance. Bimbo went on all fours with his tail in the air. As for Leo he sniffed the log once or twice and then waded through the water, stopping half-way for a drink.

On the far side of the stream was a broken-down barbed-wire fence. "Our garden ends here," Hugo remarked, as they scrambled through it. "This is Belmore Wood." All around them now were tall, silvery-grey tree-trunks, and they walked on a dry yielding matting of beech leaves and beech-nuts which crunched slightly under their feet. As they went on, the ground rose slightly and the trees grew closer together. Very soon the dell was out of sight: there was nothing to be seen on any side but trees, and fallen leaves and thickets of bramble. If only they had come here in summer, Bimbo thought, how lovely it would have been to swing from one tree to another thirty or forty feet up with the sunlight shining through the soft green leaves all around. Even now, on this chilly late autumn day he felt more at home here than in any other place since he had left that first home which he had lost so long ago and could remember only dimly.

A sudden exhilaration seized him and springing to a tree, he began to race up it: he was hardly conscious of the effort of climbing, and as he climbed he found himself singing in a low-toned chattering language that he did not understand. By chance he had chosen one of the highest trees and when he reached the top he found himself looking out over the wood at the blurred, misty outline of the hills. There, among the slender branches, his exhilaration began to leave him. He felt that something was missing. It was partly perhaps the vague damp spirit of autumn that affected him, or the desolate appearance of the country beyond the wood where bare brown fields alternated with dismal bluish-green fields that looked as if they were quietly weeping for the summer that had departed. But it was more than that. He had half expected to come out into a sunny paradise beneath a deep blue sky and to see no bounds to the forest, rich and dark, with waving tree-tops stretching in every direction to the limit of vision. There was more, too, that he wanted—a companionship that he had not found among these cold, white, undemonstrative, human boys.

"Bimbo," Hugo called, "what are you doin' up there?" And he shouted, "Bimbo, Bimbo, Bimbo . . ." till it had the insistent effect of a gong and Bimbo had to pay attention.

"I'm look-out man," he replied. "I'm spying out." And almost as if because of the words he had used, he saw something which he knew would interest Hugo. Down below, and a little to his right, was a clearing. In the very middle of the clearing was a tangled mass of briar and bramble; and in the middle of this thicket was a square, black pit. Trailers of bramble with strawberry-coloured leaves, and bright yellow leaves, and dark rough green leaves hung over the edges. Bimbo knew that it was the secret den which Hugo had been hoping to find. "I have found something good," he called down, and began to descend.

"What have you found?" Hugo demanded, before Bimbo's feet could touch the ground. "Money?"

"The seegrid den," Bimbo answered and he led the way towards his discovery. But when they reached the thicket he found that it was even denser than it had appeared, and it took them some time to reach the centre. The pit was about eight feet square and five feet deep. A half rotten wooden beam stretched across the middle of it, and at one side part of the edge had been cut away to make a few rough steps. At the bottom a broken stone jar lay on its side.

"What do you think it's for?" Hugo asked. "D'you think it's used now?"

Bimbo climbed down into the pit and began to sniff. He sniffed the steps, the stone jar, the sides and the floor. "No one's been here for years and years," he said. "It's quite safe. No one will find us."

Then Hugo, too, climbed down and sitting on the ground they discussed what they would do.

"It'll be no good till we get a roof on it," Hugo decided. "We could use the goat's house."

The goat's house was in a small paddock adjoining the Clarkes' garden. It had collapsed long ago, but the corrugated iron sheets remained. Hugo suggested that they should get them immediately and bring them to the wood.

They set off at once, but passing the house Hugo was seen, and brought in to be introduced to a visitor who was calling on his mother. Bimbo returned home. His room felt chilly, for so far this autumn the central heating had not been in use, and he was never allowed a fire. He swung on the rings and the trapeze to keep warm. It was not till the following week that he and Hugo were able to put a roof on the dug-out.

18

After this Bimbo went to Belmore Wood every afternoon. At first he went with Hugo to work at the dug-out. Later, when the dug-out had been completed, he was more often alone, or had only Leo to keep him company. He was happier in the wood than anywhere else. He felt less restrained there: he could run and jump and climb with no one to notice that he did these things differently from human beings; he spent hours at a time crawling through the bushes and swinging among the branches of the trees. He liked its smells and its sounds, and he found it more interesting every day: it appealed to his imagination: it was romantic and mysterious.

All over the wood he had secret hiding places, from which he could watch both animals and people. He liked to watch them. He liked to peer out at them through the undergrowth or crouch, silent as a cat, on a branch above their heads. As a result he was never seen by the few people who went to the wood: only by Hugo and the animals who lived there. These animals watched him, but it was in the same way as they watched one another: they recognized that he, too, was an animal, and a friendly animal at that. So they allowed him to see them, though they avoided getting directly in his way.

It had always been natural to Bimbo to move quietly; but now, on his journeys through the wood, he became even quieter than before: he concentrated on making as little noise as possible. He was careful never to tread on dry twigs, or even on dead, curled-up leaves which would crackle as he crushed them. He found out, too, that if he didn't want to be seen it was best to listen for the sounds made by others before coming into the open himself.

Leo was a nuisance on such expeditions. He didn't bark much, but he made a great deal of noise in other ways. So if Hugo was in the dug-out Bimbo usually told Leo to stay behind to keep him company.

On one of these occasions he left Hugo trying unsuccessfully to light a fire. The dug-out was cold and dark and Bimbo found it much pleasanter outside in the wood. It had been damp and misty all morning, but now, in the afternoon, the sun had come out and the air was full of smells and vapours. Bimbo knew that he would be able to find animals who had hidden and gone to sleep for the winter, for the damp and the warmth would make them give off a faint scent. He did find two, though the first was betrayed by sound more than by scent. Bimbo heard snoring and sniffed about until he discovered a hedgehog rolled up in a ball under a drift of dead leaves. A little later in a hollow oak tree he saw a squirrel; it was asleep, too, with its head completely buried in its dark bushy tail. Bimbo tried not to wake either of them, but it pleased him to have discovered their hiding-places.

He thought it strange that the squirrel had not chosen a tree in a more remote part of the wood; for the oak grew quite close to Belmore village and was only separated from the road by a narrow, rocky field, half covered with whin bushes. After he had seen the squirrel Bimbo hid for a moment on the ground behind the trunk of the tree. He hadn't decided where to go next and he didn't want to be seen by any of the village boys. As he crouched there a slight sound attracted his attention. It came from among the whins. He listened carefully. He was very patient and when the sound was not at once repeated he continued to listen. At first there was nothing but the rustling of birds in the undergrowth and the distant rumble of a train. Suddenly, however, he heard what he was listening for and this time it came again and again, almost continuously. Quite close at hand among the whin bushes someone was sobbing. It seemed to Bimbo a terribly sad sound, as if all the troubles of the world had been packed into a little box which was too small to hold them, and were trying to burst their way out. Yet the sobbing was not very loud.

Bimbo followed a winding passage through the whins where the ground was spattered with big round pancakes of dried cow dung. At the end of the passage in a small, circular clearing he found Michael curled up on the grass.

Michael didn't hear him; and for a moment Bimbo stared at him, wondering what to do. Michael's whole body was shaking. His head was buried in his arms. His fists were clenched. Bimbo noticed the end of a small piece of yellow ribbon which protruded from his left hand. He seemed to be trying to control himself, but was only succeeding to the extent of muffling slightly the sound of his sobs. Bimbo was sure that this was unhappiness greater than any he had experienced, and he couldn't imagine what might have befallen this human boy, who had his own kind all around him.

"Michael," he said, and putting out his hand timidly he let it rest on Michael's shoulder.

The effect surprised him. Michael stopped sobbing at once. He looked up at Bimbo with an expression of pure hatred. His face was red, and scratched, and tear-streaked. "Go away," he muttered angrily. "Can't you see I don't want you?"

Bimbo did see that, but at the same time he saw something else —another part of Michael which was longing to explain everything and to release itself from its burden of sorrow. "Poor Michael," he whispered. "Poor, poor Michael." At first his words had no effect. Michael continued to look at him with a curious, fixed expression as if he didn't see him, and Bimbo wasn't quite sure if Michael really understood that he was there. He ventured to stroke Michael's face very gently with one hand, but Michael didn't say anything. For a little while his face remained in the same shape, but gradually

Bimbo saw the hot, angry look disappear from his eyes. Michael didn't smile, but he relaxed a little.

"What's wrong?" Bimbo asked. "Michael, tell Bimbo what's wrong."

And presently Michael did tell. He had been going to Belmore village where he was to meet two cousins. They were to take him to see a football match in which their school was playing. It was the school to which Michael himself expected to go after he left Miss Sutton's. Its colours were red and yellow and Michael's mother had made him a red and yellow rosette. The story as Michael told it was disjointed and not very clear, but Bimbo gathered that all had gone well till Michael had come to the outskirts of Belmore village. There he had encountered Albert and Jackie who supported the rival school. They had ordered him to remove his rosette and trample on it. When he refused they had removed it themselves, trampled on it themselves, and thrown Michael into a whin bush.

At this point Michael gulped noisily. "I couldn't help it," he said apologetically. He seemed to be ashamed of what had happened, though as far as Bimbo could see there was no need for him to be ashamed.

It was all very confusing, but evidently it was not the pricks of the whins which had made him cry. Physically he was not hurt very much: it was his spirit which was injured, or his pride.

Bimbo understood that what Michael needed now was sympathy; but he didn't quite know how to sympathize with him. If it had been Leo who was in trouble there would have been no difficulty about it: he would have thrown his arms round him and hugged him. But humans were peculiar: they worried about fleas and smells. You had to be careful. "I'll go wid you," he suggested eventually. "I won't let them touch you."

"Oh, no," Michael answered. "Oh, you don't understand. It's no good any more. It doesn't matter any more. I don't *want* to go now. . . . Oh, dear, an' it's going to rain."

Bimbo had noticed this, too, and he had no desire to get wet. "Can't you go home then?" he suggested.

"No. I don't want to go home. They'd want to know why I wasn't at the match and what had happened to the wee rose Mummy made me."

"But nothing's happened to it," Bimbo remonstrated. "Isn't that it in your hand?"

"Yes, but it's all over mud."

"You can wash it," Bimbo answered him. "It'll be nice again when it's washed."

"It won't ever be the same," Michael said sadly. "Not after *they've* had it."

This attitude of passive despair annoyed Bimbo, but he didn't show his annoyance and in a way he understood what was wrong. Michael felt that while wearing the rosette he had been a sort of standard-bearer for what later would be his own school. He had been carrying its colours and he had let them be insulted. He had had its honour in his keeping and he had allowed it to be sullied.

It seemed strange to Bimbo that so much importance should be attached to a piece of ribbon. However, the rain had begun and there was no time to discuss the matter further. "Come wid me," he said. "Hugo an' me have a den wid a roof on't."

Michael got up and they went back through the whins towards the wood. With the rain the smell of cows had become stronger. Bimbo turned over one of the pieces of dung and revealed a startled, crawling mass of insect life. "Oh, look!" he called to Michael. "That's where they all live."

Michael looked and was disgusted. "Aren't they horrid?" he exclaimed.

Bimbo didn't think so: to him they seemed just another variety of living creatures like himself. He was sorry for having disturbed their home and he put the dung back as nearly as possible in its former position.

Bimbo found the dug-out as he had left it. Leo was asleep in a corner while Hugo still squatted on the floor, vainly trying to start the fire. Of the six boxes of matches he had brought with him three were already empty. He didn't say anything when Bimbo and Michael came in, but he watched them out of the corners of his eyes. Leo began to wake up. He was not an excitable dog, asleep one moment and all growls and bristles the next. He opened his eyes, yawned and grunted. Next he stood up, stretched, and gave two or three more yawns. After that he began to wag his tail. It waved from one side to the other in wide, horizontal sweeps. He advanced and pushed his nose against Bimbo's middle. He realized at once that Michael was a friend, and after a preliminary sniff or two to make sure greeted him in exactly the same manner. Michael threw his arms round Leo's neck. Quite suddenly he sat down, still clasping Leo, and buried his head in the dog's fur.

Hugo watched all this with a gradually deepening frown. When at last he spoke his voice was anything but friendly. "We don't want you," he told Michael bluntly; and, looking at him more closely, he added, "You've bin cryin'! Who hit ye?"

"I wasn't crying," Michael retorted. "I didn't cry at all—at least, not till after they'd gone."

"It was Albert and Jackie," Bimbo explained. "They were angry wid him because he was wearing a red and yellow ribbon. They took off his ribbon and trampled on it and threw him into a whin bush."

Hugo looked more interested, and it was clear that he appreciated the importance of Michael's rosette. "It's a pity none of the Blackstone chaps came along," he said. "They'd have shown them—two against one and look at the size o' them, too."

This speech seemed to have more effect than all Bimbo's comforting. "I think I hit Jackie in the eye," Michael announced, suddenly ceasing to look ashamed. "Maybe he'll have a black eye at school to-morrow."

"If he does it'll be worse for you," Hugo warned him. "And another thing, don't you dare tell anyone about comin' here, and don't you ever come back by yourself. This is my den an' no one's any right to ask you here but me."

"An' me," Bimbo said.

Hugo looked at him crossly. "No, just me," he retorted. "It was my idea havin' a den in the wood. You'd have never even come here if it hadn't been for me."

"I found it," Bimbo reminded him. "I showed you where it was. I found the way in, an' I did just as much as you at puttin' on the roof."

Hugo gave way. "Oh, all right," he grumbled. "Tell everyone about it. Bring the whole school to see it." And lighting a match he held it under one of the smaller twigs in a fresh effort to start the fire. The twig burned for fifteen seconds or so after the match had gone out. Then it, too, went out. Hugo lit another match and held it in the same position as the first. "You have to keep the place hot," he informed them.

Michael and Bimbo watched him while a further box was consumed. At last Michael could keep quiet no longer. "I can light fires," he announced.

"All right," Hugo returned, "light one. I'm not stoppin' you."

Michael looked doubtfully at Bimbo. "Will I?" he inquired.

"If you can," Bimbo told him.

"I'll need hairpins, and twigs, to start it, and. . . ."

"Hairpins!" Hugo repeated scornfully.

"I mean pine-needles," Michael corrected himself. "I always call them hairpins."

"I'll show you where to get some," Bimbo said, and they set out together. Temporarily it had almost stopped raining and except for the drops from the bushes they got very little wet. They were away about twenty minutes and when they returned Hugo had decided to give up attempting to light *his* fire. Instead he settled down with Bimbo to watch Michael.

First of all Michael arranged the fuel in three different piles according to size. Next he made a fireplace in the corner from four bricks Hugo had brought on some previous occasion. He filled the space between the bricks with pine needles and spread a framework of small twigs across the top. The first match he lit blew out, but he sheltered the second with his hands. At first only one or two pine needles caught and burned feebly with small, thin, lonely flames. Then, so suddenly that Bimbo didn't actually see the change, the whole mass flared up at once and burned away very quickly. When they began to die down the twigs had caught. Michael pushed more pine needles in below and added some slightly larger twigs at the top. These lit in their turn and soon the fire was burning away quite steadily.

Michael appeared to have forgotten his troubles. His mouth was slightly open and his eyes were fixed on the fire. Every two or three minutes he put on a few more twigs, but he did so as if he were dreaming: he didn't turn his head and his expression never altered. Hugo drew nearer, and crouching on his hunkers spread out his hands to be warmed. Both he and Michael—and Leo, too, for that matter—seemed indifferent to the smoke which was filling the den in great billows: it oozed up all round them, turning the boys' faces from scarlet to grey, and sending sooty tears trickling down their cheeks. Bimbo began to splutter and cough and his eyes smarted. He felt that he must get out at once and staggering towards the steps he scrambled up into the open air. A thin column of smoke followed him, but he pushed a little way into the bushes and hid from it. For once he didn't mind the rain: it wasn't very heavy and the drops which fell on him seemed soft, and cool, and delicious.

When he had recovered he went back and found that Michael and Hugo had been driven out, too, and were standing on the top step of the dug-out. Their faces were streaked with dirt and damp with tears. Their cheeks were scorched and their eyebrows singed. Yet they looked more happy and excited than Bimbo had ever seen either of them before. After a few quick breaths of fresh air they both dived back into the dug-out.

Bimbo remained outside watching the smoke come up through the doorway and at the edges of the roof beneath the undulations of the corrugated iron. It was cold and damp sitting still there among the bushes, and Bimbo felt lonely. He knew that the others were enjoying themselves and he hankered after their company. Why couldn't they have made a fire without smoke, he wondered, like the fires at school and in the kitchen at Mr. Browne's. *They* made no smoke: only occasionally was there even a smell of it. And suddenly he remembered: the smoke had secret passages up to the roof, and came out through the chimneys.

At once Bimbo realized what was wrong. The smoke was like *him. He* liked to get up high into the trees: the smoke liked to get up high into the air. It didn't want to stay in the dug-out: the dug-out was a prison to it. If it could find some easier way of escaping it would do so. If he made a hole in the roof just above the fire the smoke would have no difficulty at all: it would escape straight away.

He crawled across the roof to investigate, but when he reached the corner over the fire the corrugated iron was too hot to hold.

"What are you doing?" Hugo shouted. "You'll bring the roof down."

Bimbo paid no attention. He gripped the cool end of one of the sheets of iron and pulled it towards him so as to make an opening at the corner where the fire was. At first the imprisoned smoke pushed out in a mass through the gap, but soon it was all free and nothing remained but a thin streak of grey which oozed up into the trees and curled round them like a snake. Bimbo went down into the dug-out again and found that the atmosphere was bearable: at least he could breathe.

The fire was blazing up strongly, making a pleasant crackling sound. Hugo and Michael crouched one on each side of it, warming their hands. Leo was between them, sitting up straight, and blinking slowly from time to time. They all gazed at the fire as if it had entranced them.

For a moment Bimbo felt out of it; and then he realized that he only had to push in and he would be one of them. So he squeezed between Leo and Hugo and stretched out a long arm round each of them. For some time none of them spoke. They were all perfectly happy and their close physical contact seemed to enable their minds, too, to join together in a sort of communion. Hugo, Michael, Leo and Bimbo were all one. They were warm and slightly sweaty. Bimbo could smell clothes and fur and smoke and bodies. When the fire was hot the body smells were strongest, but after fresh fuel had been put on, the sharp wood smoke filled his eyes and nostrils.

When the fire blazed up the dug-out was light: the shadows darted up and down the uneven earthen walls as if the light were chasing them: but it never chased them quite away. They sheltered in corners and cracks and crevices, and when the fire died down they all came creeping out again.

At the beginning of the afternoon the doorway had been the one piece of white in the hut. Later it became a patch of pale grey which gradually darkened. Eventually it was a square of black against which the firelight beat in vain. It seemed to Bimbo as if from time to time an extra shadow detached itself from this blackness and slipped into the dug-out.

Periodically the rain had tapped on the roof and the fire had spluttered and hissed. Now this spluttering and hissing became more frequent and the tapping became a regular drumming.

Suddenly Michael seemed to waken out of a dream. "What time is it?" he asked uneasily.

"I dunno," Hugo answered. "Long after tea-time, anyway."

"It's ten-past six," Bimbo said. He was accustomed to acting as a clock for Hugo, and all the children at Miss Sutton's knew his accuracy as a timekeeper.

Michael didn't doubt him now. He was horrified. "Mummy'll be expecting me," he exclaimed. "She told me to be home at five." Yet though he jumped up he didn't go—and Bimbo knew that he was afraid of being alone in the dark.

Bimbo himself had no desire to return. No one would be expecting *him*, and he would much rather have stayed the whole night by the fire in the dug-out. At Mr. Browne's he would have to spend the evening alone, and in the dark. It was the way he had to spend every evening, and in spite of all his expedients for passing the time, he would have welcomed a change. In any case he didn't want to go back just at the moment. The dug-out was dry, while if he set out in all this rain he would be soaked and there was nothing he hated more.

Michael was obviously unhappy, and Hugo, who was watching with a sort of brutal understanding, smiled to himself. Bimbo didn't smile. He knew that Michael was terrified and he felt sorry for him. "I'm going then," Michael said. "I'm going to go home by myself." But still he hesitated, standing uncertainly at the foot of the steps.

"Good-bye," Hugo called. "We're not keepin' you."

Michael didn't answer. He went straight up the steps and disappeared at once out of the light. They heard him trying to find his way through the bushes.

Bimbo got up. "I'm goin' wid him," he announced.

"Why?" Hugo demanded.

"To be kind," Bimbo answered simply, and he followed Michael.

Hugo wasn't pleased. "What's the hurry?" he inquired, but when he found that he was going to be left quite alone he gave in. "Oh, all right," he grumbled. "There's nothing more to burn anyhow, and you needn't think I'm going to stay here all by myself."

Outside it was pitch dark and teeming with rain. Michael was on his hands and knees feeling the bushes blindly in an attempt to discover the way through to the clearing. Bimbo could hear the wind and the rain and the tossing branches rubbing one against another. He grasped Michael's arm. Michael drew in his breath sharply and shivered.

"It's all right," Bimbo said. "It's Bimbo. Bimbo is coming home wid you to keep you safe." Even as he spoke Bimbo regretted the dryness and warmth of the dug-out, but he plunged at once into the bushes and began to crawl along the passage that led to the clearing.

"Where've you gone?" Michael asked nervously. "I can't see you."

"I'm here," Bimbo replied reassuringly. "Hold on to my tail an' you won't lose me."

He waited, waving his tail slowly in circles so that Michael should be able to find it. Michael was crawling towards him and next instant he felt his tail brush against Michael's face.

Michael gave a little "Oh" of surprise, but his hand closed round the tail and grasped it rather too tightly. He gave it a little chuck. "Gee up," he said. Bimbo experienced a curious sickening sensation at the base of his spine.

A moment before he had felt the utmost benevolence towards Michael, but this treatment of his tail had an effect on him out of all proportion to the physical discomfort—it could hardly be called pain. He was filled with a sudden, furious anger. He spun round twitching his tail out of Michael's hand. If Michael had been able to hold on he would have been bitten: instead Bimbo turned first to lick his tail and in that instant his temper vanished as quickly as it had come.

"I can't hold it," Michael grumbled innocently, quite unaware of his escape. "It's got all slippy with the rain."

Bimbo had not been quite sure whether Hugo had yet left the hut, but now he heard him coming towards them, and a moment later he bumped into Michael. "Go on, can't you?" he exclaimed irritably. "What's stoppin' you?"

"I've lost Bimbo's tail," Michael replied.

"You don't need Bimbo's tail," Hugo told him. "Go on, can't you. You don't want to kneel here all night. Go on, an' you'll bump into him."

Michael accepted this advice. He did bump into Bimbo and again he grasped his tail; but this time Bimbo was prepared and did not turn on him. All the same he hated being held by the tail and he resolved that he would never again make such a foolish suggestion. As soon as he came into the open he spoke sharply to Michael. "Let go now," he said. "You can see all right."

He himself could just make out the far end of the clearing, though he could not distinguish the individual trees. He turned round and watched the others emerge from the thicket—Michael, Hugo, and behind them a very dejected and reproachful Leo. They were wet enough already but out here there was nothing to shield them. Bimbo felt his fur gathering in little lumps, while cold rivers formed courses for themselves and flowed slowly and icily over his back, and on down his tail. His tail drooped and drooped. He could feel it sinking of its own accord till it almost touched the ground. A succession of drops flowed down it towards the tip. They tickled him and made him twitch. Each time he twitched the drop at the end fell off and another took its place.

Every now and then a glimmer of moonlight shone down on them. It showed bare trees and black waving branches, and a distant, dismal sky. There was a pearly grey circle round the moon, but soon the moon would go out. Angry black clouds were rushing at it. They would cover it and the rain would come down harder than ever.

Bimbo led the way towards the dell at the foot of the Clarkes' garden. The others trailed after him and he was almost certain that neither Hugo nor Michael knew in which direction they were going. Leo, of course, must have known, but he showed no interest. He came last, and though Bimbo couldn't see him, he could hear the padding of his feet on the dead leaves.

So long as they were in the wood they were all equally depressed, but when they reached the Clarkes' garden Hugo and Michael began to recover their spirits. Hugo, of course, was the first. "What'll happen to *you* when you get home?" he asked.

"I'll get bread and milk," Michael answered with cheerful anticipation. "They'll bring it up to me in bed. There'll be a row first, but I'll have to have a hot bath and bread and milk or else I'll get a cold—and they won't want that."

Hugo wasn't quite so sure of his welcome. "I'll be all right if Father doesn't see me," he said. "He'd whale me, but I'll get Cook to tell Mummy. She'll keep him out of the way till I'm in bed. Then she'll bring up supper if she can."

Bimbo knew that for him there would be neither luxuries nor danger of trouble. Probably no one would even see him coming in. They might notice at bedtime that his supper had been taken from the scullery—that was all. He thought it strange that he should be with these two boys: in some respects he was so like them; and at the same time he was *un*like them—in his position, in his past, and probably also in his future. In one way indeed Leo came closer to them than Bimbo: he at least occupied a definite position in the human world.

It was at this point in Bimbo's reflections that he caught sight of the lighted windows of the Clarkes' house. They seemed to announce the welcome and the comfort which were waiting for Hugo. In one room where the electric light was not lit the warm flickering glow of a fire could be seen reflected on the drawn blinds. Suddenly another light was switched on on the first floor and Hugo drew their attention to it. "That's my room," he told them. "They'll be puttin' in my hot water-bottle and takin' off the quilt."

Bimbo felt a mixture of contempt and jealousy, but Michael was interested. "D'you keep the bottle in?" he asked. "I kick mine out before I go to sleep. It's a rubber one; so it doesn't break."

Bimbo realized that compared with these two he was a sort of vagabond. The comforts they spoke of were not for him—not yet at any rate. For him were the cold and the rain and the lonely darkness of the night. Perhaps somewhere a real home did wait for him—a home even better than their homes. Perhaps he was really a prince shut out from his kingdom by a curse, a lost, stolen prince who would return at last to live happily ever after like the people in the fairy stories. Not that Bimbo believed in everlasting happiness—happiness needed unhappiness and could not exist without it: otherwise it would soon forget that it was happiness. Could anything exist without being aware of its existence? A man asleep? He dreamed: an unconscious man? He, too, might dream. A dead man perhaps. . . .

"The wash-house window's open," Hugo announced. "I'll get

in that way." He said "Good night" and crossed the grass border which separated the path from the house. He climbed onto a window-sill, paused, waved, and disappeared.

The glow of the light only stretched out a little way from the house: all around was a tall, dark circle of trees—and Michael was frightened. "I wish I was home," he whined. "I wish I hadn't gone to your horrid old dug-out. I don't like it here."

"I'll take you home," Bimbo said. "I know the way. Take my hand, and you can hold on to Leo on the other side if you like. Nothing will happen to you."

He felt that as he had taken Michael under his care he would like to see him safely home, though there was little danger now of another encounter with Albert and Jackie. They wouldn't stay out in this rain if they could help it. Nor was it of them, he soon realized, that Michael was afraid: it was of the darkness and the trees. He took Bimbo's hand and the three of them went down the drive together. The drive was winding: for quite a distance it was hidden from both the road and the house, and it was very dark indeed. But on the road there were lamps, and as soon as they came into the light Michael's fears vanished: he became cheerful.

For the rest of the way neither of them spoke very much; yet Bimbo soon got the impression that Michael didn't want him. And when they arrived at Sandstone Park Michael dismissed him almost brusquely. "This is where I live," he said, and he went in, shutting the gate behind him. He remembered to say "Thank you," but immediately afterwards he turned and ran towards the hall door. Bimbo and Leo went back to Beechwood together. They were both soaked to the skin, and Bimbo was dreadfully cold. He wished he had sent Leo home when they came out of the wood. There was really no reason why he, too, should have got this additional wetting, though like Bimbo he could get dry by rolling in straw. Bimbo made sure that there was plenty of straw in Leo's kennel: then he left him and went on alone.

At first he saw only one light in Mr. Browne's house. It came from Mr. Browne's study and somehow it didn't look very cheerful. Bimbo tiptoed up to the window and peered in. Mr. Browne was alone: he had a morose expression on his face: he was reading a book. After watching him for a little Bimbo went round to the back. Lights were burning in the kitchen and scullery. He opened the back door and as he did so he came face to face with Cook. She gave a scream of disapproval. "Not a step further," she warned him. "Don't you dare to come drippin' puddles over my kitchen." On a shelf behind her were four bananas and a mug of milk. This was Bimbo's supper. She handed it to him. "Go an' eat in your own place," she said. "You can mess up there as much as you like."

Bimbo went through the cage and climbed to his sleeping box. He took handfuls of straw and rubbed himself till he was fairly dry. He ate the bananas and drank the milk and curled up to go to sleep. He was still cold. He tried to bury himself in the straw, but he had not sufficient. He thought of Hugo and Michael; by this time they would both be warm and comfortable, and probably forgiven. They would be sitting up in bed with hot water-bottles at their toes, sipping bread and milk. In making Michael happy he had made himself cold and uncomfortable. Yet Michael's happiness pleased him.

All the same he wished that there had been someone to welcome him home—even if the welcome had been combined with a scolding. However cheerful he might naturally be—and he knew that he *had* a cheerful temperament—it was hard to be happy, alone, in the dark, with his teeth chattering so that he could not stop them. He, too, wanted to be petted and scolded and cared for. If only he could live with Miss Martha. If only Mr. Browne had been someone quite different. He was sure that in Dolan's house he would have been quite happy. Well! If he went to Mr. Browne's room now he would get his scolding all right, but it would be the wrong sort of scolding: there would be no bread and milk at the end of it. Instead he would be sent back to put himself to bed.

That night was very long and in the morning Bimbo was still cold.

19

On Monday morning Bimbo was very ill. It was more than two days now since he had got wet coming back from the hut in the wood. He thought he was going to die. He lay on his straw bed trying not to cough. It hurt him to cough: it hurt him to breathe: and he wasn't afraid to die. He didn't know that there was any reason why he should be. He felt that to die would be a relief. It was so tiring, this continual struggle for breath. He didn't know why he went on struggling, but he couldn't help it.

He wished he could go to sleep. He didn't think he had been asleep for a long while; and yet he hadn't always been properly awake. Sometimes he was very hot: sometimes he shivered with cold. He knew the room was cold—and there was no fire. Since yesterday he hadn't eaten anything. Dolan had brought him a bowl of warm milk half an hour ago, but Bimbo hadn't touched it yet. It was still beside him, but though he was thirsty, he couldn't make the effort of sitting up to drink it. He didn't even feel that he had enough energy to stretch out his hand for it.

He began to cough again: the cough was something inside him trying to get out; or perhaps there were a whole lot of coughs. Sometimes a great many would get out together in single file, one after the other. They were different sizes and the bigger ones were very strong. They were all stronger than Bimbo, though with some of them he struggled for quite a long time. If only they would have come out without hurting him so much, he wouldn't have tried to keep them. But they were very violent. They threw his arms and legs about in the most extraordinary fashion. He heard a crack and knew that the bowl of milk had been knocked to the floor.

Perhaps the smoke from the fire in the hut had been coughs' eggs. They must have hatched in the warmth inside him. The others must have far more of them, because they had breathed in more smoke than he had. That would be why Hugo hadn't come to see him: he had expected him yesterday afternoon. This afternoon Miss Martha would come. He never saw her at the week-ends; so she didn't know he was ill; but she would guess something was wrong when he didn't turn up at morning school.

His coughing stopped and he hoped the last one had got out. They had made him hot and sweaty. He was exhausted and lay still, with a feeling of relief and peacefulness. He heard the door of his room open. He knew that Dolan and Mr. Browne had come in. It was the first time Mr. Browne had been near him for weeks. Their voices sounded very far away.

"He'll be dyin' on ye, if ye don't watch yerself," Dolan said, and Bimbo knew from the sound of his voice that he was shaking his head and looking grave.

"He doesn't seem to be coughing now," Mr. Browne responded a good deal less seriously.

"He must ha' worn hisself out, then," Dolan answered immediately. "I tell ye ye ought to get the doctor till him."

"What's all this mess on the floor?" Mr. Browne asked irritably. Dolan began to explain, but Mr. Browne did not give him time to finish. Bimbo heard him jangle his watch-chain and there was a snap as he closed his gold hunter watch. "I haven't time to see him now," he cut in. "I'll have to hurry for my train. I'll look in this evening and see how he is."

"Would ye not get the doctor?" Dolan suggested again. "Sure some o' them clurks would wire up for ye. Ye'd have no call to trouble yerself."

"The clerks have their work to attend to," Mr. Browne replied stiffly. "If he gets any worse I'll send for the vet, but it will be time enough this evening. Get that mess cleared up quickly and don't spend the whole morning over it. You've other work to do: the garden's in a shocking state."

"Yess, surr."

Even in this last reply Bimbo could detect a hint of defiance. Mr. Browne must have noticed it too, for he banged the door after him, and his footsteps in the passage had an angry sound. The front door opened and shut and the house seemed quite silent except for the chinking noise Dolan made as he swept up the broken china.

"Dolan," Bimbo whispered presently. There was no response and Bimbo made a greater effort. "Dolan! Do you hear me?"

"That you, Bimbo?"

"Dolan, could you get Miss Marfa?"

"I'll get her, Bimbo."

There was another rattle of the china and after that, silence. Gradually Bimbo's coldness was returning. Shivers ran up his spine and the backs of his legs: his teeth chattered. He began to cough again. This time he knew the coughs were alive: they were very angry and hot and they scratched him with their nails as they fought to get out. "I'll let you go, I'll let you go," he told them. "I can't help it." But they were so angry that they flung him backwards and forwards till the straw was tossed in every direction.

Then a little cough—it was the last one and more gentle than the others—said, "I'll take you with me: we're going to school."

Immediately Bimbo felt himself floating out through his own mouth. He saw himself lying on his bed with the straw all round him. He was quite still with his arms spread out and one of his legs gathered up beneath him. His head was thrown back and all his fur was puckered into little damp lumps.

Next moment they were out in the room gazing at the bed-box from outside. Dolan's ladder was propped against the opening and there was a shiny patch on the floor where the bowl of milk had fallen. Bimbo and the cough hovered in the air near the ceiling. The cough was like a little grey-blue bubble, paler in the centre. It had two tiny black eyes close together. Bimbo and the cough looked round the room. In the cold, pale, December light the room was dismal as if no one lived there. The tin trunk where Bimbo's school clothes were kept, seemed more battered and decrepit than usual, and it was not properly shut. A small mouse came out from behind the rusty, unblackened, empty fireplace, but seeing nothing of interest returned again to its hole.

"That's a church mouse," the cough said.

They went out through the cage and Bimbo noticed that both the trapeze and the rings were shivering a little. What a cold day! On down the drive: it had turned very grey—like the road. The trees on the road were cold, too. They said, "You're lucky, Bimbo, to have such nice fur."

There was Dolan pedalling his bicycle very slowly. "She's stiff this mornin'," Dolan was thinking. "She needs a drop of oil."

Bimbo and the cough weren't going very fast, but they passed Dolan and next moment they were at the station.

"Wait a bit," the cough said. "There's a train coming."

Sure enough the gates were closed and they climbed up the foot-bridge to watch. They were just in time to see the engine coming round the curve from Sandstone. Bimbo noticed that what he had thought before were smoke and steam were really coughs, too. But they were different from his cough and from each other, like white people from black. All the same they knew his cough and spoke to it. "What are you doing there?" they asked. "Come on up into the sky."

So Bimbo and his cough went. The sky was full of coughs. There were so many coughs that you couldn't really see the sky, nothing but grey streams of coughs rushing in every direction. But once you were up there you could look down and see everything. Bimbo saw himself lying in his straw bed, very small like a picture in a book. He turned over the pages of the book and saw Hugo in bed too, and James on another page and Michael—they were all in bed: but they were sitting up taking bread and milk out of the blue and white china bowls.

The next picture showed Miss Price's class in school. Bimbo and the cough floated round the room and Bimbo saw that his place and Hugo's place were both empty. But Michael was there after all and Miss Price was in a rage with him. She hit him over the knuckles with her ruler and he began to cough. Immediately Miss Martha came in and hit Miss Price with her own ruler so that all the straw came out of her face. She was nothing but a bundle of straw after all, and the straw caught in Bimbo's fur and scratched him.

"Poor Bimbo," Miss Martha said. "Don't worry: I'll make you all right again," and she jumped on Miss Price's bicycle and began to pedal to Beechwood. She pedalled so fast that she was there in no time and Bimbo heard her speaking to Dolan down in the room below him.

She was quite cross with poor Dolan. "You might at least have lit the fire," she told him.

"Sure ah would have," Dolan began, "only I was afeared the master. . . ."

"Oh, don't start all that again," Miss Martha interrupted. "Go and get the cook and the housemaid. I want all of you, and tell the housemaid to bring paper and sticks and coal. Hurry up now."

Bimbo heard her climbing the ladder and he knew then that she had climbed it before and looked at him before. He didn't know how he knew. She was carrying a bundle of blankets and she pushed them into the opening in front of her. Then she climbed partly into it herself, and very gently, one by one, began to spread the blankets over him.

Bimbo had begun to shiver again but there was something, a

feeling of strength and kindness in her touch, that steadied him. The blankets, too, were beautifully soft and woolly, and contact with them was in itself comforting. He sighed and did not cough.

It was dark in his bed-box and in a way he could not see Miss Martha. All the same he felt as if he *could* see her, and she knew he was watching her. "It's all right, Bimbo," she said, "*I*'m looking after you now and you're going to get better."

There was a sound of footsteps in the passage. Miss Martha climbed down the ladder. The door opened and Bimbo listened to hear what she would say to Cook and Minnie. She began pleasantly enough, "Good morning. I'm afraid Bimbo's much more ill than any of you have realized. I've telephoned for the doctor, but meanwhile. . . ." She stopped and when she went on again her voice had changed completely. Once or twice at school Bimbo had heard her speak in the same way. "You, I suppose, are the housemaid," she said.

"Yes, ma'am," Minnie answered guiltily.

"I said you were to bring paper, sticks, and coal, to light the fire. Where are they?"

"I, I, I mean. . . ."

"Go and get them now," Miss Martha ordered, "and hurry."

"Now, Cook. . . ."

But Cook had something to say on her own account. "The Master told us we wasn't to light no fires unless he gave instructions. 'Don't yez light no fires,' he says, 'without I gives the orders.' "

"The housemaid will light the fire," Miss Martha returned calmly. "Have you a chicken in the house? I think some chicken broth might do him good."

"I have not then," Cook retorted, "and I. . . ."

"Is there any brandy?"

"How would I know? Doesn't the Master keep the keys himself, but what I want to tell ye Miss. . . ."

Miss Martha ignored her. "Dolan," she said, "here's a pound. Go down to the village and get a chicken from Miss Miskelly and call in at Joe Scott's and get him to give you a half-bottle of Hennessey. Come straight back now. There's no time to waste."

"I know his way of comin' straight," Cook observed. "He'll come as straight as a dog's hind leg."

The door opened and shut again. For a moment there was silence. "The master. . . ." Cook began, but she was interrupted once more.

"While we're waiting we'll try and make this room a little more comfortable looking," Miss Martha announced. "The fire will be a help and. . . ."

"I give notice," Cook said.

Miss Martha laughed. "My dear woman, it's no good giving notice to me. I'm not your employer, and I absolutely refuse to take messages to Mr. Browne."

Bimbo could see the forest far away across the ice, very far away. In spite of the distance it was very distinct and Theodore Browne was looking out from among the trees watching for him to come. With Theodore were big, wise apes, but though Bimbo waved to them they could not see him. He tried to shout to attract their attention, but he couldn't shout: there seemed to be a blanket inside him that stifled every sound. The ice dragged at his feet, and slipped through the outer covering of skin and crept up the bones of his legs, right to his knees. He was in a half-standing position with his hands hanging down in front of him, but not quite touching the ice. It wasn't snowing now, but snow lay on his back and kept sliding down. It was heavy and each time it slipped it sent a cold tremor through his spine. He was tired. It was a long, long way to the warm forest. Theodore and the apes grew tired of waiting for him. They went into the forest out of sight of the cold field of ice. Still Bimbo toiled on. The North Pole, thin, and wizened, and blasted by many hurricanes was between him and them. It stood there, all alone in the great white wilderness, a faint grey in colour like a symbol of desolation.

In the forest Theodore and the apes came to the glade Bimbo knew so well. It was just the same as always with the huge dark trees rising up, and arching overhead to hide the sky. "This is the place," the oldest of the apes said. "We left him here."

"Yes, this is the place," Theodore admitted, and he looked down at his long white beard.

"You took him. You stole him," the apes said. They grabbed Theodore by the beard and the ice crackled and broke into fragments and crackled again.

"It's going nicely now," Minnie said.

There was a fire in the undergrowth: it leaped up and caught the leaves of the trees and consumed them; but it wasn't hot. There was no heat, but Bimbo had come to the edge of the forest and the thorn bushes began to prick his legs.

"Ah wasn't that long," Theodore Browne said. "It's the real currant jam, too, with the three stars on the label. Ah made sure o' that. Here's yer change, Miss."

"Thank you very much, Dolan," Miss Martha replied. "I think it would be a good idea if you opened the front gate for the doctor."

"It's not that I'm not fond of him meself," Cook was explaining. "I've been like a mother to him ye might say—me an' Minnie here."

"I don't know how much to give him," Miss Martha said. Cook and she seemed to be great friends now. "I'd better wait till the doctor comes: at least I'll wait for a little. If he doesn't come soon I'll try him with a little myself."

"It's the master," Cook went on. "He's that tight about everything—watches the pins you might say—pays all the bills hisself. It makes you afraid to lift yer wee finger, but of course, if *you're* takin' all the blame. . . . I don't mind I'm sure."

"Maybe you'd better put the chicken on," Miss Martha suggested.

20

During the next few days Bimbo's life was very strange. At times he lay tossing in his bed-box, hot, uncomfortable, and fighting for every breath. But sometimes the fight seemed to be carried on for him and he floated in the air watching his own body without taking any part in the struggle. Other queer things would happen, too. He would find himself passing through walls, and drifting off into space so that he could see the whole world beneath his feet. Once, in the night, he saw all the trees leave the wood and walk away along the white road over the top of the hill. He watched them till they were out of sight, but when he looked back the wood was back, too, dark and still in the moonlight. Bimbo liked the moonlight: it seemed to turn Belmore into an enchanted village. . . . And no matter how far he wandered he could always see his own body peaceful or troubled, lying in the bed-box with Miss Martha's blankets around it. He was attached to it by a long unbreakable thread, which in the end was always wound in till he and his body were united once more.

Gradually these adventures ceased. The walls of the room became solid. His body was not hot or uncomfortable, and he no longer wandered away from it. His breath began to come more easily, though at first he was extremely weak. Every day, however, he got a little better and a little stronger, and at the end of a fortnight he was allowed to sit by the fire in a deck-chair Miss Martha had brought him.

Bimbo enjoyed convalescing. It was nice, when it was cold and miserable outside, to draw in his chair and spread out his fingers and toes to the blaze. He liked receiving visitors, too. Miss Martha and Hugo came nearly every day, and once or twice some of the other children from the school. But, of course, he saw Dolan more than anyone. The fire attracted Dolan. Sometimes he would stand in front of it for an hour or more talking of his experiences as a soldier, or of Bimbo's illness. He smoked as he talked and every now and then he would send a spittle sizzling into the flames.

"It was the pewmonye, so it was," he announced on one of these occasions. "I heerd the Doctor tellin' Miss Marthy. 'It's the pewmonye,' he says. 'The pewmonye's got him.' "

Bimbo was deeply interested. "Was I bad?" he asked.

"Bad!" Dolan exclaimed. "Ye were at death's door, ah tell ye; an' it was me pulled ye out of it by the skin o' yer teeth. If I'd left ye to *him* I know where ye'd ha' been; and if ye ask me he wouldn't ha' been any the worse pleased neether."

"Where would I have been?" Bimbo inquired.

Dolan considered this question for a moment. "Pushin' up the daisies," he answered at last, "under the sod, in yer grave if you like."

Bimbo shivered, but not unpleasantly. He realized that his narrow squeak had given him a new importance, for Dolan, at least, and he liked to be important. "Do you think *he* wanted me to die?" he asked.

Dolan hesitated and looked round uneasily. "Think!" he then said. "You watch yerself, that's all I'll say. You watch yerself." He shut his mouth tightly with an odd expression of knowing a great deal, picked up the slop-pail which he had come to fetch, and went out.

Bimbo heard him going down the passage, but suddenly he stopped and there was a rattle as the pail was put down. After a moment's silence the footsteps sounded again: Dolan was returning. He opened the door and thrust in his head. "Ah tell you what ut is," he said, speaking in a hoarse whisper. "There's money at the back of it—that's what ut is—money!"

"Money?" Bimbo repeated, leaning forward in the chair. He knew very little about money, but Dolan made it sound exciting and mysterious.

"Aye, money," Dolan answered, in so low a voice that Bimbo had to strain his ears to hear him. "Ah'll tell you what ah think. Th'owld master he must ha' left somethin' behind to keep ye, and him"—he jerked his head towards Mr. Browne's study—"he wants the howld of ut for hisself. He's not as well off as he was—he's had a knock somewhere, if ye ask me."

With these words Dolan closed the door and departed again down the passage. It was a disturbing idea, but Bimbo was much too warm and comfortable to be frightened. He lay back in his chair. It was the only easy chair he had ever had and he felt very luxurious. Yet what Dolan had said seemed probable enough. Bimbo knew that Mr. Browne didn't like him: he never *had* liked him, though for a period, when Bimbo first began to talk, he had been interested in him as a curiosity: even at that time Mr. Browne had never voluntarily touched Bimbo. He seemed to have a physical aversion to all animals. Bimbo had seen him throwing stones at a stray dog who had blundered into the garden, and once he had shot a cat.

Surely such a man would never have undertaken to spend his own money in keeping Bimbo. It must be Theodore Browne's money he was spending, and if Theodore Browne were dead, and Bimbo were to die, too, no doubt Mr. Browne would be able to use the money himself.

Once or twice when he had been called in during Bimbo's illness there had been an expression on Mr. Browne's face that would have frightened Bimbo if he had not felt complete confidence in the power of Miss Martha. It was an expression of cold hostility. This, no doubt, had been partly due to the disagreements there had been about treatment—for Bimbo knew vaguely that Miss Martha and the doctor had allied themselves to triumph over Mr. Browne, and that Dolan had not been in sympathy with his master.

"Pewmonye?" What exactly was it, he wondered, and when Miss Martha came in the afternoon he asked her.

"Pneumonia," Miss Martha said, and she wrote it up on the blackboard, so that he could learn to spell it. "That's the name of the illness you had—only you don't pronounce the P. The doctor says it's amazing that you didn't have it long ago. He thinks this isn't a proper climate for you to be living in and that your body can't get used to it. In any case his orders are that you're to stay inside till the weather improves: so there's nothing for it but to obey."

"When will t' weather improve?" Bimbo asked.

"That's a difficult question," Miss Martha replied. "I can only tell you that the doctor doesn't want you to go back to school until April or at least the end of March. But it depends how March behaves. It's supposed to come in like a lion and go out like a lamb, you know, but very often it does just the opposite. Of course, there's no reason why you shouldn't go on doing lessons, and I thought we might start again next Monday. I'll come up every afternoon—or most afternoons—and teach you myself. How would you like *that*?"

Bimbo said that he would like it very much, and on the following Monday the lessons started.

Bimbo found that he got on a great deal faster than he had at school. He had plenty of time to work, and he liked working. He enjoyed finding out things and once he started to do problems it seemed that sums just turned into a game. He liked history, too. It was interesting in the same way as Dolan's conversation was interesting. Both enlarged and modified his conception of human life as a whole. Dolan's conversation was like the more lurid parts of history. He told stories—stories he had heard or read in the papers, or stories about his own life in the army.

"But why did you want to kill each other?" Bimbo asked one day when Dolan had been telling about the war. "Ah don't know as we did want to," Dolan said. The question puzzled him. He took off his cap and scratched his head. "They were decent people," he added reflectively. "Tur'ble fond of washin' theirsel's. They was always at it."

It was a virtue that both Bimbo and Dolan could admire objectively. In fact it sometimes seemed to Bimbo that when you washed you stopped being yourself for a while: certainly you didn't smell like yourself. Dolan was never the same on Sundays. Bimbo liked him better towards the end of the week: then he was really himself, and Bimbo knew who he was without the trouble of looking.

So with reading and lessons and conversations of this sort Bimbo's time passed pleasantly enough. As he got better, however, Hugo's visits became shorter and less frequent. It didn't interest him to talk by the fire in Bimbo's little room, though Bimbo allowed him to sit in the deck-chair and crouched on the floor himself. Once they played draughts on a board Miss Martha had left, but Hugo lost every game and the next afternoon he refused to play. Bimbo could beat Miss Martha, too, and Cook and Minnie and Dolan: but it was no fun playing with Cook and Dolan: they wouldn't take it seriously.

Eventually Hugo's visits deteriorated into weekly calls. He would leave two or three books and the previous week's copy of *The Magnet*; and sometimes he would talk for a little about school: but he rarely stayed more than fifteen minutes—and after the first few weeks none of the other children came to see Bimbo at all.

Bimbo understood this well enough, and he didn't blame anyone. He had come to accept whatever happened without it occurring to him that he was being ill-used or unjustly treated. For a time he had been interesting to the children: now he had ceased to be interesting. But he knew this was only temporary. When spring came and he was able to meet them at school, and to roam through the wood once more, their interest in him would return. Meanwhile he was content to live almost in solitude—particularly as Mr. Browne had at last been persuaded to allow him a light in the evenings. All the same he looked forward to the spring.

21

When Bimbo went back to school he was further on than the three eleven-year-old girls, who composed the sixth form at Miss Sutton's. It was clear that he would have to work separately and Miss Martha decided to keep him as a special pupil and teach him herself. So he was given a desk apart in her classroom and there he did his own work. This arrangement was found very satisfactory and it was continued in the summer term. It saved Miss Martha the trouble of going to Mr. Browne's house and Bimbo liked it better because he enjoyed meeting the other children at playtime. In the last year he had grown a good deal—and in particular his legs were much longer than they had been. He had been practising running, too, and now when they played Tig he found that he could get along as fast as any of them: indeed, no one could catch him unless he was driven into a corner.

In the afternoons he would usually encounter some of them again. Besides Hugo, those he saw most frequently were James and Michael: for Michael's family had moved to a house near Belmore village, and now he and James went regularly to the wood.

One very hot afternoon at the end of May, they all went together to buy ice-creams at the little shop beside Sandstone Station. Leo went with them and Hugo paid for his ice-cream and for Bimbo's as neither of the animals had any money.

When they had finished Bimbo suggested that they should go back through the grounds of Belmore House, keeping close to the railway line and coming out near Belmore Station. He wanted to avoid the dusty smelly road where every stranger they passed would stare at him. The others refused. Hugo said that he wasn't going to spend all afternoon watching Bimbo climb trees and that Leo would very likely be run over by a train. So Bimbo was forced to set off alone.

He went first across a field and reached the railway at a place where the line ran along an embankment. At the foot of the embankment were trees and Bimbo enjoyed himself climbing and exploring among them. He was struck by the curious change the heat had made in everything: the trees were not quite like ordinary trees: there was no sound of birds; everything was very quiet.

The quiet was broken by a faint singing from the rails, which changed to a distant rumble: a train was coming from Belfast. Choosing a tall straight chestnut tree Bimbo climbed it till he was ten feet or so above the level of the line. He heard the train stop at Sandstone Station. Then it started again and came on slowly towards Belmore. Bimbo was on just the right level to look through the carriage windows, and at the rate the train was travelling he was able to see quite easily what was going on inside. Each carriage was a little section of life by itself. It was astonishing to see moment after moment in the same place quite a different set of people. Bimbo gazed at them in turn with a sort of surprised fascination—men reading newspapers, a man taking a case from the rack, a woman gathering her parcels together, two youths writing on the walls. . . . Bimbo had known for a long time now that a train was a piece of machinery; but he had never looked into one before and seen its interior life, and he couldn't efface his earlier impression that trains were powerful animals with violent emotions, animals who only kept to the track because it did not occur to them to leave it.

The third class carriages were full. In one of them a baby was being smacked. It was across its mother's knee with its little red bottom exposed to the gaze of its fellow-travellers and of Bimbo. Bimbo saw the mother's hand raised and he saw it begin its downward journey, but both mother and baby were flicked away before the hand actually fell.

The train disappeared from view. Bimbo heard it slowing down: it stopped and started again. Gradually the sound of it died away in the distance.

Bimbo descended to the ground, and going through the belt of trees which bordered the railway found himself at the edge of a grassy slope running down towards a little glen. In the glen there was a heavy stillness as if this particular spot were eternal and cut off from the changes of the world. The grass was a thick solid green and the shadows of leaves lay scattered over it like splashes of black paint. Bimbo crossed the grass and went along a narrow path which descended in a series of curves deeper into the glen.

"I smell water," Bimbo thought, and almost at the same moment he heard quite clearly the sound of a stream. The path joined the stream and followed it along a deep shady course at the foot of the glen. There was no grass down here, only masses of bluebells which seemed to float between the roots of the trees like bonfire smoke in November. The Path wound on and Bimbo dragged his feet to hear them rustle through the soft dead leaves which covered it. In time the path would moulder away like the leaves till one day the bluebells would grow there, too, and the place where it had been would be forgotten.

Then the space between the trees widened, the sun shone through and in a gap among the bushes Bimbo saw the dark gleam of a broader sheet of water. It was Melville's pond, and the stream he had been following flowed out of it. He remembered Hugo telling him that a man had once been drowned in the pond, and that no one dared to go near it at night.

It was an artificial pond, perfectly round, its banks shored up with masonry like the banks of a waterworks. The trees grew down almost to the edge, and the bushes stretched out beyond it. The water was filled with their shadows and reflections except for patches here and there which showed the dark blue summer sky, with one big white cloud creeping across it. In the centre was a small stone island where, half hidden by bushes and brambles, Bimbo could see vaguely a group of grey figures. He felt puzzled by them and a little frightened. One at least was like a man and some of them seemed to be looking at him. Their attitudes gave an impression of movement, but their positions never seemed to alter. Bimbo climbed a tree to get a better view and immediately discovered that the figures were really only stones—a stone man driving two stone horses. For a long time he stared at them wondering why they were there. He had a curious feeling that they might suddenly come to life and gallop out to him across the water. There was a rustle in the bushes and for a moment he held his breath. But instead of the man or the horses a small, bright blue bird shot from the island and skimmed across the pond towards the opposite bank. For a moment Bimbo forgot his usual caution.

He clapped his hands with delight. The bird was a magic bird. It was visible for only an instant, but its flight changed the pond to a pool in Bimbo's own remembered forest. He stared at it and as he stared the water grew darker and thicker, and the light shining down on the unshadowed patches grew brighter. The yellow water lilies grew bigger and their buds, which had been floating on the surface demurely closed, burst open to allow new flowers of complicated form and various colours to emerge from them. They grew and grew till the whole pond was covered with flowers. The grey stones of the island disappeared under a mass of creeper and hairy beings came out from the undergrowth and lay down to drink. Bimbo recognized them. He had seen them before. They were the creatures out of his dream forest, creatures like himself, only much bigger. "They're the Bimbos," he murmured. "They're all Bimbos there, grown-up Bimbos. Like me only grown-up." And he knew that it was a real pool at which he was staring: that what he saw was really happening, or had really happened in some forest far away. That was where he had to get to, that mysterious dark forest where he had been long ago, before Theodore Browne had captured him and taken him away. He knew that Theodore Browne had returned there, and he felt certain that he was still alive. Some day Bimbo, too, would return and find a father and a mother and brothers and sisters. . . .

And then there were footsteps and Bimbo knew that the world of Hugo and Michael and Dolan—the world of Mr. Browne and Miss Martha—was about to break in upon him. He took a last look at the pool and drew back among the leaves.

It was Hugo, and Bimbo startled him considerably by dropping suddenly out of the tree on to the ground beside him. "What d'you think you're doin'?" he exclaimed crossly, and he wouldn't listen to Bimbo's suggestion that instead of returning to the others they should spend the rest of the afternoon on the banks of the pond. "It's too quiet," he objected. "I don't, I don't like it—and anyhow I came to hurry you up."

So together they went by the way Hugo had come till they reached the other end of the pond, where the stream trickled into it with only the slightest of murmurs. Here, too, the stream was overhung by trees and bordered by a path; but neither Hugo nor

Bimbo used the path. Hugo said it was dangerous and scrambled along the bed of the stream, slipping into pools and balancing uncertainly on stepping-stones. Bimbo looked down on him from the trees above. He could go three or four times as fast as Hugo, swinging from branch to branch, but he didn't mind dawdling to let Hugo catch up. As he went he sang to himself a peculiar song. He knew it was peculiar because he didn't know the meaning of the words, or even if they had a meaning. But the song itself had a meaning. It meant, "Bimbo will return, return to the trees of the forest. Bimbo will return to his own people. Bimbo will be happy in the tall trees. Bimbo will be happy swinging through the branches. Bimbo will have friends and parents and brothers. They are waiting now. The sunlight is for Bimbo, and the dark leaves and the pale leaves, and the red flowers which grow on the trees, the red flowers which only Bimbo can see." He liked these red flowers: he delighted in making them spring to life in unexpected places. He plucked them and dropped them lazily down on Hugo one by one. Yet he didn't expect Hugo to see them and Hugo didn't see them, not even when they dropped down straight in front of him, brushing his hair as they fell. Their scent was sweet, like the scent of old-fashioned cabbage roses, but it was heavy, filling the air and wrapping itself round the leaves and the branches in little spirals of pink smoke.

"I can make my world," Bimbo thought. "I just have to think and I can grow trees on the roads and make grass and flowers grow over the houses." So he thought of the railway and the plants growing between the sleepers and at the sides of the track. He put new life into them so that they spread and spread. A train came and the green things gathered round its wheels so that they couldn't turn. The engine stopped with a little sigh of despair; but its despair became contentment when it found itself changed into a lovely green bower with beautiful red flowers growing out of its smoke stack. The passengers leaned out of the carriage windows to see what was happening, but the creepers stretched up and entwined them also till there was nothing to be seen, but a great green caterpillar asleep in the sun. Bimbo looked at Hugo and sent down a long trailing wisp of creeper which caught round him, and blew aside, and fastened to him again.

But Hugo said, "This river's full of spricks. There are millions and millions of them—billions. I wish I'd a jam-pot to put them in."

The trees ended: the garden ended. They climbed out on to the road close to Belmore Station.

As they reached the clearing it began to rain: at first there were only a few heavy drops, but soon they came faster and thicker. Bimbo and Hugo dashed at full speed to the dug-out where they found James and Michael and Leo. They all squeezed in together and listened to the rain hammering down on the iron roof. Bimbo felt warm and clammy. He was wet from the rain and sweaty from exercise.

"It's a thunder shower," James said. "P'raps we'll be struck by lightning."

As he spoke there was a flash, which made them jump and look at each other. James began to count and after a little there was a long crackling roll of thunder. "It's twenty miles away," James announced, "but trees attract it. Maybe it'll come closer."

It did come a little closer, but not very close and before long it died away altogether. For a time the boys talked about people being struck by lightning. Then Hugo asked, "Bimbo, you don't ever have a bath, do you?"

"No," Bimbo said, in some surprise. "How did you know?"

"You don't smell as if you bathed," Hugo answered simply.

There was a pause and Michael put in rather shyly, "It's quite a nice smell when you get accustomed to it. I don't mind it."

"It's all right," Hugo agreed. "Only I wonder Mr. Browne doesn't make you bath. They usually do."

"Make me!" Bimbo exclaimed. "Sure he'd be mad if he found me in the house at all—except in my own room. Of course I could go when he was in town. Cook lets me go where I like, now she's friends with Miss Martha: but *he* doesn't know, and anyhow I've never been upstairs: it doesn't look nice. I was in the hall once, and I didn't want to go further. Miss Martha wanted to bath me, but *he* says brushin's good enough for any animal, an' I just brush."

Bimbo scratched himself. The rain and the sweat drying on his fur gave his skin a prickly, sticky sensation. He was content and self-confident.

He looked at the others reflectively with a curious feeling that was almost compassion. He felt he knew his own future now. Whatever difficulties and troubles might lie in the way he would at last reach his real home. There was great happiness in store for him, happiness such as these boys could never know, happiness such as could only come to one who had been lost and in trouble.

22

Hugo's remarks about baths remained in Bimbo's mind. He was curious about them and would have liked to take one as an experiment: it was something more than lack of opportunity which for a long time prevented him from doing so. It was a certain deep down reluctance, a dread of getting completely wet, which he could not altogether explain.

At last his curiosity overcame his doubts. He consulted Hugo, and one afternoon when Mr. Browne was safely in the office, they set off for the bathroom together. Bimbo had never liked passing through the hall with its tiger skin and deers' heads—and upstairs the decorations were just as bad: there was even a stuffed spaniel on the landing. By the time they reached the bathroom Bimbo had the creeps and the hair was bristling all up his spine.

The bathroom itself was free from these decorations. It was a narrow room with faded brown woodwork and an old-fashioned, sloping-backed bath. Hugo put in the stopper and turned on the taps. When the bath was sufficiently full Bimbo got in reluctantly. He wished now he hadn't been so curious. Lots of animals and some human beings got on perfectly happily without baths: why couldn't he? Dolan never took a bath and he was one of the nicest people Bimbo knew. If Hugo had not been there to give directions Bimbo would have stepped straight back onto the bathroom floor, with the feeling that the experiment had been carried far enough. Instead he had to wet himself all over, and soap himself all over, and finally rinse all the soap off again, till the colour of the water had changed from its original, faint steamy green to a thick oily black. At last Hugo allowed him to get out and he jumped joyfully over the side. He was immediately seized with a most violent twitching. He shook and shook, and as he did so tremors ran up and down his back like particularly violent shivers.

When the shivering stopped he found that he was alone and that Hugo was speaking to him through the keyhole. "I'll go home an' leave you," Hugo said, "unless you promise to stop."

"I can't help it," Bimbo returned, and taking the towel Cook had given him he began to dry himself vigorously. As he dried his fur became fluffy and soft. It had never felt like that before: it was delightful and exhilarating. He wanted to laugh and sing. So he did laugh and sing. He was soaked in happiness.

Yet when they went into the wood afterwards he was uncomfortable: his body seemed strange. All the time he was with Hugo he felt unnatural, and when Hugo had gone home he wandered back to his cage, lonely and disconsolate. He climbed to his bed-box and his own familiar odour rose up around him like an old companion. Then he knew what he had lost. He threw himself down and rolled and rolled, till he was warm, and a little sticky, and his complete self once more.

Thenceforth Bimbo bathed regularly once a week and soon he learned to enjoy it. After every bath he rolled in the straw of his bed-box till Hugo discovered what he was doing and stopped him. Hugo said that he was making himself dirty again and doing away with all the good of his baths. The first time Bimbo did without rolling he was afraid he had lost his smell permanently, like the musk which Miss Martha had told him about; but in a day or two he found that it had stolen back to him of its own accord.

Bimbo's journeys to and from the bathroom eventually led him to explore the whole house systematically. It was no nicer than it looked from the hall, and in different rooms Bimbo discovered additional relics of the chase—a bear-skin rug in the dining-room and a stuffed alligator in the study, besides stuffed birds on stands and, in glass cases, stuffed fish who still preserved a slightly indignant appearance of life. Bimbo often reflected that he was lucky not to be a member of this funereal company. He could imagine the little plaque, black with white letters, which might have been attached to his stand.

Ape—Immature male.
Species Unknown.
Shot by Theodore Browne, M.B.
? Forest, South America.
October 1912.

He wished he could fill in the name of the forest. If only he knew where he had been found he could start to make plans. But it was difficult to make plans for a journey if you had only the vaguest idea about the destination. Somewhere in South America—that was all he knew. Mr. Browne probably knew more: perhaps even he knew all about it, though Bimbo didn't think so. Yet if he asked Mr. Browne, Mr. Browne would inquire why he wanted to know and most likely tell him nothing. Bimbo decided that he would find out as much as possible by other means.

He learned from Cook and Dolan that Theodore Browne's belongings were packed away in metal trunks in a certain locked room at the top of the house. Bimbo had never seen the door of this room opened, but Dolan had helped to carry up the trunks when hope of Theodore's return had been abandoned. Dolan said they had been very heavy, and that one which had burst open had been crammed with books and papers. Bimbo believed that among these books and papers there was almost certain to be some clue to his identity.

So one wet day he collected the keys from all the doors in the house and tried them one after the other in the door of the locked room. The key of the dining-room fitted. Bimbo opened the door and went in. The room was airless and dusty, with a mass of cobwebs over the window. Bimbo remembered the story of Bluebeard, but he knew Mr. Browne wasn't due home for another two hours and he thought it would be safe to examine the trunks: there were eight altogether and he was able to open three: the rest were locked. Of the three two contained clothes and one books. Bimbo wasn't interested in the clothes, but he began to pull out the books one by one, reading the titles as he did so. *Fauna of Asia Minor*, *Extinct Species of Southern India*, *New Discoveries in Java*, *The Great Apes*. This last was illustrated by photographs and drawings and Bimbo turned over the pages slowly in the hope that he might find a portrait that resembled himself. But he didn't. On the whole, indeed, it seemed that most of these creatures bore more of a likeness to humans than to him. There was only one young orang-utan which did have something of Bimbo's expression. That was as far as it went. Bimbo's head was quite a different shape, and he did not have the orang-utan's protruding, snout-like mouth.

Suddenly Bimbo remembered the time. The two hours had nearly gone: Mr. Browne would soon be back from town and if he found Bimbo in the house there would be trouble not only for Bimbo himself, but probably for the two maids and Dolan as well. Bimbo looked round hastily and tried to decide what book he should take away to read. *The Origin of Species*—that sounded as if it might explain the whole problem. He opened it and read on the fly-leaf, "Theodore Browne, '92. Re-read '95, '97, '01, '14". And when he turned over the pages he saw that the margins were filled with notes. He set it to one side and packed the other books back in the trunk. Then he picked it up again and went out. He locked the door and returned to his own room, replacing the various keys on his way.

After this Bimbo continued to visit the locked room at intervals. Each time he brought away a different book, and when the holidays began he was well launched on a study of anthropology. If it was fine he sat in trees and if it was wet he went to the dug-out or stayed in his own room at home. There was no one to disturb him for Hugo and Michael were at the seaside and James never went to the wood by himself. Leo, too, had temporarily disappeared with his family, and no one had told Bimbo where he had gone.

At first Bimbo encountered many words in Theodore Browne's books which he did not understand, and he had to wait till Mr. Browne was out of the house to look them up in the big Webster's Dictionary in the study. This, however, was not a great hindrance as Mr. Browne was in his office most of the day: besides Bimbo could memorize not only the words he had to look up but the context in which they occurred—and he never had to look up the same word twice.

He enjoyed himself. It was the first time he had undertaken a course of reading entirely on his own, and he felt a satisfaction in the steady acquisition of knowledge. But what interested him far more than the books themselves were the innumerable notes on the fly-leaves, end-papers and margins. Always they seemed on the verge of revealing something about himself; always they stopped short as if designed deliberately to tantalize him. One in particular gave him a great deal of trouble: it read, "See my memoir re Specimen 'Bimbo'." Bimbo wished he *could* see it, but though he searched the three open trunks from top to bottom he could find no trace of any such work either in print or in manuscript. He considered bursting open the five remaining trunks with a poker, but he didn't. He knew that if Mr. Browne ever discovered that he had been in the room at all he would never be allowed to see any of the books again.

23

In Ulster the 12th and 13th of July are holidays. On the 12th the Battle of the Boyne and the Battle of Aughrim are commemorated by a procession of Orangemen: on the 13th the mock battle of Scarva is fought. The object of these proceedings is to strengthen the Protestant spirit in the province and to warn the Protestants to be on their guard against the designs of the Roman Catholics. Dolan was an Orangeman and walked in the procession every year.

On this occasion "The Twelfth" was on a Friday. So when Dolan departed on the night of the 11th Bimbo did not expect to see him again till the following Monday morning. Mr. Browne was not an Orangeman, and Bimbo found out from Cook that he intended to spend the two days' holiday at home.

Bimbo decided to keep out of his way as much as possible, and early on the morning of the 12th he went to the wood. He climbed to the top of the highest tree he could find and settled down to read and enjoy the sunshine.

The heat delighted him. He could feel his whole body drinking it in. From time to time he stopped reading and glanced at the dark green tree-tops around him. They, too, were absorbing the sunshine, pushing one another aside in an effort to steal more than their share of it. Even when there was no wind at all they didn't look quite still: there was no wind now and they seemed to be moving. A cloud drifted across the sun and a ripple like a slight shiver passed through the trees. In the distance Bimbo heard the sound of drums.

The drums made him think of Dolan. He wondered how Dolan was getting on in the middle of the crowds and the noise and the dust. Surely he would have enjoyed his holiday more if he had spent it in the wood with Bimbo.

This reminded Bimbo that he had brought a book and he began to read again rather idly: but in two or three minutes he was looking at the trees once more, counting how many different shades of green he could distinguish: there were dark greens that were nearly blue, coppery greens, greens that were already beginning to wither and fade, and the fresh pale greens of leaves which were still unfolding.

He turned over a page and immediately a pencil note in Theodore Browne's handwriting caught his eye. It ran all down one margin and across the bottom of the page:

"But why should Man be the ultimate achievement? It would be sad indeed to think so. Perhaps God is always experimenting, *has* always been experimenting. Is there really any proof of the Darwinian theory of evolution? Might it not be that God, when he creates a new species, places it first in some garden of Eden where it can go through the nursery stage unmolested by other creatures, who would naturally wish to destroy beings better than themselves? What definite evidence is there that any of the main species are descended from former species, that the primates have a common ancestor? The whole case for evolution is circumstantial. Might it not be more reasonable to believe that God studies the defects in one species, and then makes new creatures without some of those defects? Why should not God be an experimental scientist, with the world as only part of His laboratory? It may even be that man is not His most up-to-date handiwork, that an improved species is already in existence. Some day I may be able to prove that this is so. If only I can get past the angel at the gate of the garden!"

Bimbo didn't read the note a second time. He didn't need to. It was fixed in his mind as firmly as if the sheet itself had been cut out and filed in some minute cabinet inside his brain. Did I come out of the Garden of Eden? he wondered, and pulling from his pocket the small steel mirror which Dolan had given him he stared critically at his own reflection. There was no doubt about it, he thought—so far as appearance was concerned he was a definite improvement on Man: his chin was finer, his forehead higher, while the nose, often an ugly feature in human beings, in Bimbo was small and unobtrusive. As for brains. . . . Why it was only necessary to think of how he had got on at school, to compare him with Hugo or James or Michael, or any of the children for that matter.

It was queer, Bimbo reflected, how long it had been before he had attempted to get in touch with the human world, before he had realized how like himself in many ways they all were. It was as if his brain had been asleep for years and had suddenly come to life. Were all the Bimbo people like that? He thought not. Probably in his natural surroundings he would have come on gradually and evenly. He would have learned to speak quite early, and after that knowledge would have flowed in upon him. Very likely even now he was more backward than other Bimbos of his age—if there were any others. But perhaps there weren't: perhaps he was a little Cain or a little Abel or a little Seth. Yet he didn't fancy he had been banished from the garden because of a sin. If he had he would surely remember the sin and be haunted by it. No: he had been snatched away by mischance, and the scientific fervour of Theodore. Somehow, sometime, he would have to get back. That would be his object in life, and when he did get back he must bring with him as much knowledge as possible. Possibly it might be part of God's plan that Bimbo should go out of the garden, and learn about human beings, and return. It would enable him to help the rest of his family or clan or tribe or nation—or species as Theodore Browne would have called it. The Bimbos might be in danger from man and need to be forewarned about human weapons and human machines.

Bimbo found this idea rather disturbing. It had never occurred to him before that he had a mission in life. Of course he had heard Miss Sutton say that everyone had a mission to perform, but somehow he hadn't thought that he was included. He had thought his circumstances were an accident, his ambition to return to the forest a private plan of his own. Even now he didn't feel certain that it was anything more, but he realized that no matter whose plan it was it was important—so important that it seemed dreadful to think of all the time he had wasted—playing here in the wood, telling stories to Hugo, gossiping with Dolan. . . . He would have to stop all that, to concentrate on acquiring serious and useful information. "Let me see now," Bimbo said to himself, "there are all sorts of things they probably don't know. Maybe they just *are* in the Garden of Eden stage, picking fruit from the trees, without knowing anything about spraying or pruning. They won't have doctors, or engineers, or understand chemistry or any of those things either. And then there's farming: I suppose I'll have to learn all about it." Bimbo realized that in spite of all his cleverness he had so far acquired very little really useful knowledge. Anything practical he did know he had picked up from Dolan. He knew how to prepare a seed bed, how far apart to put different vegetables, which of them got thinned and which were transplanted. But of agriculture, medicine, engineering and chemistry he knew nothing whatever. And even if he had somehow mastered these subjects the main difficulty would still have been to find his own country and return to it so that he could impart his knowledge to his kinsfolk. In the meantime, however, he must concentrate on packing his mind with knowledge. Considering how much he had to learn there was not a moment to waste: he'd be an old, old Bimbo before he knew where he was. Almost guiltily he forced himself to stop dreaming and go on reading. After all he could think just as well at night before he went to sleep. He would make further plans then.

So that night, as soon as he had climbed into his bed-box, Bimbo arranged himself in a comfortable position for thinking. But before he had time to think anything important he heard Dolan's voice just outside his window and his attention was distracted. It wasn't Dolan's usual voice either. It had a quality in it that Bimbo had never heard previously, a quality he didn't like—a mixture of cheerfulness and brutality. . . . It gave Bimbo an uncomfortable feeling. He felt a little nervous: it was as if he had suddenly come face to face with something new and dangerous. He listened and Dolan began to sing:

Dolly's Brae, and Dolly's Brae,
And Dolly's Brae No More,
The tune we played was Kick the Pope
Right over Dolly's Brae.

Dolan stopped: he coughed and spluttered, and hiccoughed once or twice. Bimbo slid down the rope from his bed-box to the floor. He crossed to the window and sat there listening. Dolan began to sing again:

Bein' on the Twelfth day of July, eighteen an' forty-nine,
The papists of this country to. . .

His voice tailed away, and Bimbo heard the front door opening. "Ev'nin', sir," Dolan said jerkily. "We'd a grand day for the Twalth."

"What do you want?" Mr. Browne asked stiffly. "What are you doing here?"

"Jus' dem'shtratin' loy'lty," Dolan answered, "an' ah brought ye somethin' to drink it in, somethin' spashel. 'Ah want somethin' spashel,' says I. 'It's for the gen'leman ah works for,' ah tol' him. So he gives me some real good rum, real Black Tom so 'tis. You take a pull o' that, sir. Make your toes open an' shut so 'twill. Black Tom'sh a boy."

"No, thank you," Mr. Browne responded, and his voice had just enough expression to sound unfriendly. "I don't think there'd better be any more drinking to-night. You go home, and we can discuss this again on Monday morning."

"Will ye no drink King Billy's health?" Dolan urged. "Ye'll surely drink a health to King Billy."

"No, thank you," Mr. Browne repeated coldly. "In fact you may take it that I don't wish to drink any healths with you, either now or at any other time."

"An' why not then?" Dolan demanded. "Are ye not *for* King Billy?"

Mr. Browne, however, did not answer this question. "If you make a nuisance of yourself any more," he said, "if you don't go straight home, I'll telephone for the police."

Far from frightening Dolan this seemed to make him all the bolder. "I know what y'are," he exclaimed. "I see ye in yer true colours at last. Ye's one o' them peaceful penetrators they're talkin' about. I heerd all about ye, you an' the likes o' ye, at The Field, ye papish. . . ." But at this point Mr. Browne stepped inside and quietly closed the door.

For an instant there was silence. Then Dolan began to mutter to himself. Bimbo heard Mr. Browne cross the hall and turn the handle of the telephone. Bimbo knew how the telephone worked, and he determined to put it out of order before Mr. Browne could get through. He sprang to the grate and, picking up the poker, raced through the cage to the nearest corner of the house where there was a down spout from the roof. He climbed it and worked his way along the edge of the roof till he reached the place where the telephone wires joined the house. Thrusting the poker between them he twisted them together so as to cause a short circuit.

Leaving the poker in that position he climbed down again and went to Dolan, who was still gazing stupidly at the closed front door and grumbling a little to himself. "Do go home," Bimbo begged him. "He's trying to telephone for the police. I've crossed the wires but he may have got through first."

At this news Dolan seemed to come partially to his senses. He stared at Bimbo and was overwhelmed with emotion. "Real pal, Bimbo," he exclaimed, with something between a sob and a hiccough. "I won't never forget it to ye, Bimbo, no, ah never will."

"If you go home quick," Bimbo told him, "there'll be no trouble."

"I'm goin'," Dolan answered. "Ah'm goin' now," and sure enough he started rather slowly down the drive.

Bimbo knew he was drunk. It was the first time he had seen a drunk man, but he knew how drunk men behaved. He had read about them in books. Besides Dolan himself had a whole series of anecdotes about men who got drunk. Once even he had described to Bimbo what getting drunk felt like. Without a doubt he was renewing that experience to-night.

By this time Bimbo had got over his feeling of discomfort. He was observing Dolan with friendly detachment. He wanted to prevent him getting into trouble, but he was more interested in his condition than embarrassed by it. He didn't think any great harm had been done, though very likely Dolan would be in disgrace on Monday morning. Mr. Browne would probably give him a talking-to and Dolan would say he was sorry. It was nice to think it would all be over by Tuesday.

Even now Dolan was gradually getting more normal. At the end of the drive he stopped and straightened himself up. "Ah'm all right," he said, turning slowly towards Bimbo. "Ah'll go straight home. Don't ye trouble. You leave me, ole chum Bimbo."

He went through the gate without difficulty and set off steadily along the road. Bimbo got up into the trees and kept abreast of him as far as Belmore Station. After that he let him go out of sight: Dolan now appeared quite capable of looking after himself. Certainly there was nothing in his manner to attract anyone's attention.

When Bimbo got back the only light in the house was in Mr. Browne's bedroom. Evidently the police had not come. Bimbo climbed back to the roof and retrieved the poker. The wires returned to their normal positions with a thin whinging sound. Bimbo went to bed and curling up in the straw was soon asleep.

But on Monday morning Dolan did not reappear and Bimbo learned from Cook that he had been dismissed. "He'll be hard put to it, too," she added. "The master'll stop his buroo sure as eggs is eggs. It wouldn't be him if he didn't."

Bimbo was sorry. He was really fond of Dolan. Dolan had been his friend from the very beginning, before Hugo, before Miss Martha. . . . He couldn't remember when he had first seen Dolan—it must have been very soon after he first came to Belmore. And in the last two years he had often spent hours at a time watching him at work and listening to his stories. Surely he would make it up with Mr. Browne and come back in a week or two.

This gave Bimbo an idea. If Dolan did return he would find himself terribly behind in all he had been doing. He would have a hard time catching up. Bimbo decided that there were some things he could do to make things easier for Dolan when he returned. It pleased him to think of the pleasant surprises Dolan would get when he found things weren't so bad as he had anticipated. So on

Tuesday afternoon he got out the lawn-mower and began to cut the grass.

It was a bigger job than he had thought and he was still at work when Mr. Browne returned from business. For some time Mr. Browne stood at the edge of the lawn and watched without speaking. Then he called in his sharp, dry, peremptory voice, "Bimbo!" Bimbo went to him. "Why are you doing that?" Mr. Browne asked.

Bimbo explained and ventured to add, "I don't think Dolan meant to be bad. I'm sure he'd do his best and never say anything bad again."

Mr. Browne gave a little shrug of impatience. "No doubt," he agreed.

"I'm sure he would," Bimbo declared.

Mr. Browne ignored this. "I'm informed you can read," he said.

"Very well indeed," Bimbo assured him. "I haven't had to learn for more than a year now."

"All the better," Mr. Browne responded drily. "Wait here a moment." He went into the house and returned a minute or two later. He handed Bimbo Mrs. Beeton's book on gardening. "Now," he proceeded, "here is an opportunity at last for you to do something towards earning your keep. You're strong, you're on holiday, you've nothing at all to do. I don't know how long it'll be until I engage another gardener—or bring back your friend Dolan. In the meantime I shall expect you to keep the garden, and keep it well. That book will tell you what to do. If you've any doubts you can ask me. Now you'd better go on with the grass. You'll find your bananas will taste better to-night. Food honestly earned always does: so I'm told." He gave a little laugh and went back into the house.

Bimbo put the book down on a garden seat and began to push the lawn-mower again. He liked the exercise but he didn't like the idea of working all the time. He wanted to go on with his reading, specially now since he had decided it was so urgent. He wished Miss Martha had been at home so that he could talk the question over with her. Unfortunately she was at the seaside and wasn't expected back till almost the end of August.

24

At the end of a week Bimbo decided that he liked gardening. The weather was fine and by starting early and going on till dusk he got a great deal done. He began with the intention of keeping everything in the same order as Dolan had left it, but before long he discovered that Dolan had been neglecting his work. All the out of the way parts of the garden were thick with weeds, and even the beds near the gate which had been "made dacent for the Twalth" had actually only been turned over.

At first these discoveries made Bimbo feel disillusioned about Dolan, but when he thought of his friendliness and his kindness nothing else seemed to matter. So he tried to hide Dolan's faults from Mr. Browne in the hope that some day Dolan might be forgiven and brought back. How much Mr. Browne saw it was difficult to know. Since Dolan's departure he had been taking a great interest in the garden. He gave Bimbo instructions every morning, and when he returned from the office in the evenings would follow him round watching everything he did. Sometimes he praised Bimbo's work: sometimes he merely remarked that he must be glad to be making a small contribution towards the cost of his keep. Once or twice he lent Bimbo further books on gardening and advised him to read them. Bimbo read them on Sundays—it was the only day he was not expected to work. He read them with no intention of pleasing Mr. Browne, but in the hope that the knowledge they contained might be useful when he returned to his own country. . . .

He didn't care indeed whether he pleased Mr. Browne or not: for he was convinced that Mr. Browne's present friendliness was nothing more than part of a scheme to make him gardener in Dolan's place. He didn't want to be a permanent gardener, and he didn't want to deprive Dolan of his job. Besides, he intended to go back to school in the autumn. Meanwhile he thought it better to do everything Mr. Browne required. His objections would be all the more effective if he waited for Miss Martha's support and advice. He was expecting her to return from her holidays on the 25th of August and on the evening of that day she did in fact come to see him. She found him cutting the hedge beside the gate. He had chosen to do this partly so that he could look out for her, partly to give her an immediate demonstration of his new duties. He had expected to surprise her, but at first she was far too busy remarking how much he had grown during her absence to pay particular attention to what he was doing. Then she assumed that he was cutting the hedge for fun or to please Dolan. Bimbo explained what had really happened. "Dolan's left," he told her. "I'm the gardener now."

At this she did look surprised. "Not permanently, surely?" she said. "I don't suppose it'll do you any harm for a week or two."

"He *says*, till he gets a new gardener," Bimbo replied, "but I don't believe he's trying to get one."

"And d'you like being a gardener?"

"Yes," Bimbo confessed. "I do like it, but I don't want always to be one. I want to go on going to school—or having time to read books so that I can learn everything that's any good. I'd like to go to a university when I'm older."

"Well, it was about your education I came to see you— Come down off that ladder. I've a crick in my neck already trying to talk up to you." Bimbo came down and put the hedge-clippers on the bottom step. "I suppose you've realized," Miss Martha went on, "that so far as teaching's concerned my sisters and I can do very little more for you."

"You mean you've no time," Bimbo said.

"I mean I don't know any more," Miss Martha admitted candidly, "or at least, not very much. For one thing I've forgotten most of the work I did at Queen's when I was taking my degree—and *nearly* everything I was taught in the higher forms at school. I'm afraid my education is now at just about the same level as the education of one of my best pupils—and only in my own subjects, too. Goodness knows where I am in the others: the kindergarten would reject me with scorn. So far as learning goes I'm no more than a sort of glorified prefect. In another month or two I won't know what you're talking about when you want something explained—it was bad enough last term—and as for your private reading I lost track of that long ago. I was thinking about you while I was away—we all were. We think the best possible thing would be for you to go to a proper boys' school, where you could do science and higher maths, and Greek, if you liked. You really need someone who knows more than you know yourself, and besides, I think competition's a help—yes, even for you, Bimbo. We thought of St. Patrick's—you've heard Hugo and the others talking about 'Paddy's', I expect. How would you like to go there?"

"Would they have me?" Bimbo inquired doubtingly. "And what would Mr. Browne say? I'm sure he wouldn't pay the fees. You see I know it was only because you were kind and took me free that I got going to school at all."

"You needn't worry about them having you," Miss Martha assured him. "As it happens Mr. Travers, the new headmaster of St. Patrick's, was at Ballycastle when we were and I told him about you. He was very much interested and would be delighted to get you."

"And the governors?" Bimbo asked. He knew from storybooks Hugo had lent him that all big boys' schools had governors. "What'll the governors say?"

"Oh, blow the governors," Miss Martha exclaimed, with quite unusual violence. "Mr. Travers will fix them. What's the good of the man if he can't? Governors are only a nuisance anyhow—lot of silly old men, who aren't half educated themselves, most of them. Do you want to go? That's what really matters."

Bimbo would have preferred to remain at Miss Sutton's. He hated crowds and strangers, and if he went to St. Patrick's he would encounter both. It was a big school and to get to it he would have to pass through the centre of Belfast every day. On the other hand it might offer opportunities of learning he would never get at Miss Sutton's.

"Yes, please," he replied. "Anyhow I think I'd better go."

"Of course you'd better," Miss Martha said, "and that means there's no time to be lost. Their term starts on the second. I'll have to see Mr. Browne immediately."

With that she marched straight towards the house. She rang the bell, and after a moment Minnie opened the door and took her inside. Bimbo picked up the clippers and mounted the steps: but he worked more slowly than before, and the next time he stood back to look at what he had done he discovered a distinct dip in the line of the hedge, which before had been perfectly level. "Oh, blow the hedge," he said, imitating Miss Martha's voice, and though he had originally intended to have it all beautifully even he made no attempt to straighten it out.

It was nearly dark when Miss Martha reappeared an hour and a half later. Bimbo had stopped work, but he had not put away the ladder and clippers for fear she should come out while he was in the tool shed. As it was she only stayed with him long enough to give him one further piece of advice. "Remember, Bimbo, you've made up your mind. Don't pay any attention to what Mr. Browne will say to you. Good night." And she went home.

Bimbo expected that when he got in he would immediately be summoned to Mr. Browne's study: but it was not till the following evening when he was closing the lights in the greenhouse that Mr. Browne spoke to him. Then he came to the door and stood for an instant watching. "Well," he asked, "do you like gardening?"

Bimbo was puzzled by this question. In the ordinary way he would have answered it truthfully, but he couldn't be sure that Miss Martha had been truthful. He didn't want to let her down. "No," he replied emphatically.

Mr. Browne gave a little, dry smile, and Bimbo knew he had fallen into a trap after all. "That's strange," he commented. "Only last night Miss Martha Sutton, who declares she is wholly in your confidence, assured me that you were devoted to it, that indeed it was your chief pleasure."

"Only if I've nothing better to do," Bimbo answered. "I wouldn't like it to keep me from going to school and learning things." He felt that he had escaped, though not, perhaps, very neatly.

Mr. Browne, however, showed no signs of being put out. "Oh, indeed," he said. "So you want to go to school again, do you? You've still something to learn, even after two years of hard work?"

"Yes," Bimbo told him, "lots and lots."

"Look here, Bimbo," Mr. Browne said in an altered and much kinder tone, "what on earth's the good of it? Have you thought this matter out? Suppose I let you go to school—to St. Patrick's as has been suggested—what's going to happen? You don't know, but

I'll tell you. We'll imagine that you do exceptionally well at school and go to a university and repeat the performance there. If you were an ordinary normal, human boy you would be able to get a job of some sort, or you might go into one of the professions, but you're not. I'm not trying to hurt your feelings—you know you're not as well as I do."

"Yes," Bimbo interrupted, "and I'm glad I'm not. I'd. . . ." but he checked himself.

"Oh! So you're glad, are you?" For a moment Mr. Browne seemed a little disconcerted, but he evidently decided that Bimbo was lying and he went on again quickly. "Glad or sorry it's going to cause you a great many difficulties. You don't imagine that any business house is going to put you on its staff, or perhaps you were planning to go in for medicine? I'm afraid Doctor Bimbo would not have many patients. Or the Church. . . ."

"I don't want to go into the Church," Bimbo said.

"Well, that *is* a disappointment," Mr. Browne exclaimed. "How well the Reverend Bimbo Monkeyface would sound—or Dean Bimbo—that's even better."

"It would be Archbishop Bimbo," Bimbo retorted. He felt that he might as well enter into the spirit of this game. There was no sense in letting Mr. Browne have all the fun.

It seemed, however, that for Mr. Browne the fun was over. "Well," he continued stiffly, "you can at least see that the whole idea is rather ridiculous. Now I have an alternative suggestion to make, and if you think about it sensibly I believe you will see that it offers you your best chance of living a happy and useful life."

"You mean to go on gardening?" Bimbo asked.

"Yes, to go on gardening. It has been your misfortune, I think I may say, to have spent most of the last year or two with boys who considered themselves of a class superior to gardeners. As a matter of fact most of them are nothing of the kind. Why old Clarke, your friend's grandfather. . . . However, that doesn't matter at the moment. Suppose you went on looking after this garden, you would in a year or two—with a little advice, which I would see that you got—become quite an expert gardener. I've been watching you during these last few weeks and you've really done remarkably well, shown a distinct aptitude I may say. Well, let us presume that some years have passed. You are an *efficient* and industrious gardener. I can assure you that you would have no difficulty in finding a home. Indeed I should probably be very loath to part with you."

"I expect you would," Bimbo agreed, "—specially if. . . ." but there was no sense in annoying Mr. Browne any further.

"Specially if what?" Mr. Browne inquired, and his voice sounded vaguely suspicious.

"Specially if I turned out as well as you expect," Bimbo answered glibly.

Mr. Browne smiled reassuringly. "If you put your heart into it I'm sure you will," he said. "Now think it over and I'll ask for your answer in the morning."

Bimbo, when he was left alone, wondered why he was asked at all. Mr. Browne didn't want him to go to school, didn't want him to be taught anything, didn't want him to play with Hugo. Why couldn't he just lock the cage door and have done with it? It was queer: sometimes it seemed as if Mr. Browne lacked full authority, as if he were acting on the instructions of some invisible third party. Bimbo remembered Dolan's suggestion that Mr. Browne had wanted him to die when he had pneumonia, that Mr. Browne would benefit financially by his death. Bimbo couldn't understand it all, but he took advantage of Mr. Browne's behaviour whenever he could. So the next morning when the question was put he said at once, "I've decided. I want to go to school."

Mr. Browne was surprised. "You do, do you?" he exclaimed. "This is most interesting. May I ask who is going to pay the fees—or perhaps you have been awarded a scholarship?"

"I don't know," Bimbo answered, "but I want to go."

"You don't know," Mr. Browne repeated, "but they won't take you without payment. I should think its the first thing you'd need to find out."

"I s'pose Miss Martha'll pay them then," Bimbo responded.

Mr. Browne shrugged his shoulders. "You think so? You've a wonderful confidence in human nature."

25

Yet though Mr. Browne gave his consent Bimbo never went to St. Patrick's. The day before the school was due to reopen a letter came from the headmaster: Mr. Browne showed it to Bimbo and Miss Martha. This is what it said:

Dear Mr. Browne,

I am sorry to have to tell you that we shall not be able to take the ape-boy after all. Someone informed the governors that he was coming and they held an emergency meeting this morning. When it was over I was instructed that on no account must your protégé be entered as a pupil here. I cannot give you any reason for this decision: none worthy of the name was given to me.

Believe me I very much regret what has happened.

Yours sincerely,

Ernest Travers.

26

So long as there was sufficient light Bimbo worked. Then he put away the tools he had been using, said good night to Leo who had kept him company all afternoon, and finally washed the earth off his hands in the wooden tub outside the greenhouse. Just a month had passed since the failure of Miss Martha's plan to send him to St. Patrick's. Dolan had got a job at the docks and Mr. Browne showed no sign of engaging a man to take his place. Bimbo was to be the gardener: there seemed to be no hope of his continuing his education except by private reading—and the only times he could read were on Sundays, and in the evenings when his work outside was finished. This evening, however, he was going to paint.

He was in a hurry to start: so he dropped on all fours and ran as fast as he could to the house and in by way of the cage to his own room. After brushing himself vigorously for five minutes, to get the earth out of his fur, he felt refreshed and comparatively clean; so he went round to the back door to see what Cook had for his supper. Cook gave him a bunch of bananas, an orange and a bag of nuts. Bimbo carried them back to his room, and putting the orange aside to be eaten last, began with the bananas. As he was eating he got his tins of paint and brushes out of the cupboard. He had found the tin of red paint and the tin of blue paint on the top shelf of the potting shed, and Hugo had brought him the tin of yellow paint and the brushes. By experimenting Bimbo had discovered how to mix the paints to get the different colours he required.

Having arranged paints and brushes along the edge of the table, he stared at the wall. While he was staring he went on slowly eating a banana. At some time in the past the walls must have been papered; but they had been stripped and bare for as long as Bimbo could remember. The plaster was greyish white with a number of large and small watery brown stains. Only one corner was different and that was the corner where Bimbo slept. He had painted the four supports of his bed-box in various shades of brown, and black, and green, so that they looked like tree-trunks covered with masses of green leaves; and on the wall behind he had painted more trees, gradually disappearing into a bluish-green distance.

Eventually he intended to paint the whole room to look like a glade of his forest. He knew every flower, every leaf, the smallest plant that grew there. When he stared at the wall he could make the soiled, stained plaster disappear, and see instead sunlight shining through trees, casting bright patches on the shadowy ground beneath. The scene was clear and brilliant—the leaves, the flowers, the gaily coloured birds that perched on the branches and watched everything through blinking, sleepy eyes. It was all vivid and definite. . . . But to produce it needed an effort of imagination. Bimbo had to call it up out of the void. What he wanted was to make this vision permanent, to make his room so like a part of the forest that when he looked round it he would only know by reason and memory where he really was: that was why he had begun to paint—and once he had begun he found a dreamy pleasure in the occupation, a pleasure he had never experienced through any other means. It was as if he cast aside his body and became a spirit or an angel. It was like a foretaste of immortality, or a harking back to some pre-corporeal existence. When he thought of it afterwards it always seemed that with a little more effort, a little more imagination he might have abandoned his body altogether and become completely free. Yet somehow, when he was in this mood he never thought of making any such effort, but painted on, hardly conscious even that he was happy.

When the idea of this painting had first occurred to him, Bimbo had considered two methods of work. He could either paint the picture as a whole, or he could divide the walls into sections and complete a section at a time. This latter was the method he had chosen and already the first section was nearly finished.

To-night he was going to do flowers, red flowers, those small brilliant red flowers which grew in such profusion and seemed the very symbol of the dark forest of his dreams. So far the only occasions when he had used the red paint had been in mixtures with blue paint and yellow paint to make the brown trunks of some of the trees—not that they all had brown trunks; some of the trunks were a bluish-green, and some were black as ebony.

Before he began he peeled another banana; and he ate it while he was painting the first flower. Though he was thinking of his picture he remained completely conscious of the banana, of its sweetness and richness, of the satisfying sensation it created as it passed down his throat. In a way it helped to take him back to the forest. He imagined himself after his return being fed with bananas by the other Bimbo people. How they would gather round him and listen once he had learned their language, or they had learned to understand *him*. They would call him, "Bimbo the Wise", and so, before he returned to them, he wanted to become as wise as he possibly could. In particular he wanted to get some practical knowledge of medicine. He had read all Theodore Browne's medical books, but they were bound to be out of date: besides he knew that he could never understand the subject properly without seeing doctors at work in hospitals.

It was the hope of acquiring further knowledge, the hope that he might after all be able to spend a few years at a university and have access to a good library, which kept him from trying to escape. He knew, of course, that to escape would be difficult; but he had already made a plan and believed that when the time came he would be able to carry it through.

This led him to wonder, as he had often wondered before, how true his memories of the Bimbo people really were: he knew that he was practically certain to have idealized them. Most likely he would find them living an extremely primitive life: but that was no reason why they shouldn't be both intelligent and nice. They would not, however, be in a condition to come in contact with civilized Man. They would have to remain hidden in the jungle a little longer—a few hundred years perhaps—perhaps a few thousand—and then, when civilization had destroyed itself, they would emerge: and in time they would inherit the chief place in the world. They would be better than Man: they would advance a little further: and eventually, probably, they too would be replaced, as the Divine Artist approached one step nearer to His vision of perfection—or did that vision always draw back a little as the Creator advanced?

Since he had begun to paint, it had pleased Bimbo to think of God as an artist. He would have liked to have been an artist himself, painting all the time; but actually he only painted two evenings a week. Every other evening, and during the day on Sundays, he read. From now on his chief difficulty would be to get books. Last week he had finished *The Golden Bough* and there were no books left belonging to the house which he had not read.

This week he was reading *Huckleberry Finn* and *Die Grundlage der allgemeinen Relativitätstheorie.* Both these had been sent to him by a cousin of Miss Martha's who was a lecturer on physics in an American university. In addition he had sent Birtwhistle's *Quantum Theory of the Atom*, which Bimbo had not yet begun. To-night, however, he didn't mean to do any reading at all.

He painted continuously till eight o'clock: then, having finished all his bananas and nuts, he stopped to eat his orange. After that he worked on till almost eleven when he began to feel hungry again and a little sleepy. So he went to the kitchen to get his supper. In the kitchen he found Cook sitting up alone. She told him that Minnie had been given notice. "He wants me to stay on as general," she added. "I told him I'd consider it if he got you to do the boots and the brasses."

27

One evening about three weeks later Hugo came to visit Bimbo. Though it was long after tea-time he had his schoolbag with him. He carried it like a soldier's pack, across his shoulders.

"Are you moving houses?" he asked. "There's a furniture van outside the gate."

"Not at this time of night," Bimbo answered. He was cleaning one of Mr. Browne's boots and he held it up to the light to see if it were sufficiently polished. "I expect it's going on somewhere and has just stopped there for a minute." He gave the boot a few more rubs with the brush and picked up the other one of the pair. Hugo unhitched his schoolbag, opened it, and took out a Latin grammar.

On a table were four brass candlesticks, a brass gong, and a brass kettle on a stand: underneath were two sets of brass fire-irons and a copper coal scuttle. Hugo looked at them. "I say, Bimbo," he remarked. "You can't half make them shine. Will you hear me when you've finished?"

"What have you got?" Bimbo inquired.

"Second declension—principal parts of moneo, and the present and perfect."

"You mean second conjugation," Bimbo told him. "You decline nouns and adjectives, but you conjugate verbs. What's the second person plural, perfect tense of moneo?"

"I don't see what difference it makes," Hugo grumbled. "What did you say?"

"Moneo, perfect tense, second person plural."

There was a pause. "Monevimus," Hugo replied at last. "We have advised or we advised."

"You'd have been better to have *been* advised," Bimbo told him, and he put the boots under the table with the fire-irons and the scuttle. "You're wrong in two ways. It should be monuistis. The endings are the same as amo. You just put monu– instead of amav–."

But Hugo hadn't been paying attention. "I hate Latin," he

announced. "What's the good of it, anyway? His gaze had been wandering round the room and now it was fixed steadily on the wall beside the door. "What's that?" he demanded. "I don't like it."

Bimbo looked. "Just an experiment—something I put there for fun."

"I don't like the way it's looking at me," Hugo objected, with a nervous smile that was quite unlike him. "It's not like a real picture: it's like something there."

"Of course it's there," Bimbo said. "Would you like me to cover it up?" He took a sheet of paper and attached it to the wall with a drawing-pin. "Is that what you want? Does that make it all right now?"

But Hugo didn't seem satisfied. "It's trying to see me through the paper," he asserted. "It's no good coverin' it up."

Bimbo was pleased; for all he had painted on an otherwise perfectly blank wall was a single eye, a green eye with a red pupil. He had painted it not as part of his picture, but merely to satisfy a passing fancy. He was flattered. Then he remembered Hugo's Latin. "What are the principal parts of moneo?" he asked.

But before Hugo had begun to answer the door opened and Mr. Browne came in. "Bimbo," he said—and it was clear he hadn't noticed Hugo, "come to my study. I want to have a little talk with you." Suddenly he caught sight of Hugo and was, it seemed to Bimbo, slightly disconcerted. But he was the sort of man who never behaved naturally with boys. "Oh! How d'ye do?" he greeted him. "There's no hurry. It'll do when you've gone. I suppose you'll be going in a few minutes."

"Yes," Hugo answered meekly, though Bimbo knew he had intended to stay all evening. "I'll go now."

This obviously was what Mr. Browne wished, though he still appeared to be slightly uneasy. "There's no hurry," he repeated, but added, almost in the same breath, "I'll expect *you*, Bimbo, in five minutes." He stepped out and closed the door behind him.

Hugo waited till the footsteps had died away in the passage. "Is he always like that?" he inquired.

"Like what?" Bimbo said. "He seems nearly the same as usual—he's a little upset about something perhaps. Maybe he's lost more money in business. I don't think he's much good at business."

"Father says times are bad," Hugo responded. He was frowning, but suddenly he seemed to remember something. "I know what he's like," he announced. "He's like a wicked uncle."

Bimbo laughed. "He'll have a job losing me in the woods," he said.

Hugo had been packing his schoolbag and now he picked it up. He hitched it on his shoulders and prepared to leave. At the door he turned. "Does he often do that—have you into his study, I mean?"

Bimbo shook his head. "Only when I've *done* something, or when he's got some plan for me to do more work. I wonder what he wants this time."

He walked to the front door with Hugo, let him out, and crossed the hall to Mr. Browne's study. He knocked.

"Come in," Mr. Browne called.

Bimbo went in and found him alone, but he knew at once that he hadn't been alone for very long. There had been a visitor, a strange man—and there was a fainter smell also, a smell of animals. The visitor had been a man who worked with animals, a groom perhaps, or a cattle dealer: but the smell was not of horses and not of cattle. Mr. Browne, surely, had been in strange company.

Bimbo looked at him more closely. He *was* slightly upset, slighly on edge; but it was with an unusually hospitable gesture that he waved Bimbo to a chair which was drawn up to the fire on the opposite side of the hearth to his own. "Sit down there," he said kindly. "It's a night for the fireside." On the right of Bimbo's chair was an oval, dark oak table with corkscrew legs. On the table was a dish containing a large bunch of purple grapes. Bimbo loved grapes. Miss Martha had brought him some on two or three occasions, and so had Hugo. He had once got Cook to suggest to Mr. Browne that he should be supplied with them regularly, but Mr. Browne had said they were too expensive. He knew now, at once, that these grapes were intended for him. He decided to eat them all before the interview was over, but not to allow them to affect in the slightest his reception of whatever it was that Mr. Browne had to say. He sat down. "Help yourself to grapes," Mr. Browne told him.

Bimbo thanked him coldly and took some. He remained alert

and suspicious as he ate them, spitting the stones and skins into the fire. The damp skins bubbled and sizzled on the hot coals. Mr. Browne let him eat quite a number of grapes before he spoke at all. It was only when Bimbo stopped and looked at him inquiringly that he rather hurriedly began. "Perhaps you don't know it, Bimbo," he said, "but at the moment this country is passing through a very serious financial depression."

He paused and Bimbo, because his mouth was full, at first could only nod his head. "I know," he answered, with a gulp. "Times are bad."

"The slump is affecting almost everyone," Mr. Browne went on, without taking much notice of Bimbo's response. "It's making everyone poorer. In my case—I am taking you into my confidence—it acts in two ways. I find there is less business to do—people are less litigious, if you know what that means—and secondly my income from investments has decreased considerably. Some of my investments have stopped paying altogether, among them those on which I relied for your support."

He paused again, but this time Bimbo remained silent, watching him steadily, with brown, unblinking eyes. He was wondering what exactly was going to be demanded of him—perhaps more work, perhaps the acceptance of smaller rations—and also, vaguely, in what way the taste of the grapes was peculiar. They had a faint secondary taste that was not a grape-taste at all.

Mr. Browne looked at the floor and spoke again: "I have been forced to consider my position. I can't continue to live on my capital. I have to get rid of Cook or you, and you. . . ."

"Why can't you let me go to Miss Martha?" Bimbo demanded. "*She* wouldn't have to get rid of me—or of anyone."

"It's all very well for her," Mr. Browne replied stiffly. "I don't suppose she has the faintest idea what it costs to keep you. Besides I can't shirk my responsibilities like that."

"You want to use me, that's what it is," Bimbo retorted angrily. "You don't care what happens to me otherwise. I'm cheaper than Dolan and cheaper than Minnie. . . ."

"And cheaper than Cook," Mr. Browne added softly. "I want you to learn to cook. It's not any more difficult than gardening, I'm sure, though I have never tried it myself. It'll mean that you'll have less time for the garden, but I'll expect you to do something in the garden, too—a gardener-housekeeper, we'll call you. I'll always expect to find you doing something."

"I won't do any more than I'm doing at present." Bimbo detached some more grapes from the bunch in the dish and began to eat them. "You want me to be just a slave, but I won't be. . . ."

Mr. Browne smiled—it was a genuine smile of satisfaction, Bimbo noticed, and he was a little puzzled. "I think, Bimbo," he said, "you forget your position. If you displease me, you know, I have always my remedy, the remedy one always has with unsatisfactory animals."

Bimbo knew what was meant; nevertheless he asked, "What remedy?"

"I could have you put down," Mr. Browne answered coolly.

Bimbo wasn't frightened. "Do you not think that at the very least you'd make yourself unpopular?"

"At the very most," Mr. Browne returned. "You must remember, Bimbo, that whatever your amazing talents you are no more than a monkey in the eyes of the law."

Bimbo reached lazily for more grapes, but with his hand in the dish he stopped. It occurred to him that all this talk was irksome and confusing; and besides it was getting nowhere. Mr. Browne and he had reached a deadlock. He had meant to eat all the grapes just to get the better of Mr. Browne, but that was silly. They weren't really nice grapes: their peculiar secondary taste lingered about his throat: he felt slightly sick. "There's always monkey law," he remarked profoundly. Monkey law—it had never occurred to him before. He felt that he had surprised Mr. Browne.

"Ah, yes, monkey law," Mr. Browne agreed. "Of course there's monkey law. . . ."

Bimbo sighed and closed his eyes. Mr. Browne could say what he liked. Bimbo just couldn't be bothered to listen. "Monkey law, monkey law," he murmured to himself. "That's what we need—more monkey law."

He was almost asleep, but a slight noise attracted his attention for a moment. Somewhere behind him a window was being opened. Mr. Browne was no longer in his chair by the fire. It must have been he who had opened the window. The cold draught from outside revived Bimbo a little, but only for an instant. He saw a man with a coarse pink face, blue eyes, a sandy moustache and sandy eyebrows. This man was watching him. Bimbo knew at once that it was the animal man, the man whose smell he had noticed when he first came in. Mr. Browne, too, was watching him very gravely.

The animal man smiled and looked at Mr. Browne. "'E won't give you no more trouble," he said, "not 'im."

Bimbo went to sleep again.

28

Bimbo knew that he was falling: he awoke in complete darkness and found the floor slipping away from beneath him. Next instant it rose and crashed into him, jarring every bone in his body. An English voice shouted angrily, "Careful, you fools—there's val'ble chiney in that box." It was the voice of the animal man.

From the background came many noises, the sound of horses' hooves, iron-rimmed dray-wheels on the square-setts, men shouting. . . . A goods train was shunting with a slow clank-clank of buffers and a subdued swishing of steam from the engine. Bimbo was bruised and dazed. He felt a bump rising on the side of his head: his left knee was sore, and his left hip-bone was beginning to throb: the inside of his mouth was like leather: something sharp was sticking into his right hand. For a moment he lay still. There was a smell of newly sawn wood. The darkness was absolute.

With great difficulty he succeeded in making himself think. Trains, horses, carts, a paved street, the smell of wood. . . . He must be at a railway station in some sort of a box or crate. He understood now why Mr. Browne had brought him into his study, why the grapes had tasted queer. But if Mr. Browne had taken such precautions to have him removed quietly would he not be certain to send him really far away—out of Ireland at least? In that case he wasn't likely to be sent by train. Suddenly the engine whistled and at the same time a ship's horn blew a long, harsh blast. Bimbo knew he was at the docks.

"Here, Mister, where d'you want her put?" This question was

asked by Dolan. To Bimbo his voice was unmistakable. He was standing close beside the box and next moment his smell became perceptible.

Bimbo's head was still muzzy. He could not understand why Dolan should be here, apparently working in conjunction with the kidnappers. It was several seconds before he remembered that Dolan had become a dock labourer, several more before it occurred to him that Dolan might be able to help him to escape.

The engine whistled again and Bimbo did not hear the Englishman's reply. Whatever it was, he and Dolan, and a number of other men who had been standing round the box, began to walk away, and were very soon out of earshot.

Bimbo sat up and felt around cautiously. The box was about four feet square and on the floor was a thick layer of hay which must have broken his fall. In the sides and roof were a number of small, bright discs. When Bimbo realized that they were air-holes he got up and looked out through one of them.

He saw an expanse of paved street crossed by railway lines. About thirty yards away was a row of dock sheds stretching for as far as he could see in either direction. It was nighttime and electric lamps placed high up along the edges of the sheds threw dim patches of light on the damp, greasy square-setts and glistening rails.

Bimbo sniffed. He could smell oil and water and tar and fish. . . . also, more faintly, the lingering, mingling, human scents, that the Englishman and Dolan and the other dockers had left in the moist air. The only person in sight was a policeman, who stood between two sliding doors at the entrance to one of the sheds. Bimbo wondered if he could force his way out of the box without attracting the policeman's attention. Using all his strength he pressed against each of the sides in turn. The boards creaked a little, but he realized at once that he would not be able to break them. So he sat down to try and think out some other plan of escape.

If he had been human all he would have had to do would have been to call the policeman to his assistance. As it was, the policeman and the whole vast organization of human society were against him. But need they be?

In a rush Bimbo's optimism returned. If he shouted from inside the box no one would believe he wasn't human. Once out of the box the hardest part of his escape would be over. Surely he was clever enough to think out further plans; surely he would be able to deal with fresh difficulties as they arose. If he wasn't too closely pursued he would try to find Dolan. Dolan would help him if he could—he might even be able to provide a disguise of some kind.

While Bimbo was considering all this, and gently rubbing the bump on his head, he heard the sound of Dolan's footsteps returning—and this time he was alone. He stopped beside the box and Bimbo could just see him licking a sticky label. "Dolan," Bimbo said softly.

Dolan jumped and looked round. "That you, Bimbo?" he inquired, with a puzzled expression on his face.

"Yes: I'm in the box."

"What are you doin' there? Ye'll be catched on if ye don't watch yerself."

"I'm 'catched' already," Bimbo responded, and in a hurried whisper he explained what had happened and how he intended to escape.

"After I get out," he concluded, "I'll have to trust to luck for a bit—but if I'm not caught again I want to meet you somewhere as soon as possible. What time do you stop work?"

"Ah stop at ten. When the boat sails ah'm finished."

"As soon as you've finished," Bimbo asked, "would you go home and get an old skirt and an old shawl of your mother's and bring them back here?"

"An'ah suppose *she'll* have nothin' to say to that," Dolan commented derisively. "*She* won't give me ony shawl nor skirt neether. She'd be askin' what ah wanted them for."

"Could you not tell her?" Bimbo suggested. "Tell her, Mr. Browne doesn't get paid for me if I escape. Would that not make her want to help—after the way he treated *you*?"

"Aye, she'd like to get back on him right enough," Dolan admitted. "She'll let me have all ye want if ah tell her that. Where'll ah find ye again?"

"That's what I want *you* to decide," Bimbo said. "Could we not meet in the sheds somewhere?"

Dolan shook his head. "They close them as soon as the boats go."

"*You* think of a place then," Bimbo told him. "You must know of somewhere. *I've* never been here before—think!" Dolan thought for so long that Bimbo began to despair of there ever being any result: but at last the result came. "Ah tell ye where ye'll go," he began. "Ye know the railway line. Well, if ye follow it back for a wee way ye'll come to a tunnel. The tunnel takes it under the Queen's Bridge and on the other side there's a wee station they don't use now—ye can bide there till I come."

At first everything went as Bimbo had planned. The box was put on a flat truck and Dolan wheeled it towards the shed with the animal man, whose name turned out to be Higgins, walking beside him. Bimbo peered out again through an air-hole. A thin mist was settling on the docks, blurring everything and winding dewy, rainbow-coloured veils around the lights. The truck jolted and rattled over the square-setts and Dolan told Higgins that he would have a smooth crossing. Bimbo kept his eyes fixed on the policeman, who was a mild-looking man with a benign expression. When they were within a few yards of him Bimbo began to sob. Dolan pretended not to hear the first sob, but Higgins seemed alarmed. The second sob was much louder and Dolan stopped the truck with a jerk. "What ha' ye got there?" he demanded roughly.

Higgins smiled uncertainly. "I told you there was china in it," he explained, "an' so there is, too, but that in't all. I've souvenirs in that box there—mementoes I'm takin' 'ome to the wife. One of them 'appens to be a parrot—wonderful bird," he went on more confidently, "very val'ble—believed to be the best mimic hever captured. I wish it'd just start now and let you 'ear it. W'y you'd swear there was a 'uman bein' in that box—you couldn't 'elp it. Come on now! Pretty Polly—there she goes."

"I wanner go home to Mammy," Bimbo wailed. "Take me home to Mammy."

The policeman looked puzzled and Higgins managed another desperate smile. "Wot did I tell you?" he inquired. "Realistic, in't it?"

Bimbo let out a howl. "He's takin' me away to kill me," he sobbed. "The howwid man's goin' to kill me."

The policeman scratched his head. "I think I'd maybe better see thon' bird," he decided at last. "Would any of yiz have sich a thing as a hammer an' chisel handy?"

"Aye," Dolan volunteered. "Bide there a wee minute an' I'll fetch them till ye."

"Mammy! Mammy!" Bimbo yelled. "I want to go home to Mammy!"

"God save us!" the policeman muttered. "Will ye get that chisel an' lose no time about it. It's all right, sonny. We'll have ye out in no time." He scowled at Higgins and there was an angry murmur from the crowd which was gathering round them.

"He's got a wee girl in the box there."

"Ah tell ye it's a wee boy. Didn't ye hear what the peeler said?"

"He should hang for it an' no option, if ye ask me. That's what I think."

Bimbo felt pleased with his success and Higgins burst out nervously: "I'll tell you what it is, constable—an' this is the 'ole truth so 'elp me. It's the talkin' ape I've got there—you know, chum, the famous talkin' ape you all read about in yer pypers. . . ."

"I'm fwightened of the dark," Bimbo whined. "Don't let him get me."

"Ach don't worry yourself any more choild dear," the policeman said kindly. "Sure haven't I a wee lad o' me own? *I'll* take ye safe home to Mammy. Where d'ye live now, could ye tell me, and what do they call ye?"

"I live with Mammy," Bimbo answered, and he broke into a fresh paroxysm of sobs.

"Aisy now, aisy," the policeman comforted him. "We'll have ye out in no time at all."

Bimbo liked him. He felt certain that any policeman would have been taken in, but he felt sorry to think that he was getting such a nice one into trouble.

The crowd had begun to get angry and Higgins was watching them apprehensively. "Throw him in the tide," someone had suggested, and it was only Dolan's return which prevented violence from being done.

Dolan had brought a hammer and a cold chisel and set to work at once to prise off the top boards of the box.

"Stop!" Higgins called dramatically. "I warn you, one an' all, chums, if that hanimal escypes you'll be liable for 'eavy damages. Open a small 'ole first an' you'll see it ien't a kid—w'y it's no more'n a bloomin' monkey to look at, but it isn't 'arf val'ble. W'y it'll be worth a thousand a week in Brighton."

Dolan did his best to drown this outburst by hammering with particular violence. Nevertheless it had an effect.

"Aisy now, me boyo," the policeman said. "There's no call to kill yerself. Aisy now till ah get a wee peep within."

Dolan, however, continued to work at top speed. "Ach, constable," he returned good-humouredly, "ah'm not that easy killed yet. Don't worrit yerself about me."

"Take it aisy now, take it aisy," the policeman said, his voice gradually growing more irritable. "Will ye not heed what I tell ye?"

Bimbo crouched in the hay at the furthest corner of the box and watched the boards gradually springing up. He wondered how much Dolan would be able to do before someone stopped him.

"Will ye sace that hammerin'?" the policeman demanded, "or will I have to lift me hand till ye?"

Dolan gave one or two more mighty blows and the hole widened. There was a scuffle and a curse, and the hammer fell softly into the hay at the bottom of the box.

"*You* done that!" Dolan exclaimed. "Ye done it yerself. Ye can't blame me."

Bimbo seized the hammer and with tremendous bangs forced plank after plank upwards. Crash! Crash! Crash! He had a full view of the policeman's horrified face, a furious Higgins and a grinning Dolan. "Devil take it," the policeman gasped. "I declare it's an ape after all. Don't let it away for God's sake."

But Bimbo was too quick for them. He forced apart the broken boards and giving a great yell sprang towards the crowd, swinging the hammer round his head. They scattered before him and he ran into the shed, his tail upright and twitching with excitement. In the shed were piled goods of all kinds, but there was a pathway up the centre. To the left, the opposite direction from the Queen's Bridge, this pathway was clear for as far as Bimbo could see. So he turned to the left, and dropping the hammer, ran on all fours as fast as he could go.

When he had gone twenty or thirty yards an uproar broke out behind him. A moment later he glanced round and saw that the whole crowd was in pursuit. Higgins and a young policeman whom Bimbo had not seen before were leading.

Bimbo ran on. His plan was to draw the chase after him; then hide, climb one of the spouts and make his way back to the Queen's Bridge along the roof. Out in the fresh air his headache had gone, his bruises were forgotten. He ran fast and easily. The cries of the pursuers grew fainter. They weren't nearly fast enough to keep up with him let alone to overtake him. He began to enjoy himself. He felt as if he could go on for miles without getting tired. When next he looked round neither policeman was in sight and Higgins, though still leading, was much further behind and obviously flagging. The rest looked a little indistinct, not so much on account of the distance perhaps, as by an effect of the lighting. The electric lamps were high up and rather far apart: below them were circles of light, which looked like huge yellow pancakes on the concrete floor. These circles did not quite meet, and between them and around them were dim areas; and dark patches where bales of goods were piled. The one or two dockers Bimbo passed stared at him in amazement, but they were all too much taken by surprise to make any serious effort to stop him.

Before long he saw in front of him a stretch of shed which was not lit up. Here, surely, he could hide for a few minutes and let the pursuers run past him. Once more he glanced back at them. They looked like black, tailless mice all bunched together, with four or five scurrying round the edges as if to keep the others in order. Suddenly he realized that they had stopped chasing him. Bimbo stopped, too, and climbed on to a large wooden crate to get a better view and to try and find out what they were doing.

He saw that the two policemen were organizing the crowd in a particular way the reason for which he could not at first understand. They were forming them into a long line which eventually stretched obliquely across the whole breadth of the shed. The end of the line furthest from Bimbo terminated at one of the sliding doors which was very slightly open. Bimbo guessed that they intended to drive him through it. A second party must be working down the shed from the other end. They had either been organized by telephone or else had passed him by driving in motor cars up the street outside. At first Bimbo was frightened, but his fear was swept away by a surge of excitement that was altogether pleasant. This was going to be fun, much more fun than if the opposition had had no plans at all.

He remained still for a moment thinking. One of the crowd shouted, "There he is. D'ye not see him—on top o' thon box thonder."

Bimbo jumped down. He went some distance further till he reached a place where the darkness was almost complete. Then he crossed to the side of the shed nearest the water: but he found that all the doors leading onto the edge of the quay were shut.

Suddenly he heard a voice some distance ahead of him. "Get into a line across the shed, but keep touching each other. Go slowly and examine everything carefully. There's plenty of time." He had been right in his guess about a second party—and whoever was in charge of them sounded fairly close. He pushed hard at one of the sliding doors. It would not budge. He pushed harder, bracing his legs and putting all his weight against it. It remained stationary.

The second party drew nearer: he could hear them talking to each other.

"Silence." It was the same authoritative voice which had given the order to spread out. "There's no need to talk. As soon as anyone sees him let me know. We don't want to help him any more than we need."

The murmur of voices ceased.

A cold wind swept through the shed. It made a hollow sound among the girders of the roof.

Bimbo felt his way slowly along. He must find a way out of some kind: if not he would have to burst through the cordon and make another dash up the shed.

There was a faint shuffle of many footsteps coming slowly closer—too close.

He went back. Quite unexpectedly he found his eye opposite to a long narrow slit, running from floor to roof. On the other side was a grey-blue glimmer of light. He heard a distant tumbling crash. After the crash came a rattle and a clang, followed by a pause, during which the faint lapping of water against the quay-wall became audible.

Somebody coughed.

Bimbo tried first one door and then the other, but neither would move. They were either stiff or jammed, or worst of all, locked. He was about to make a further effort, when his hand, groping for something to push against, came in contact with a small knob. He turned it and found that it opened a narrow low wicket door leading on to the quay. He looked round quickly. On one side of him was a stack of wool bales: on the other a huge packing case. The door was screened from both directions: no one would see it opening. He slipped out quickly and shut it after him. The quay-side was deserted. He crouched down against the door and listened.

The wind was stronger out here and colder. He shivered. The crash he had heard before was repeated, followed by the same rattle and clang. The noise came from a crane which was discharging a coal-boat on the far side of the river. Inside the shed two voices were whispering. After a moment Bimbo was able to make out what they were saying.

"Aye, I heered it right enough."

"It's my belief he's not far off."

"What'll ye do if ye do see him? Will ye try an' lay a howld on him?"

"Nar."

"What'll ye do then?"

"Sure ah'll stand stull an' holler on the peeler."

"He's good meat for it."

"Aye. Isn't he paid for it?"

Their whispering faded away.

29

The Albert Memorial Clock had just struck twelve when two figures came out of the disused Central Railway station near Queen's Bridge. One was Dolan: the other, who was short and slightly bent, was dressed in a long skirt and a dark shawl, both of which seemed too big for the wearer. The couple walked slowly towards the end of the bridge; but instead of crossing it they turned to the left down Ann Street. At the corner of Victoria Street Dolan spoke for the first time since they had come into the open. "Where do ye want took?" he inquired.

"Longcourt Road," Bimbo answered. "Anywhere on Longcourt Road would do, but tell the taximan number twenty-three—it's the Andersons' gate lodge. It might sound suspicious if we didn't know exactly where we wanted to go. We must make everything we do seem as ordinary as possible."

"What d'ye want wi' the Longcourt Road?" Dolan demanded curiously.

"I'd rather not tell you," Bimbo replied. "It's a secret."

But Dolan wasn't satisfied. "If you're goin' to see *him*," he persisted, "I'd like to come wid ye."

Bimbo wouldn't agree. He intended to talk to Mr. Browne alone. "It's silly for you to have another row with him," he pointed out. "I can manage all right by myself."

There was no taxi on the stand at the Albert Memorial, but Dolan was certain that he would find one at the Junction. Bimbo thought it better not to go with him. "Say it's for your mother," he suggested, "and that she's missed the last tram. Say she's very old and feeling poorly. . . . And mind, when you've left me in Longcourt Road don't let him drive you to your own house. If there are questions asked afterwards I don't want anyone to know who *you* are. Make him drive you back into town. Tell him you live on the Shankill Road. Now I'll stay here till you come—I'll walk slowly up and down. If I stood still someone might speak to me."

So far as the journey to Longcourt Road was concerned everything happened exactly as Bimbo had intended; and as soon as the taxi was out of sight he crawled through a hole in the hedge and took off the shawl and skirt. He rolled them into a bundle, which he tied on his back, and set off by a route of his own to Beechwood. By one o'clock he was in Mr. Browne's kitchen garden. All the back of the house was in darkness, but he could see that there was a broad streak of light shining across the lawn at the front. He went slowly round the house keeping close to the wall and found that it was from Mr. Browne's study that the light came. The curtains were drawn fully back and for a moment Bimbo hesitated to look in. Then he crawled to a flowering currant which grew at the edge of the grass a few yards from the window and slowly raised himself behind it. He found himself staring straight into Mr. Browne's eyes.

After the first shock of surprise he realized that Mr. Browne didn't see him. He was sitting in an armchair which had been pushed back against the wall opposite the window. The arms were low and most of the cushions in the room were propped behind his back to keep him comfortably in an upright position. Across his knees lay a large double-barrelled shotgun. His right hand rested on the stock. His left hand was on his knee beside the barrels. All the furniture had been ranged round the walls, with the object apparently of leaving an unobstructed field of fire, should he wish to shoot in the direction of the door or of the windows. His expression was one of weary alertness as if he were fighting against sleep. Bimbo watched him for quite a long time without moving. Was Mr. Browne afraid of being attacked himself or was it that he had decided to kill Bimbo if he should return?—or perhaps he was just guarding the safe which stood in the corner to his right. Bimbo's object in coming back was to get some information about his own origin. He knew that Theodore Browne had written various papers about him, though none had ever been published. He was almost certain that some such papers had been left with Mr. Browne for safe-keeping. Bimbo intended to ask Mr. Browne to show him these papers: if he objected Bimbo was prepared to use force: but he had not expected to find Mr. Browne armed, and for a moment he did not know what to do.

He saw at once that as long as Mr. Browne remained in his study he was unassailable. The problem was to make him leave the study voluntarily and without suspicion. After some thought Bimbo decided upon a plan which seemed to him satisfactory. First of all he would have to go to the potting shed—but as he was about to slip away he heard someone walking quickly up the drive towards the front door. It was Hugo—Bimbo recognized his footsteps, and as soon as his eyes got accustomed to looking away from the light he was able to see him as well. In his right hand Hugo was carrying a large revolver. Bimbo was very surprised, and for a moment he just stood still and watched. Then he guessed that Hugo must have found out something and be coming to his rescue. Possibly he intended to shoot Mr. Browne, possibly only to threaten him: in either case he would have to be stopped.

Very reluctantly and very quietly Bimbo went to meet him. It was not a dark night: there was a moon somewhere, though it was hidden behind the clouds; and besides the light from Mr. Browne's window there was a lamp on the road which shone faintly through the trees. The house could hardly be said to throw a shadow; but close to its walls there was less light than elsewhere. For a little Hugo didn't see Bimbo: when he did he jumped and swung round suddenly, pointing the revolver straight at Bimbo's chest. Bimbo hoped he wouldn't fire.

"Hands up!" Hugo ordered, and Bimbo obeyed: as he did so he recognized the revolver. It was a toy which Hugo had received as a Christmas present. Hugo's voice was shaky and hardly seemed to belong to him. "Who's that?" he asked.

"It's me, Bimbo."

Hugo gave a little sob of relief. "Oh, Bimbo!" he said, and burst into tears.

Bimbo was touched. He caught Hugo by the shoulders and held him tightly. "Where were you going?" he inquired presently, "and what were you going to do?" But it was some little time before Hugo could answer. "Come into the bushes," Bimbo advised. "If we stand here he may look out and see us." So they went behind some laurels and crouched down on the ground.

"I couldn't help thinking about the wicked uncle," Hugo began at last. "So I didn't go home. I just hung about. And for a bit I just watched the furniture van backing up the drive. After a while a man came to the door—not Mr. Browne—he had sort of riding trousers on."

"Did you hear him speak?" Bimbo inquired. "Was he English?"

Hugo shook his head. "I wasn't very close. I was hiding in the bushes. I expect he just beckoned or something. Anyhow two men took a sort of great big wooden box out of the back of the van an' then I saw Mr. Browne was at the door, too, an' Mr. Browne an' the other man took the box from the two men; an' they went away. An' after a while they brought it back again an' gave it back to the two men, an' I wondered if you were inside. An' the two men put it into the van again and drove away, an' the other man went with them." He yawned. "I'm awf'lly sleepy now, Bimbo."

"No wonder," Bimbo said. "It's nearly two. You should have been in bed ages ago, but how. . . ."

"I *was* in bed ages ago," Hugo burst in, "but I had to wait till the others had all gone to bed, too, in case they heard me gettin' out."

"What made you think I was in the box?" Bimbo asked.

"I don't know. I didn't at first, but while I was waiting I made a pretend that you were and that I rescued you. Then I thought Mr. Browne might have finished talking to you an' I went to see if you were back in your room, but you weren't. So I went to see if I could see in the study window, an' I could, an' you weren't there. Mr. Browne was there by himself. Then I thought you really were in the box, an' I didn't know what to do at first." He stopped suddenly. "Where were you, really?" he demanded, "and what are you doin' now?"

"I *was* in the box," Bimbo told him, "only I've escaped. You go on and tell *your* story. I'll tell you what happened to me afterwards. What did *you* do?"

"I didn't know what to do at first," Hugo repeated. "I was going to tell Miss Martha, but I thought I'd better find out first in case you were really just in the house all the time. So I went to the front door an' rang the bell. At first no one came and then Mr. Browne came himself."

"It was Cook's night out," Bimbo put in. "I suppose that's why he chose it."

"Anyway," Hugo went on, "I said, 'I want to see Bimbo, please. I've remembered somethin' I forgot to tell him.' An' he said, 'You can't see Bimbo to-night.' I said, 'Why not? Where is he?' An' he said it was none of my business an' when I said he'd *haf* to tell he just got very cross and shut the door. So then I thought I'd make him tell me—an' I would have, too. That's why I brought my revolver—I was goin' to tell him that I'd shoot him if he wouldn't."

"It was very brave of you," Bimbo said. "I want to ask him questions, too, but I don't know if I'll be able to make him answer or not."

"I'll come with you," Hugo volunteered immediately. "I'll

frighten him with my revolver. He'll never know it's not a real one."

Bimbo, however, didn't want Hugo's support in his interview with Mr. Browne any more than he had wanted Dolan's. "I don't think you'd better," he responded. "He'd be sure to tell on you in the morning." But what he was really afraid of was that there might be some sort of a scuffle in which Hugo would get shot.

Hugo sighed. "What do you think I *should* do?" he asked.

"You'd better go home," Bimbo said, "and get to bed before you're found out." He knew this sounded blunt and unkind, but it was the only sensible course. Besides he wanted to get his interview with Mr. Browne over as soon as he could. At any time the police might decide to put watchers round the house—and it was obvious that Mr. Browne was already expecting him. Yet suddenly he realized that Hugo was frightened to go home alone. His courage had been strained to the utmost in coming; it wasn't fair that he should have to go through the whole ordeal a second time. "I'll come with you," Bimbo said, "and on the way I'll tell you what happened to me."

But it wasn't easy to talk crawling through trees or darting across the road from one hole in the hedge to another. So when they came to the Clarkes' house Bimbo climbed in too, by the window Hugo had left open. "I'll tell you the rest when you're in bed," he promised.

They crept upstairs to Hugo's room without disturbing anyone. Hugo got into bed and Bimbo crouched down on the floor beside him. Hugo lay at the edge of the bed and they talked in whispers. "But how are you going to get there?" Hugo asked, when Bimbo had finished, "even if he does tell you everything."

"I don't know yet," Bimbo answered, "I've an idea." But he would say no more.

Hugo had got very sleepy. "You'll say good-bye before you go, won't you?"

"I don't think I'll be able to," Bimbo said. "You see I can't stay at Mr. Browne's. He would just hand me back to the animal man and if I went to Miss Martha the police. . . ."

He broke off. Hugo was asleep. Bimbo looked at him for a minute. A faint streak of moonlight was shining into the room and Bimbo could see his face. It was a brown, freckled, very weary little face. Hugo was a plain boy with a lower lip that stuck out too much, and a snub, turned-up nose. He had dark blue eyes and wavy black hair. He was lively, but not at all intellectual: in the subjects which recently had most occupied Bimbo's mind he took no interest whatever. Yet Bimbo found great pleasure in his company and felt very sorry to leave him now.

It was nearly three when Bimbo got back to Mr. Browne's. He peeped in the window and saw that Mr. Browne was still in almost the same position. He had sunk a little lower down in the chair and his face looked very drawn; but he was awake and watchful.

Bimbo had hidden his bundle in the bushes. He found it again, and carrying it round to the potting shed put it on the bench and picked up a black-handled jack-knife which Dolan had sometimes used for pruning. From a shelf above the door he took a parcel of putty which had been left behind by some workmen three or four weeks before.

He left the putty outside the back door and holding the jack-knife between his teeth climbed up the creeper at the side of the house to the window of one of the bedrooms which he knew to be empty. As he had expected the window was closed and latched, but he had no difficulty in pushing the knife through the crack between the upper and lower sashes and forcing back the snib. Cautiously he opened the window and entered the room.

The door was not locked and he was able to go out into the passage and down the stairs. In the hall he paused to listen, but the house was silent except for a faint whistling of wind in the chimneys. The only light was a thin golden line, which showed beneath the door of Mr. Browne's study. Bimbo disconnected the telephone, fetched the putty from the backdoor step and went upstairs again, but this time to the bathroom. He put the plugs in the bath and the basin, stuffed the overflows with putty and turned all the taps on full. Closing the bathroom door after him he returned to the hall and squatted down outside the study. The bathroom was directly above the study, and except for a bath-mat the floor was uncovered.

The hall was cold. A draught stirred the carpet slightly and

Bimbo shivered. For a little while he could hear the water flowing into the bath, but as the level rose nearer the taps the sound grew fainter and died away. At the end of five minutes Bimbo was sure the basin must have overflowed: but fifteen minutes later there was still no sign of anything happening. Another five minutes passed and Bimbo began to feel impatient—he heard a slight splash close beside him: there was another splash and another. . . . It became a steady drip, drip, drip. The water had begun to flow out of the bathroom and was dropping from the edge of the landing above. Bimbo found that he was getting wet.

Suddenly, from inside the study, he heard a loud thud, followed by the sound of water falling and an exclamation from Mr. Browne. Mr. Browne came quickly across the room towards the door. The key rattled: the lock clicked. Bimbo got ready to spring. The handle turned and the door opened. There stood Mr. Browne, with his gun ready. He blinked and tried to see into the darkness beyond the patch of light which shone out from the doorway.

He swung the gun to the left and to the right. Then he pointed it at the foot of the stairs and remained motionless, peering in the same direction. "Is there anyone there?" he inquired nervously. His left hand was on the stock of the gun just below the barrels: the forefinger of his right hand was on the trigger.

Bimbo sprang. With his left foot he grasped Mr. Browne's wrist so that his fingers were dragged away from the trigger. With his right hand he covered Mr. Browne's mouth to prevent him from shouting. Mr. Browne staggered and his head hit the door-post with a thud. Bimbo snatched the gun from him and forced him back into the study. "If you make a sound," he whispered, "I'll kill you. Now go back to your chair and sit there." Mr. Browne did so. Bimbo shut the door and put the gun down in front of it. Mr. Browne's study was in a terrible state. A large slab of plaster had fallen from the ceiling: through the hole a steady stream of water was flowing, and already a large puddle had formed on the floor. There was plaster dust everywhere. . . . Bimbo came forward slowly and looked at Mr. Browne. His dirty fingers had left marks on Mr. Browne's pale cheeks.

"What do you want?" Mr. Browne asked. He looked very frightened.

"I want to see all the papers your brother left behind which have anything to do with me—particularly those that tell where he found me and how to get there."

Mr. Browne hesitated. "I'm not sure that they're all here," he said.

"Get me all that are here," Bimbo replied, "and mind you don't miss any. I'm going to go through the safe and the desk when you've finished. Open the safe first."

"And if. . . ." Mr. Browne began.

Bimbo stepped forward and caught his wrist: at the same time he again covered Mr. Browne's mouth. Then he twisted Mr. Browne's arm in the way he had learned at Miss Sutton's. Mr. Browne winced. "Open the safe," Bimbo repeated, and let him go.

Mr. Browne went to his desk and, pausing for a moment, looked uneasily over his shoulder at Bimbo. "The key's in here," he said, and unlocked a drawer. He took out a bunch of keys, and crossing over to the safe, unlocked it too, and pulled the door towards him. He produced a bundle of papers tied with a pink tape and tossed them to Bimbo. "Those are some of them," he announced. "You can see what's there while I'm hunting for the rest." He began to rummage through the safe, while Bimbo sat down on the floor and undid the tape.

The papers were all enclosed in long, legal-shaped envelopes. On the envelopes were notes in Theodore Browne's handwriting:

"Bimbo. Settlement in event of my non-return. Trustee Sebastian Browne, Esq."

"Bimbo. Instructions regarding diet, accommodation, etc."

"Bimbo. Possibility of Education."

"Bimbo. Details of finding. Miscellaneous notes, etc."

"Letter to be delivered to Bimbo should he be capable of understanding and reach years of discretion—being in the nature of an apology."

Several times Bimbo looked up to see what Mr. Browne was doing. But Mr. Browne seemed to have learned his lesson and was sorting through the papers in the safe most industriously.

"Bimbo. Details of finding. Miscellaneous notes, etc."

That looked really interesting. The envelope was not closed. Bimbo began to pull out the papers.

"Here are some maps," Mr. Browne said. "Catch."

He flung a thick bundle tightly tied with red tape towards Bimbo. It fell short, but Bimbo leaned forward and just managed to catch it. As he did so he saw something glitter. Mr. Browne was raising a revolver and taking aim. Leaning forward had brought Bimbo from his hunkers on to his toes and without a moment's hesitation he sprang.

He managed to catch Mr. Browne's wrist and force the revolver upwards. They both toppled towards the floor, and while they were falling the revolver went off with what seemed a tremendous report close to Bimbo's ear. As they hit the floor Mr. Browne gasped with pain, but Bimbo was on top of him and was not hurt. He snatched the revolver and, jumping to his feet, pointed it at Mr. Browne's chest. "Don't move an inch," he panted.

Mr. Browne writhed on the floor and groaned. He was winded. Bimbo listened for a minute, but he could hear nothing except the steady splash of the water. He went to the door and opened it: there was no sound of anyone coming. Cook was probably lying in bed quaking with fear, but if he went upstairs to reassure her she would most likely think she was going to be murdered. The sooner he got away the better, though first of all he wanted to search the safe. However he couldn't risk leaving Mr. Browne free. It wasn't likely that he would have any more firearms; all the same it would be wiser to tie him up and Bimbo looked round for some rope or cord. He couldn't see any: so he cut strips of leather from the covering of an armchair: with these he tied Mr. Browne's wrists and ankles and gagged him.

He listened at the door again. Perhaps the revolver report hadn't been as loud as he had imagined: at any rate there was still no sound of anyone coming. He began a quick examination of the safe. It contained title deeds, stock and share certificates, insurance policies. . . . Everything was neatly arranged and docketed, but Bimbo could see nothing further regarding himself—and there was no money. Bimbo thought he would need money and rolling Mr. Browne over he searched his pockets. Mr. Browne wriggled a good deal and tried to kick, but his efforts were ineffectual, and Bimbo got eleven pounds fifteen shillings and fourpence.

He was about to go when he remembered Cook and decided to

leave a message for her. He sat down at the desk and wrote:

DEAR COOK,

Mr. Browne is tied up in the study. He's quite all right, but you'd better untie him as soon as possible. I hope the noise didn't wake you and that if it did you weren't frightened. I have to go away. Good-bye.

Your loving friend,

BIMBO.

There was a crash and Bimbo jumped up. All that had happened, however, was that another lump of plaster had fallen from the ceiling. He saw, too, that the pool of water had spread considerably: three-quarters of the floor were covered. Mr. Browne was quite wet. Bimbo realized that if Mr. Browne were left there with the water still on there was a danger that he would be drowned. He lifted him into a chair and ran upstairs to turn off the taps.

When he returned to the study nothing remained to be done. So he picked up the maps and papers Mr. Browne had given him and, leaving his note on the hall-table, hurried to the kitchen. He took a candle and a box of matches from the kitchen cupboard and went on out by the back door. On his way to the toolshed, where he had to collect his bundle, he met Leo. They had been together most of the afternoon: nevertheless, Leo was delighted to see him: he didn't bark, but wagged his tail joyfully, so that it thumped against the toolshed door and rattled it as they were going in. Bimbo knew that Leo was a bad sleeper—there were so many bones buried in the straw of his kennel that he could hardly have been anything else—and that he was in the habit of wandering about at night in the hope of meeting someone who would keep him company. They set off for the wood together.

Bimbo found Leo's presence rather comforting. He was large and solid and placid, and Bimbo felt reassured every time he pushed his fingers into Leo's soft woolly coat. They reached the wood without adventure. It was very dark, but to neither of them was this a disadvantage. They knew their way too well to get lost and were able to feel where the trees and bushes and fallen branches were, without either seeing them or touching them. What Bimbo did not like were the noises. The wind, slight though it was, rubbed the branches together and rattled them. And several times they heard birds and small animals moving in the undergrowth. Once a rat scurried across the path just in front of their feet. They heard it and smelt it, but did not see it. Leo made no attempt to chase it, but there was such a stir already that Bimbo had to strain his senses to the utmost for signs of human beings: there *were* none, but he was kept unpleasantly on edge.

His immediate intention was to go to the hut and examine the papers he had got from Mr. Browne. He did not mean to remain there long, for he expected that the wood would be searched as soon as it was known that he had returned to Belmore.

So he left Leo in the clearing to act as sentry and crawled alone through the undergrowth to the hut. Down in the pit it was very sheltered, and though he could still hear the wind in the trees overhead, the candle, which he now lit, burned steadily: it seemed very quiet and cosy.

The second bundle of papers Mr. Browne had thrown to him proved to be merely maps of an estate in County Down, but the others were all genuine. First of all Bimbo read the description of how he had been found and the miscellaneous notes.

These occupied altogether ten pages of foolscap and were mostly quite uninteresting to Bimbo. They contained descriptions of trees and shrubs and notes on the tribes which the expedition had encountered. On the fourth page, however, was the following:

"This morning when we were all ready to start I found that Suner had returned to his sleeping-bag. He had made no preparations and quite refused to get up. He was evidently ashamed of himself, but none the less obstinate for that. He has been frightened by the talk of 'Hairy men of the forest'. Fortunately he has not communicated his fears to José or Miguel, our two bearers, and neither of them has picked up the dialect of this tribe. With Suner it is the old story of a little learning being a dangerous thing. Well! I was against taking him from the beginning. I have always found that paid guides are unsatisfactory in the long run. Besides it turns out that he had never been beyond Santa Caterina in his life before. The others agree now that I was right, but of course the harm is done. Rawlinson and I have agreed to give out that Suner has twisted his knee. The circumstances, I believe, justify this small subterfuge."

The next page was devoted to a minute description of a new variety of wild lupin which apparently grew in great profusion. Then, after several entries regarding the climate, came this note:

"October 16th. We buried Rawlinson this morning. The poor fellow had been ailing for some time, but bore up with remarkable fortitude, so that none of us guessed that he was seriously ill. He must have died in his sleep. Miguel and José dug the grave, but the ground was so hard they could not make it very deep. As I had a Prayer Book in my kit I was able to read the burial service over the remains. We all found the simple words very moving.

"About noon startled a number of small creatures which vanished quickly among the trees to our right. They were pretty little things and seemed to be some variety of lemur. Unfortunately I was at the rear at the time and was unable to get a shot for fear of hitting José who behaved most foolishly. I have instructed both of them to crouch down and remain still on any future occasion of this sort, but they are very irresponsible and most likely will have forgotten my instructions by to-morrow. So far as possible I intend to take the lead myself in future.

"I am writing this by the light of our fire. The others have all turned in. The death of poor Rawlinson has cast quite a gloom over our little party. His unfailing gentlemanliness was an inspiration to us all. He will be sadly missed.

"October 18th. So much happened yesterday that I had no time to write. Our outward journey is ended. Like so many expeditions of exploration we have failed to attain our object. We have, however, made a discovery of extreme value and in that way accomplished more than we had any right to anticipate. For that reason I have no cause to repine. Still I find it disappointing to have to turn back at the very moment when the exceeding richness of the field has first been revealed to us, when for the first time we have had a glimpse of a promised land whose existence we did not even suspect. Some day, if God spares me, I shall return. At any rate we have the proof with us. Thank God he seems strong and healthy. I believe he will survive.

"Early yesterday morning we began to notice a change in the

composition of the forest. We had hardly set out when I remarked a new variety of conifer and the change of climate I mentioned on the fifteenth was more distinctly noticeable. We took some branches and foliage for the specimen box—not without complaints and sulky looks from José and Miguel who declare that this box is already above the stipulated weight: also two cones of which there was an abundance lying on the ground beneath the trees.

"This conifer was, however, but a forerunner of what was to come. By midday we had given up taking specimens. I can only state that it was as if we had entered a new world—a world where everything was on a gigantic scale. The trees in particular were immense, though owing to the fact that we were always in among them, and never able to look at them from a distance, I can give no reliable estimate of their height. It is sufficient to say that the foliage proper did not begin below at least 100 feet.

"In accordance with my decision of the previous day I remained at the head of the column almost continuously, and at about two o'clock in the afternoon when we made our great discovery I was leading. Since noon we had been proceeding with great ease along a path which was remarkably smooth. We supposed it to be a passage regularly used by wild animals of one kind or another, and remained constantly on the alert. Nevertheless, I had the feeling that there was something artificial about it, though such a feeling was quite unaccountable, there being absolutely no signs or trace of any human agency having been at work.

"The path had many bends, but kept a general southwesterly course which suited our purpose well. Rounding one of these curves I suddenly saw before me an immense glade. It was surrounded by huge trees, with straight black trunks, whose boughs met overhead. Through the leaves the sun was shining suffusing the whole space with a pale green light which made a strange contrast to the dim twilight through which we had been walking. I had the impression of a great natural cathedral, far greater than the largest of the cathedrals of our civilized world—only it was not natural: of that I am convinced.

"Disappearing through the trees at the far end, into an avenue similar to that by which we ourselves had arrived, were two large figures, whom if it were not for subsequent information I should descibe as belonging to some species of anthropoid ape. It was only after they had gone that I remarked that they had left behind them a smaller figure of about the same size as a normal human child eighteen months old.

"After a moment's hesitation I led the way in only to find after a pace or two that the others were no longer following me. I turned, not I must confess without myself feeling a certain uneasiness, and inquired what was the matter. For a moment there was no reply. The two Indians were plainly terrified, while Jackson and Melville merely looked sheepishly ashamed of themselves. The queer thing was that none of them had seen what I had seen: it was the atmosphere of the place which had overawed them. I tried to persuade them to continue, but nothing I could say had any effect. They did not reply. They just stood there looking foolish.

"I was reasonably certain that the apes, as I then thought them, had not seen us, but I was afraid they might return at any moment. So I determined to capture the young one while there was yet time. With this object, I set off across the clearing alone. With every pace I took the feeling of uneasiness I had felt at first increased, but before long I was able to recognize from what it sprang. This recognition, though it did not in any way lessen my discomfort, enabled me to continue sufficiently master of my movements to fulfil my purpose.

"I can best describe it as an acute realization of my own insignificance. Thus might an ant feel setting out to crawl up the nave of St. Peter's in Rome—not that difference in size was so great as that—the feeling was spiritual—the fear was spiritual—not physical or superstitious.

"At any rate I reached the young creature, gathered it in my arms and returned. As I returned I had the odd notion that I was committing a sacrilege. I was very much tempted to return him to the place where I had found him and believe indeed I should have done so after showing him to the others had it not been that at the moment of my return Melville gave a gasp of astonishment. I looked round and saw that the two adult creatures had re-entered the clearing. Without more ado we all fled.

"The specimen we still have with us. I have nicknamed him

Bimbo. He appears likely to survive. This is not the time or the place to set down a detailed description of him. It is sufficient to say that he is too young to make any attempt to escape, and that if anything were to happen to him I should feel more guilty than if he were a human child.

"October 20th. In spite of the entreaties of the others that I should leave him behind I still have my Bimbo. It is curious the effect he has had on me. I have given orders that nothing is to be shot. All are extremely nervous. We are travelling twice as fast as on the journey up."

Bimbo was puzzled. In all the notes there was no clue as to the route the expedition had followed: there wasn't even a sketch map. He stopped reading and blew out the candle. The hut was not a safe hiding-place, and if bloodhounds were used they could easily trace him to it. Bimbo had another hiding-place in view. He intended to go to it through the trees so that he would leave no scent which could be followed. First of all, however, he meant to lay a number of false trails so as to lead the police astray if they *did* use dogs.

He went out into the clearing and found Leo still patiently watching. "Go home," Bimbo told him. "Dear good dog, go home." He put his arms round Leo's neck and gave him a hug. He felt that he would not see *him* again either.

Leo licked Bimbo's face; and Bimbo licked Leo. Then, with his tail between his legs and his head drooping, Leo went back by the way they had come.

30

Bimbo's next hiding-place was an empty house not far from Miss Sutton's. It was still dark when he climbed in by an upstairs window which had been left unsnibbed. He didn't dare to light his candle in case it should attract attention; anyhow he was very tired. So deciding that he would wait for daylight to look at the rest of the papers, he curled up in a corner and went to sleep.

When he awoke it was nearly half-past twelve, and a broad

streak of autumn sunlight was shining through the dusty, cobwebbed window. He was stiff and rather cold from lying on the bare boards: he was hungry, too. He stretched and went out into the garden where there was an orchard. It was warm and sheltered and the long damp grass was thickly speckled with yellow apple leaves. All the pears and most of the apples had been pulled, but there were still a few pale, rain-washed pippins left on some of the higher branches. He took half a dozen and returned to the house to eat them. So far as immediate discovery was concerned he was fairly safe. The garden was not overlooked by neighbouring houses and he was sure no one had seen him getting in. Nevertheless Bimbo did not feel very cheerful. He had always known that he would have great difficulty in returning to his own people: but he had thought that with a certain amount of help from Miss Martha and Dolan he might make the journey either as a stowaway or in disguise. He had counted, however, on being able to discover the exact position of the place where he had been found: and in this respect Theodore Browne's papers had so far given him no help at all. The writer seemed deliberately to have avoided all mention of place names and there were no map references. It seemed hardly likely that the remaining papers would contain anything useful. As he munched his apples Bimbo turned them over again—Settlement, Diet, Education, Apology. . . . He might as well see what Theodore Browne had to say for himself—a great deal it would seem. He shied an apple core into the fireplace and ripped open the flap of the envelope.

To his surprise he found it contained nothing but another envelope which he had some difficulty in drawing out from the first. On this envelope was written, "To be opened by no one but Bimbo. If not opened by him within twenty years after First August 1914 to be destroyed unopened in the presence of two clergymen of the Church of Ireland in default whereof my brother Sebastian, his heirs and assigns, shall lose all claim to inherit my property or any portion thereof in accordance with the terms more particularly set forth in the codicil to my will dated this first day of August 1914, this being the envelope referred to therein."

Bimbo's spirits rose. Hastily he opened the second envelope only to find that it contained two more envelopes. These also were directed in Theodore Browne's handwriting. On the smaller was written simply:

"Letter of Apology":

on the larger,

"Exact instructions to Bimbo should he desire to return to his own people.

"Map showing route to place of finding.

"Deposit receipt from Belfast Banking Co. Ltd. for £500 to be used by Bimbo to pay whatever amounts may be required for his journey.

"N.B.—Much of the information given herein was known also to my companions, Henry Jackson and Loftus Melville, who in spite of my objections intended to make them public in a paper to be read before The Royal Society. The fact that they both perished of yellow fever before this intention could be put into effect strengthens my belief in the propriety of my own silence. Should any unauthorized person open this in spite of my instructions let him therefore BEWARE!"

Bimbo opened this envelope also. First of all he unfolded the map and spent ten minutes studying it carefully. By the end of that time he could have re-drawn it in every detail, including even the exact shape of the blot at the bottom left-hand corner. He spent a little longer in reading the instructions. Then he took them to the grate and burned them: he burned the map also.

The rest of the papers were less interesting, but Bimbo read through them all carefully, in case they should contain any information that would be useful to him. When he had finished he knew that he had no longer anything to fear from Mr. Browne, provided he could get some responsible person to take charge of his papers. Indeed it was Mr. Browne who had reason to be fearful; for it was evident that he had embezzled the money set aside by his brother for Bimbo's upkeep. The only danger now was that Bimbo might be caught before he reached Miss Martha and the papers handed back unexamined to Mr. Browne.

Nothing of the sort happened, however, and at eight o'clock that evening Bimbo was standing on the step at Miss Sutton's ringing the bell. The maid who opened the door gave a cry of amazement, "Miss Martha! Miss Martha!" she called. "Will ye look who's here?"

Bimbo heard a chair pushed back and Miss Martha's footsteps hurrying across the dining-room. "Who? Who?" she replied. "Don't be so excitable, Kate!"

"Wait till ye lay yer eyes on him," Kate retorted good-humouredly. "We'll see who's excitable then."

"Why, Bimbo!" Miss Martha exclaimed. "I've been trying to find you all day. What's this I've been hearing about you?—the paper's full of your gallivanting. Is it true?—and now Kate's got some story that she had from the milkman. Come along in here. I'm sure you're starving."

She brought him into the dining-room where they were all just finishing supper and made him sit down by the fire. In a few minutes Kate came in with a large bowl of bread-and-milk and between spoonfuls he began his story.

It was ten o'clock before he had finished; afterwards they all examined the papers he had brought with him. "It's quite clear that Mr. Browne can't do anything," Miss Sutton remarked, "but I think we'd better get a solicitor to go over them all in the morning just to make sure there's no mistake. If they're in order it'll be only fair to inform the police. It'll bring the reporters again, but that can't be helped and the sooner you get them over the better."

They were all smiling at him and Bimbo felt extraordinarily happy. "I'd like to tell Hugo and Dolan," he said. "I'm sure they'd like to know."

"I'm sure they would," Miss Martha returned, "but you're not seeing anyone till we've fixed up with the solicitor and know that the police are satisfied. After that you can hold a reception if you like. As it is I've already put both the maids on their Bible oath not to say squeak, though they're simply bursting to talk. You'd better go and tell them how you tied up Mr. Browne before you go to bed: they don't seem to like him for some reason and they've got a sort of inkling of what happened through the milkman."

"I hardly think he ought to," Miss Sarah objected. "It encourages them in. . . . in wrong ideas."

"Nonsense," Miss Martha declared. "If they don't get the truth they'll hear something far worse."

"I think perhaps," Miss Sutton began gently, "what Sarah. . . ."

Miss Martha gave in cheerfully. "All right," she said, "I don't care. What I want to hear is what Bimbo means to do next."

"I want to go back," Bimbo told them, "but the instructions say that I ought to have someone with me as far as Santa Caterina—after that I can disappear into the forest and find my own way. . . ."

"No, Martha, you simply can't," Miss Sutton interrupted suddenly. "It's the middle of term for one thing—besides this Santa Caterina is right in the jungle. You've no idea what the people are like there—pueblos, or whatever you call them."

"I expect they're very nice," Miss Martha asserted boldly, "and no doubt we could arrange for an escort. There are lots of British people in all these places. What I was going to ask was if Bimbo'd wait till the summer holidays."

"And then you'll come with me?"

"We won't decide anything now," Miss Sutton said emphatically, "except, of course, that Bimbo's to stay here till he does go."

"He can take a class," Miss Martha suggested—and with that they all went to bed.

31

I have told nearly all I know of Bimbo's story—nearly all, I suppose, that ever *will* be known.

For eight months he lived with the Miss Suttons in Belmore and it was generally thought that he had settled down there for good. People didn't know exactly what had happened on the night Bimbo was kidnapped—and Mr. Browne didn't dare to say anything for fear of getting himself into trouble. There were rumours of course, and some of them came pretty near to the truth; but the contents of Theodore Browne's papers remained secret.

So it caused great surprise when it was realized that Miss Martha and Bimbo had disappeared. They must have gone some day in the first week of the summer holidays, but there had been no preparations that anyone saw or heard of. Towards the end of August Miss Martha returned alone.

As far as I can discover she has never spoken to anyone about her journey, or told where she parted from Bimbo: certainly she has never told me. I do know, however, that she did not go the whole way to his destination.

The last time I was with her, a few days before Christmas, I managed to get one additional fact from her. I asked if she thought it likely that Bimbo had ever really got there.

"I know he did," she answered.

I shrugged my shoulders and pretended to feel sceptical. "But how?" I demanded.

"I had a message from him," she said rather crossly. Then she shut up completely, and no wiles of mine could induce her to divulge any more. Before I left, indeed, I saw clearly enough that she wished she had kept this secret, too, to herself.

ALSO AVAILABLE FROM VALANCOURT BOOKS

Michael Arlen	Hell! said the Duchess
R. C. Ashby (Ruby Ferguson)	He Arrived at Dusk
Frank Baker	The Birds
Walter Baxter	Look Down in Mercy
Charles Beaumont	The Hunger and Other Stories
David Benedictus	The Fourth of June
Paul Binding	Harmonica's Bridegroom
Charles Birkin	The Smell of Evil
John Blackburn	A Scent of New-Mown Hay
Thomas Blackburn	A Clip of Steel
	The Feast of the Wolf
John Braine	Room at the Top
	The Vodi
Michael Campbell	Lord Dismiss Us
R. Chetwynd-Hayes	The Monster Club
Basil Copper	The Great White Space
	Necropolis
Hunter Davies	Body Charge
Jennifer Dawson	The Ha-Ha
Barry England	Figures in a Landscape
Ronald Fraser	Flower Phantoms
Gillian Freeman	The Liberty Man
	The Leather Boys
	The Leader
Stephen Gilbert	The Landslide
	The Burnaby Experiments
	Ratman's Notebooks
Martyn Goff	The Youngest Director
Stephen Gregory	The Cormorant
John Hampson	Saturday Night at the Greyhound
Thomas Hinde	The Day the Call Came
Claude Houghton	I Am Jonathan Scrivener
	This Was Ivor Trent
James Kennaway	The Mind Benders
Cyril Kersh	The Aggravations of Minnie Ashe
Gerald Kersh	Fowlers End
	Nightshade and Damnations
Francis King	Never Again

FRANCIS KING	An Air That Kills
	The Dividing Stream
	The Dark Glasses
C.H.B. KITCHIN	Ten Pollitt Place
	The Book of Life
HILDA LEWIS	The Witch and the Priest
JOHN LODWICK	Brother Death
KENNETH MARTIN	Aubade
MICHAEL NELSON	Knock or Ring
	A Room in Chelsea Square
BEVERLEY NICHOLS	Crazy Pavements
OLIVER ONIONS	The Hand of Kornelius Voyt
J.B. PRIESTLEY	Benighted
	The Other Place
	The Magicians
	Saturn Over the Water
	The Shapes of Sleep
PETER PRINCE	Play Things
PIERS PAUL READ	Monk Dawson
FORREST REID	Following Darkness
	The Spring Song
	Brian Westby
	The Tom Barber Trilogy
ANDREW SINCLAIR	The Facts in the Case of E.A. Poe
	The Raker
COLIN SPENCER	Panic
DAVID STOREY	Radcliffe
	Pasmore
	Saville
RUSSELL THORNDIKE	The Slype
	The Master of the Macabre
JOHN WAIN	Hurry on Down
	The Smaller Sky
	A Winter in the Hills
HUGH WALPOLE	The Killer and the Slain
KEITH WATERHOUSE	There is a Happy Land
	Billy Liar
COLIN WILSON	Ritual in the Dark
	Man Without a Shadow
	The Philosopher's Stone
	The God of the Labyrinth

WHAT CRITICS ARE SAYING ABOUT VALANCOURT BOOKS

"[W]e owe a debt of gratitude to the publisher Valancourt, whose aim is to resurrect some neglected works of literature, especially those incorporating a supernatural strand, and make them available to a new readership."

Times Literary Supplement (London)

"Valancourt Books champions neglected but important works of fantastic, occult, decadent and gay literature. The press's Web site not only lists scores of titles but also explains why these often obscure books are still worth reading. . . . So if you're a real reader, one who looks beyond the bestseller list and the touted books of the moment, Valancourt's publications may be just what you're searching for."

Michael Dirda, *Washington Post*

"Valancourt Books are fast becoming my favourite publisher. They have made it their business, with considerable taste and integrity, to put back into print a considerable amount of work which has been in serious need of republication. If you ever felt there were gaps in your reading experience or are simply frustrated that you can't find enough good, substantial fiction in the shops or even online, then this is the publisher for you."

Michael Moorcock

www.ingramcontent.com/pod-product-compliance
Lightning Source LLC
Chambersburg PA
CBHW012207030726
47494CB00023B/2551

* 9 7 8 1 9 4 1 1 4 7 0 4 7 *